'Tough, genuine, racy – serving up London hard-boiled. Chris Niles is a fresh voice. *Spike It* is the beginning of a distinguished criminal career.' Andrew Klavan

'A light touch and sparkling dialogue make this the most promising first for some time.' *Irish Independent*

'Sam Ridley is a likeable hero, and Niles provides a sharp and funny portrait of life in a low-rent radio station.' *Daily Mail*

'A pacy, entertaining read, a murder mystery of the old school where the prose is hard-boiled . . . This is a highly promising debut which bodes well for the future.' *Oxford Times*

'Sam Ridley is the stuff that hard-boiled heroes are made of. A slick and cheeky debut.' Val McDermid, *Manchester Evening News*

'An excellent debut, with hopefully more in a similar vein to follow.' *Crime Time*

Chris Niles was born in New Zealand. She has worked as a television and radio journalist in New Zealand, Australia, Britain and Eastern Europe. She is currently with CNN in London.

Spike It is her first novel. Her new Sam Ridley novel, *Run Time*, is now available in Macmillan hardback.

Chris Niles

Spike It

PAN BOOKS

First published 1997 by Macmillan

This edition published 1998 by Pan Books
an imprint of Macmillan Publishers Ltd
25 Eccleston Place, London SW1W 9NF
and Basingstoke

Associated companies throughout the world

ISBN 0 330 35053 6

1 3 5 7 9 8 6 4 2

A CIP catalogue record for this book is available from
the British Library.

Typeset by Intype London Ltd
Printed by Mackays of Chatham PLC, Chatham, Kent

Acknowledgements

I am indebted to the following people for their professional expertise: Anthony Richmond, Danielle Whelton, Tom Grantham, Randi Epstein and Frances Hughes.

I would especially like to thank Drew and Ellen for their friendship and support. And Roderick – for helping me through.

Chapter One

I hadn't planned to go to work drunk. It was just the way things worked out.

It was Monday night. I was at my local, can't remember with whom. Some guy a lot like me.

'Know what?' my friend said to me as we huddled over our Scotch glasses. The pub was full, and clogged with smoke and smokers. The jukebox played some lovelorn ballad by Dire Straits. We were hoarse from the shouting and the smoking. And we were drunk. Quite drunk.

'I love this town . . . love this town. Lodda people godda lodda bad things to say about London. But not me, mate.' He paused, picked up his drink and gulped from it. 'I love this town.'

I nodded. He was right, of course. Why had I never seen it quite this clearly?

'Yurright,' I said. 'London. Less drink to London.'

We drank to London.

'I mean, people talk about Paris, Rome. Livable ciddies they say to me. Livable ciddies, but I'm asking you.' He held a whisky glass and a cigarette in his hand, but he was still able to release one finger to stab at me. '. . . Nah. Nah, I'm *telling* you . . . What have they got that London hasn't?' He paused. A reply was expected. I thought carefully before I gave it.

'Nothing,' I said. 'Not a goddamn thing.'

'Exactly,' he said triumphantly. He paused again and looked around, as if what he were about to reveal was not for general consumption. He leaned closer. 'Lived in Birmingham once,' he said.

'Izzatrigh?'

He nodded, lips pinched. Evidently the memory was still painful. 'Longest three months of my life, I don't mind tellin' you. Longest three months of me bleedin' life.'

'I can imagine,' I said solemnly. 'Only too well.'

He regarded me through squinting eyes. 'You lived anywhere else?'

I waved my non-drinking hand insouciantly. 'All over.'

'Really?' His face filled with pity.

'All over. A stranger in a strange land, that's me.'

'Stranger in a strange land. Yeah, that's good. Like sorda poetry. Godda remember that one. Tell the wife.' He looked at his watch, pushing his sleeve back laboriously. The watch confirmed his worst fears.

'Godda go,' said my friend. 'Or the wife'll be waiting with the cleaver.'

'Right,' I said. 'Godda go.'

He stood up unsteadily, pawing his pockets for keys and wallet. 'Whadiya say your name was again?' he asked me when he'd located both.

'Sam Ridley.'

'Well, Sam Ridley. It's been a privilege to talk with such a cul . . . cullivated gennilman,' he said before lurching out the door.

2

I collected my belongings but not my wits. The keys I found easily enough on the table top. My overcoat, draped over the back of the chair, took a little longer to extricate and transfer to my person. My wallet, thankfully, was still in my back pocket. The drinking had been vigorous, and conducted on an empty stomach. It was shaping up into one of those nights I would wake to regret.

It's a short walk from the pub to my flat. I took it slowly: partly because there wasn't any particular hurry, but mostly because I didn't seem capable of walking in a straight line. The cold air had had an accelerating effect on my inebriation: unseen hands jostled me from one side of the pavement to the other.

I found my flat after a couple of embarrassing attempts to let myself in on neighbours. In the dark all the houses on my street look alike.

The phone rang as I inserted the key in the front door to my flat. I wrenched the door open and sprang for it. Fumbled the receiver, caught it again.

'Simon?'

'Sam? It's Ted. From work. Were you expecting a call?'

'Oh, no. Not especially.'

'Sorry to bother you. I know you're probably doing something, but I've been listening to the police radio. Some woman's been killed near you. It was nasty by the sounds of things. Wondered if you could check it out. That is, if you're not doing anything.'

I was too drunk to tell Ted that I was too drunk to do anything. 'I, uh. Sure,' I said, trying to sound like my usual sharp self.

Ted sounded relieved. 'Great. You know, if we don't

3

check it'll turn out she was playing sexy bondage games with a gerbil and a Cabinet minister.'

'If she was then I'll be sure to get the gerbil on tape.'

'As long as he doesn't want too much money. Our gerbil budget is low.'

'I'll apply my famous powers of persuasion,' I said.

Luckily I hadn't taken my coat off.

The ten-minute walk did little to sober me up, but I was able to put one foot in front of the other in a satisfactory manner. The address that Ted had given was on Mulberry Avenue, which runs parallel and north of Ladbroke Grove. It was half of a nice neighbourhood; the mid-Victorian terraces on the south side of the street were forced to look on to a poured concrete housing estate on the north. If I had to hazard a guess, I would say that they didn't like what they saw. The estate was ugly, no other word for it.

Detective Inspector Charlie Hobbs was on the case. He was just getting out of his car as I arrived.

Hobbs and I go back a long way.

'Have you been drinking?' he asked suspiciously.

'Just a nightcap,' I said. I held the gate open for him and we walked down the side path to the basement flat. I was getting the hang of my pretend sobriety. This walking business was no trouble whatsoever.

We reached the door of the flat. Hobbs was just about to tell me to hoof it when a young woman rushed out. She was sobbing. She went to push past Charlie, but he's a large man, and the way was narrow. She crashed into him, they danced together briefly, unsteadily, and then collapsed, as if in slow motion, on the floor. The woman landed on top. Flapping like a landed fish.

I looked through the door. There was a cop inside the flat, another three outside. None of them had ever seen their superior officer in such a position. Hands reached out to help them both up. The woman was still crying, but confused now, knowing that it somehow wasn't such an appropriate response any more.

I saw my chance. I stepped deftly round and into the hallway.

The body lay in the middle of the living room floor. A blonde woman wearing a black dress and make-up. One patent leather high-heeled shoe was on her foot, the other lay some distance away. She was tall and slender and someone had tried to hack her head from her body with a blunt instrument. Her neck was a pulpy mess, bones and tissue spread out on the floor. There was a lot of blood and the room smelled of it – metallic and salty. She looked young – late twenties at the most. I looked at her and her deathly beauty and felt instantly sober and quite sick.

Looking around the flat, it seemed as if there had been a struggle. Books lay scattered on the floor, knocked off shelves. Lamps had been knocked over and a small portable filing cabinet ransacked. The video recorder was unplugged but sitting on the arm of a chair. In contrast to the mess, a stack of children's toys stood neatly in the corner. A tube of Chanel lipstick lay beside a plastic dump truck.

I didn't want to stay there with her. In an effort to quiet my protesting stomach, I went into the kitchen. It was small – a table took up most of the space and a bench along two walls. It was extremely tidy. Even

5

the notices on the board – reminders of sales, business cards from local tradesmen, bring-and-buy sale fliers – were pinned neatly on two corners. Nothing appeared to have been touched, except that the tea caddy was open. All it contained was tea.

'Ridley!'

Charlie was back on his feet, trying to pretend that he'd been like that all the time. He stood in the doorway to the kitchen. Had he come all the way in, there wouldn't have been room for anyone else.

'Where's the baby, Charlie?'

'Ridley, do I look like the bloody fount of knowledge to you? Now get out, I've got work to do.'

I didn't need much persuading. I went. Outside, I looked around for the woman who'd brought the respectable Detective Inspector Hobbs to his knees. She'd gone, probably spirited away in one of the many police cars that stood to attention. The cold night air reminded me that I had a hangover in the making, but I ignored my throbbing head, and phoned in a story.

I rescued a limp cigarette from my top pocket and smoked it. More reporters and TV crews arrived. Well-dressed female reporters with heavy make-up conferred with sloppily attired urban cowboys in boots and Puffa jackets. We stood in the chill making idle chat. A large crowd of neighbours gathered, pressing in along the police lines. An officer made half-hearted attempts to disperse them, but they weren't budging. A cop came out of the flat looking like he might have something to say, so several strong television lights were immediately turned on him. Blinking in the whiteness, he told us that Detective Inspector Charlie Hobbs would be with us soon. I couldn't be sure, but

I thought when the young officer mentioned Charlie's name he suppressed the ghost of a smile.

Charlie came out with two officers.

'Good evening, ladies and gentlemen of the press.'

'Media,' grumbled a young woman with a microphone.

Charlie ignored her. 'We have a fatality, as you probably know. A white woman, mid to late twenties.'

The reporters shouted questions in unison, but Charlie continued without heeding them. 'A neighbour found the body. We're not releasing any names yet. The next of kin haven't been notified. We'll let you know as soon as that happens. That's all we know for the moment. Now, if you'll excuse me.' He knew that none of the reporters would be waiting for the morning press conference; they had deadlines to meet tonight, but that wasn't his problem.

More cops arrived. Forensics, fingerprints. The people who would seek out the how, when and where. More time passed. Then Charlie came out again, got into a car. Some reporters started to follow him, asking more questions, but then somebody noticed that the body was being taken out of the house on a stretcher. The TV crews and newspaper photographers scrambled to get the shot. I stood back. Radio doesn't depend on pictures, which is one of the reasons why I like it. The eye can be a deceitful organ.

I went after Charlie, who was fastening his seatbelt like the good citizen he is. I leaned in the window.

'You sure you don't have anything on the baby, Charlie?'

'Press conference. Ten o'clock tomorrow.' He pushed a button. The window slid up.

'Did someone take the baby, Charlie?' The window closed. Charlie made what looked like an obscene gesture as the car drove off.

I was home at one thirty.

I live on Ladbroke Grove. Grove is too flash a term for it. It's a busy road that explores the great social variety to be found in London. At the southern end it's spruce, smart and expensive. At the northern end it's sleazy, noisy, dirty. I live at the northern end. On the weekends it's jammed with tourists who come in search of high-priced bargains at the Portobello Market. Week days are quieter but what with the crack dealers, prostitutes and inter-gang squabbles, it's inner-city living at its most challenging.

I found my flat, stumbled over two bicycles in the entrance, walked up one flight of steps and let myself in.

My place is small – two bedrooms, a living room, a kitchen, that sort of thing. There's a narrow balcony overlooking one of the city's more vital thoroughfares. I rarely sit out on it, but I like to know it's there if ever I feel the urge to take in brain-numbing amounts of carbon monoxide.

I surveyed my domain. It didn't take long. My furniture is post-divorce minimal; a fold-out sofabed of indeterminate colour, a stereo system that only plays records, a rented TV set.

There was one message on my answer machine. I hit the button. A young voice, sounding a bit uncertain.

'Hi, it's me. Just calling to say that I . . . that I miss you . . . and, I'll call back.'

*

I had been starting to sober up, but it wasn't too late to do something about it. I went in search of the bottle of Black Label that I keep in the kitchen, strictly for emergencies. I grabbed some ice cubes from the freezer and poured myself a drink. Then another. And after I'd got into the swing of things, a few more just for the sake of it. I suppose I should have stopped after that first one. Read a book, relaxed in front of the telly, called a friend for a chat. But with what's been happening to me lately, there doesn't seem any point in living a rich and varied life.

I drank some more. My problems started to fade. Alcohol really does do that.

Some time later I heard a ringing that didn't appear to be coming from my brain. It sounded like the phone. I sat up, which was almost certainly a mistake. The room swooped and swirled and my stomach did a few arabesques to accompany it.

I grabbed the phone. 'Hello?'

Nothing. The ringing continued. I noted that I was still wearing the clothes I had put on the day before.

My brain plodded through a mental checklist of things in the flat that were capable of sound. Eventually it came to rest upon the entryphone.

I edged forward on to the seat, bracing myself for the wave of nausea that would follow when I stood up. I pushed myself up to standing and stumbled to the entryphone, tripping over the nearly-empty bottle of Scotch. It spilt on the carpet. I leaned my head against the wall as I picked up the phone. It seemed easier that way.

'Hello?'

'Yeah, it's the cab company. You're supposed to be at work, remember?'

I buttoned up last night's shirt and grabbed the jacket from where I'd hurled it. I scrabbled round on the floor looking for my tie and shoes and found them under a pile of magazines. I dashed down the stairs of my flat and on to the street, shoes in hand. The taxi driver stood opposite, leaning nonchalantly against the passenger door. He opened the door and I hurled myself inside. It was five thirty-five. I had to be sitting in a studio in Tottenham Court Road, three miles away, in twenty-five minutes. I had an appointment to read the news.

Chapter Two

'I've been leaning on that buzzer for a bleeding 'alf hour,' said my driver.

I ignored him. London cabbies, they love a good whinge.

'I know you can make it.'

The cabbie, chewing on a matchstick, shrugged modestly. He spat the matchstick out, got into the driver's seat, cracked his knuckles and pulled out on to Ladbroke Grove.

I prayed to the god of traffic as that humble black cab hurtled through the dark and deserted streets. Down Westbourne Park Road we went and on to the A40, a short hop across that and on to Harrow Road and then Marylebone Road, me praying all the while. Thanks to my intercession, and an impressive turn of speed, I arrived at work with five minutes to go before the six o'clock bulletin. I dashed into the building, waved at the security guards, who buzzed me in, and made for the lift. It was out of order. Cursing, I turned to the stairs. The newsroom was on the second floor. Three minutes to go. Ignoring my rebellious stomach, I ran up the stairs.

Breathless and giddy, I sat down gingerly in front of the sub-editor Lyall Williams' desk. A tall, thin man with a monk's ration of hair, he sat calmly at his computer terminal. Lyall is a calm person. He doesn't need to tell me that punctuality is prized among news-readers.

'Sam, so good of you to take time out of your busy schedule.' He pointed at a pile of pink scripts and about four cartridges sitting on the corner of his desk.

I picked up the scripts. I breathed deeply, trying to quiet my pounding pulse. I stared at the page. The words, I'm fairly sure, were written in English, my first and only language, but they were in a playful mood. They danced. They skipped. All that dancing and skipping made me feel quite ill. A walk is what I need, I thought. I'll walk to the studio and then I'll feel better. I took the scripts down the corridor to the studio.

'Carts!' Lyall said. He came after me with the stack of cartridges, the single-loop tapes that have the snappy, ten-second soundbites electromagnetically encoded on them.

'You're going to need these,' he said. 'Feeling OK?'

'Fine,' I said. I felt like shit.

I handed the cartridges to Gary, the engineer in the control room.

'You look like death,' he said.

'I'm fine,' I said. I felt like death. I went next door to the newsreading booth.

I tried not to think about how much like death I felt as I seated myself in the studio. I carefully put on the headphones. The station news sting throbbed in my ears. I hadn't realized until then how much it sounded like 'The Ride of the Valkyries'.

The music stopped suddenly. I looked at the

engineer through the thick glass window that separated my studio from his. He held his left hand up, and waved his fingers and thumb, as though he were playing shadow puppets. The cogs in my brain turned slowly, but when they did eventually fit into place I recognized the gesture. He wanted me to say something. I put hangovers out of my mind. I launched into professional mode.

'Good morning. Samuel Ridley for City Radio morning news. Top stories this hour are . . .'

The god that had got the taxi to work on time was still with me, because I got through the first two stories no trouble whatsoever.

So far so good, I thought.

Then the cartridges started to play up.

I read a story about a pile-up on the motorway. The cart was supposed to have a soundbite with an eyewitness. It didn't fire. I paused, waiting for it to come up. It left an uncomfortable gap in the bulletin. Dead air, we call it. It's not every broadcaster's dream but it's not the end of the world, either.

I plunged into the next story, which was about last night's murder. The cart for that one didn't fire either. More dead air. I looked through the glass. Gary, the engineer, had his hands around his throat. I was starting to wonder if the taxi god was in fact an autocratic petty-minded avenger, getting me back for not really believing in him. But I could handle it. There were other stories in the bulletin that appeared not to harbour a personal grudge against me. Then I was nearly at the end. And, after all, I am a professional.

I passed smoothly to the last story. The 'and finally', which is usually a lighthearted laugh at someone else's expense. The sort of story that sends you out into the world with a spring in your step, a song in your heart. This morning's tale was something to do with a parrot. He'd been a pretty clever Polly and had won a community service award. The enterprising reporter, obviously his first day on the job, had interviewed the bird, who was supposed to say something cute like 'Aw shucks, it was nothing' or 'Get me Spielberg on the phone', when the first cart that had failed came up instead, describing in graphic detail what happens when five speeding cars collide.

It's strange, but when I thought about it later even I wondered what came over me. I mean, I'm not exactly a raw recruit. I've been in the broadcast news business for nearly twenty years. And the first thing they impress upon raw recruits, or at least they did in my day, is to never ever say anything near an open mike that you wouldn't want your grandmother to hear.

I switched the mike off, switched on the intercom to Gary and said, 'Now I know what it's like to be fucked by a bird.'

Only the mike wasn't off.

I'd flicked the switch upwards to the 'off' position all right, but it hadn't disconnected the circuit.

Gary had removed his hands from around his throat and was now holding his head in them, rocking it from side to side.

I finished the weather and traffic reports with as much dignity as I could muster.

'Oh well,' I thought as I closed the studio door. 'There's always PR.'

I went to the bathroom and threw up. I felt better, but not much.

Chapter Three

The City Radio newsroom is a dynamic combination of high-tech and squalor. Imagine a space ship that has crashed in a rubbish dump and you'll get the general idea. A shiny computer terminal stands on every desk and banks of television monitors are set into one wall. But every surface is covered. There are coffee cups, old newspapers, scripts, tape recorders. The carpet bears a complex pattern of stains of indeterminate origin.

This morning, as always, the room smelt of old, overbrewed coffee. I made straight for the machine and poured a cup, poured another and made my way to the desk in the centre of the room where the balding head of Lyall could just be seen over a mountain of files, polystyrene coffee cups and an eclectic collection of portable radios. He was calm. If anything he was calmer than when I'd last seen him.

'Career hara-kiri. Interesting concept.' He logged off on his computer monitor. It was a sign that I had his full attention.

I cleared a space for the cup on Lyall's desk. 'I need a holiday.'

'As soon as Delaney gets in, you're going to get one. He's just got off the phone. It's still scorching.

The board chairman rang Marlowe, Marlowe rang him, he rang me. Had to get it off his chest. Thanks for the coffee.'

I took a sip. 'Think they're trying to poison us?'

'Why bother? You're digging your own grave.'

Lyall and I have been friends a long time. Words aren't always necessary in mature relationships. I sipped my coffee and said nothing.

'I hardly need tell you that you won't be going back into the studio this morning, or in fact any time soon. I'll put in a word for you – again – but you'll be lucky to keep your job after this.' Lyall, who was a Zen master in a former life, looked the closest he would ever be to angry.

I nodded. 'Thanks. If you want me I'll be at the morning presser.'

'I wouldn't. Delaney will be here at eight. He's come in extra early to have a meaningful interface with you. I think I'm right in saying he's in touch with his anger here, and he'll be frustrated if he can't share that.'

I nodded. 'Then if you want me I'll be cowering under my desk.'

'That's the spirit.' Lyall turned his attention back to his computer.

I picked up my coffee cup, a large ceramic bowl with 'I play to win' written on the side, a relic from a time when I was younger. Come to think of it, my whole life was a relic from a time when I was younger.

I went back to my desk, sat down and stared at my terminal. I read through the wires, checked for messages, all of which took up a full twenty-five minutes. Then there was nothing to do except sit around like a chump. I looked at my watch. It read quarter to seven. I indulged in a few useless recriminations. I tried not to think of the worst that could happen. That used up a good five minutes. My head still hurt.

I decided to minister to my hangover. I went out to the coffee bar, bought a bacon sandwich and a cappuccino, and sat outside at a wobbly plastic table, ate the sandwich and smoked a cigarette. It was a sunny day. The sky was big and the air smelt new. The pain that had been piercing every pore eased slightly. I went back to the newsroom at eight o'clock, Delaney's scheduled hour of arrival.

He came in. He strode purposefully through the newsroom to his office, which is in one corner. The newsroom is open plan for the common folk, but the offices of the managers are on two sides. They have glass walls, so we can look in and they can look out. At City Radio we have no secrets.

Lyall was summoned, then Felicia Randall, editor of the morning women's issues programme. I rearranged the pens on my desk and wondered how long it would be before I was doing it in the comfort of my own home.

'Sam. My man.' The deliberately powerful voice penetrated the low-density hum of the newsroom. I looked up with what I hoped was insouciance. Rick Brittan, a fellow reporter, although I use the term in its loosest sense. Tall, square-jawed, dressed like an estate agent. Sharp suit. Sharp hair.

He sat on the edge of my desk, smoothing his hair behind his ears. He then arranged his facial features in a manner which he imagined simulated concern. Rick has no direct access to sympathetic emotions.

'Too bad about this morning, mate.' He tried, not very hard, to keep the grin off his face.

'Brittan, your concern touches me deeply. Now go away.'

Rick smiled broadly. 'Sam, Sam.' He inspected his fingernails and tutted. 'The f-word. On air. In peak time. Whew!' He wiped his brow in an exaggerated manner and lightly punched me on the arm. 'Too bad.'

I picked up the newspaper, rustling it briskly. 'You make it very hard for me to like you.'

Rick laughed. It was the jolly, uninhibited laugh of a man who's about to get the job of a person he hates. He stood up, he turned, he walked away and I thought I heard him say something that sounded like 'Polly wanna cracker.' Rick has looks, and a cool sense of how to dress. He wants to be in telly, and I think that would be a very good idea indeed. Hell, I want him to be controller of BBC1 – anything to get him out of my sight.

'Sam?'

My boss, Alan Delaney, stood at the door of his office about ten feet away from my desk. He wore a smart suit and a pained expression. I could see that he wasn't looking forward to confronting me. For one thing, it would require a level of energy that he had become unaccustomed to investing in his job, for another he thought I was a dead loss, a washed-up piece of shit, a warning of what could happen if you didn't hustle.

'Can I see you in here?'

Chapter Four

I put down the paper and followed the expensive suit into the glass-walled office. For a minute, all eyes were on us, then, as if remembering their manners, people turned away. Pretended they were getting on with their work.

The glass door banished the busy office sounds outside. I sat down on the firm two-seater couch and studied a row of ice-cream-coloured crystals that Delaney had lined up at the front of his desk according to size.

Alan Delaney was a relatively new addition to City Radio. He'd given journalism the best months of his life and with the use of mirrors and cunning sleight of hand had convinced the board of City Radio that they were getting a hotshot young administrator. What they had got instead was someone who expressed his contempt for his salary by spending most of his time organizing a sideline business selling water filters. It wasn't strictly illegal, just dodgy. A lot like Delaney himself.

I, along with most of my colleagues, didn't mind. Delaney's avarice kept him from having too close a grip on what happened in the newsroom, and that suited everybody. On a few occasions, apropos of nothing in particular, Delaney would call staff into his office and hold forth about his half-baked New Age theories. His proselytizing zeal would have embarrassed a television evangelist.

Delaney looked with distaste at my unkempt condition. He sat down carefully in his orthopaedically designed chair. I wondered why it was only executives who ever got proper chairs. Surely back pain was no respecter of status?

Delaney rested both elbows on his desk and put his palms together. He breathed deeply.

'Let me explain something to you which, despite your years at this station, may have escaped you. We do not say the f-word at City Radio. We do not say it, we do not think it. We do not think of saying it. Are you with me so far?'

I nodded. It seemed important to maintain eye contact, so I did.

'Good.' Delaney relaxed his position, leaning back in his chair. He changed tack. His face crumpled. He sighed like a father who's just caught his son in the booze cabinet.

'Why, Sam? Why are you doing this to me? Do you hate me? Do you take pleasure from the fact that I'll have to go in front of the board and explain this away? How am I going to tell them that one of their most senior reporters doesn't know his arse from a hole in the ground?'

That was a tough one. I still couldn't think of anything to say.

Delaney sighed again, the disappointed sigh. 'Sam, I've tried to give you leeway. I know you've been having personal problems, and I understand all that.

But you mustn't let it affect your work. You let us all down when you do that.'

Brazenly going for the sympathy vote, I nodded sadly. I thought about tears but rejected them. Even hacks have their standards.

'We'll take those problems into account in deciding what your future with City Radio is to be. You've committed an extremely serious offence.' He looked at me for confirmation. Grovelling was called for.

'I know,' I said. It seemed better than nothing at all.

'There's no excuse for what you did.' He looked at me again, expecting penitent. I did penitent. Hell, I didn't have to act.

Delaney drew a deep breath – Was it to savour the moment? I couldn't be sure. He picked up a very sharp pencil and tapped it on a small white pad.

'For a month you'll be on probation. You will be taken off the police beat.' He marked the points off, tapping the pencil against his fingers. I said nothing. It was better than the sack. He was probably going to put me on the sub-editor's desk for a month, and I could stand a bout of sub-editing. The hours weren't great, but it would be bearable.

Delaney continued. 'You're going to be working with Felicia on *Female AM*.'

'What?' I sat bolt upright. Remembered the delicate condition of my neural region, and sat back again.

'She's short-handed. Marianne has gone off on maternity leave, and she needs someone who can do a bit of everything.'

I had been prepared to do penance, but this wasn't punishment, it was sadism.

'Alan, this is not a good idea. Apart from the fact that Felicia and I can't stand each other, I can't do stories about fashion and aerobics. Put me anywhere else but there – I'll even do sport.'

'Sam, I don't think you understand the gravity of the situation. We have a franchise renewal coming up. Something like this, like what you've just done, could jeopardize the future of the whole company. You're getting off lightly because of the great respect we have for your years of service.' He made 'years of service' sound like a socially communicable disease. 'I don't want to do this, but I have no choice. Your situation will be reviewed in a month. But I'm going to recommend to the board that you seek professional help if you are to remain with us.'

Delaney's face was set, challenging me to deny him. Personally, I thought he was overdoing it a bit. What I had done would hardly threaten a franchise bid. Those sorts of things are all about money and programming and knowing the right people, but it didn't seem like the appropriate time to bring up my views on the subject.

'I'm sorry, Sam. I know that things are hard for you right now. But you stepped way over the line this morning.'

He was right. I hate it when that happens. I stood up and turned to go. But Delaney had one more barb.

'Could you tell Rick that I want to see him?'

'Delaney wants to see you,' I said to Rick.

Rick put down his paper, took his feet off his desk. He smiled. Actually, it was more of a smirk.

'Well, gee, Sam. I wonder what that could be about?'

'Drop dead, Brittan.'

'A little hint, Sam? Go on, give it your best shot.'

'It would land right across your nose, Brittan. And we both know we don't want that.'

But he just laughed.

Back at my desk I massaged my neck and stared at the sludge in the bottom of my cup.

A fat file landed on my desk from a great height.

'Don't ask me why they're punishing us both for your cock-up,' said Felicia Randall in her mid-Atlantic accent. 'And frankly, I'm not in the mood to discuss it.' She pushed long red nails through carefully blonded hair. 'I have three hours of live radio to put out every day, and not enough people to do it with. A civilized station would have at least five people on the job. We have three. By my reckoning, this means you have to work as hard as two people. So here's what you have to do today: set up two on-air interviews – one on cosmetic surgery for children, the other on sex for septuagenarians. I'll also need you to produce a five-minute package about twins. You'll find all the information in the file. Any questions?'

She was staring at me belligerently, but I didn't take it too personally. Felicia's been in a bad mood from birth.

'So, let me get this straight; the septuagenarians have sex and the kids have surgery. Are you sure it's not the other way around? And where do the twins fit in?'

She spun away. Then she turned round, stood about five feet from me, feet planted, hands on hips.

'You may not approve of my show, you sanctimonious gits in news. I know what you say. But the fact is, it rates. People listen. They call in. My show means something to them. And that's what radio is supposed to be about. So you'll just do the stories I give you. Just do them, no backchat. No questions. OK?'

People were looking. In one morning I'd supplied enough gossip to keep the office buzzing well into the next millennium. I nodded. 'OK.'

Felicia growled and strode off.

It was only eight thirty in the morning, but it felt much, much later. I took my workload out to the front steps.

The newsroom was a smoke-free zone. Those who'd refused the company's offers to sign up for the break-the-habit programmes were forced to take their guilty pleasures outside. I sat, smoked and read over my day's assignments. Then I smoked another cigarette, because what I read depressed me so much.

I blame Mary, my ex-wife, for it all. Not the divorce, of course. I'm grown-up enough to know that it takes two to really screw something like that up.

She left me and our ten-year-old son, Simon, for an Australian stockbroker who lived in leafy Kew. *I can't lie to you*, she said. *I don't love you and the marriage isn't working*, which was true. Mary, who is also a broker, had been eyeing this chap up for quite some time. One Friday she packed and was gone. A van came a couple of days later for the big stuff. She took most of our furniture, but Simon stayed with me.

There wasn't room in leafy Kew or in the new romance for him. I consider I got the better end of the deal.

But then, about six months later, the stockbroker got a transfer to Sydney. The angel Gabriel visited Mary and she had a vision. It spoke to her of happy families frolicking in the antipodean sunshine, and it included Simon. *Australia's a better place to bring up a child*, she said. *All that sunshine and fresh air. He can learn to surf and play Aussie Rules football*. But I wasn't giving up without a fight. *What about skin cancer and snakes and dingoes that steal babies?* I said. *It's downright dangerous for a kid out there*. We fought about it. She was determined. She took me to court, hired an expensive scuzzball of a lawyer and she won. I wasn't a suitable influence, he said, with my unsociable hours, my unsuitable job. I could visit him on holidays, the judge said. Well, big fucking deal.

Simon left a month ago for the sunny shores of the southern hemisphere, and I was a lost cause. Hence the drinking, hence everything.

I sighed, I extinguished my cigarette on the steps and I went back inside.

Old habits die hard. I called Charlie at South Kensington police station, where the incident room for the murder case was located.

'He's not here,' said the callow youth masquerading as an officer of the law.

'When will he be there?'

'Who is this?'

'His sister.'

'All press enquiries are going through Roger Fitzgerald.'

'Why him?'

'Hobbs isn't in charge any more. He let a reporter into a crime scene. The chief super is not happy.'

'Oh dear. What is the world coming to?'

'No respect,' said the kid. 'It were different in my day.'

With my best contact out of the running, I was forced to get information from the wires. Last night's murder wasn't my story any more, but it's hard to teach an old police reporter new tricks. I learned the girl's name. She was Elaine York, and she had lived twenty-eight years. She was a single mother with a two-and-a-half-year-old kid whose name was Albion. She did part-time work for a trendy environmental organization called Roadblock, which, as the name suggested, co-ordinated protests against road-building campaigns. That night she'd dropped the kid off with her mother before going out for dinner with her boss, Mark Matheson. It was an all-night stay because Elaine didn't pick her daughter up on the way home. It was just as well. She got there at about ten thirty and was attacked from behind as she opened her front door. The police didn't have much in the way of evidence – no weapon, and, thus far, no witnesses. Some cash and a few pieces of jewellery were stolen, the value of which didn't amount to much at all.

'Twins.' I looked up. Felicia stood over me, in the same take-all-comers stance.

'I put a call in, waiting for them to get back to me,' I said. It was partly true. She snorted like she didn't believe me and walked away. I picked up the phone. As soon as Felicia had gone, I went back to reading the wires. Another story had just been filed and it mentioned City Radio. The woman who'd been killed had a famous sister, Anna York-Baines. She was a psychologist who'd recently started a regular phone-in on City Radio. The story said that Anna was taking care of her recently orphaned niece.

'See this?' I wandered over to Lyall with a printout of the story.

'I'll get Rick right on to it,' he said in a strangled tone. Lyall doesn't like Rick much more than I do.

Five o'clock rolled round slowly, but arrive it eventually did, and a drink seemed like a good idea. Lyall and I stepped out of the office and across the road to Hanway Place and the Huntsman, an establishment which could only charitably be described as 'ungentrified'. I bought a beer for me and a Coke for Lyall. We sat at a small table with one leg shorter than the others, and watched two eighteen-stone truckers play darts.

He fished the lemon out of his Coke and put it in a dirty ashtray. 'Now that I don't drink, I find myself wondering why I come to these places at all.'

'The company, perhaps?' I ventured. We looked at the truckers, who were playing in singlets, the better to display their eclectic tattoo art collection.

We were silent for a moment. The truckers started arguing over the score in their game. It looked ugly. We turned our backs.

'How's Rick doing?'

Lyall snorted. 'Guy wouldn't know a news story if it came up to him wearing a laminated name tag.' He glared at me.

'Yeah, well,' I said. Not only had I destroyed my career and family, I'd let down my best friend as well. I didn't have much to say for myself these days. 'Fancy another drink?'

'Got to go, promised Kate I'd be home. Sure you won't come over for a bite?'

'Thanks, I'll head off.'

Lyall and his wife Kate presided cheerfully over a large, unmanageable tribe of teenage children. I loved them all, but they were the last people I needed to see.

I took the tube home to Ladbroke Grove, stopping on the way to buy food, a six-pack and some headache tablets. I went into the bathroom and had a long and overdue shower. I felt better. I sat down with a beer in time to watch the early evening news, and wolf down my prefabricated pasta dinner, heated in mere seconds in the microwave. I used to like to cook, but like sex, I can seldom get excited about doing it on my own. I have a couple of books extolling the virtues of 'solo cuisine' but really, who are they kidding?

I watched the news for a bit. There was a story about Elaine, which didn't say anything new. I watched the reporter standing outside her flat, explaining that the neighbourhood where she lived, which was just around the corner from me in North Kensington, was a violent and drug-ridden part of town. Then she brought up the riots. The Notting Hill riots were decades ago, but mainly because of reporters like the one I was watching the neighbourhood is still struggling to live down its media reputation as the South Bronx of London.

There was a knock at the door. I got up to answer it. A small, rotund man stood outside in a silk dressing gown. He looked like a rugby ball wrapped in paisley. My downstairs neighbour, Everard Montgomery, waged a constant and largely ineffectual campaign to tart up our building. He wanted paint. He wanted windowboxes with cheerful plants in them. He wanted welcome mats in the lobby and embossed wallpaper in the common parts. I had no intention of planting geraniums in my boxes. As far as Everard was concerned, I was Public Enemy Number One.

'Mr Ridley.'

'Everard, do come in. Care for a drink? I have beer, beer or beer.'

'Thank you, no.' Everard came in, but stood right inside the door. He sniffed unobtrusively, probably smelling the whisky that I had spilt that morning.

He drew himself up to his full five and a half feet. 'Mr Ridley, we have been over this before. You know that I'm a light sleeper, and the walls in this building are very thin. Well, this morning you woke me up with your crashing and banging. And it was five thirty in the morning.'

'I'm sorry, Everard. Big story, important breaking news. I had to rush.'

'I mean, it was different when your son was living here. Children, well, you don't expect them to be quiet all the time. But adults . . . Surely we can come to some agreement?'

'I'm very sorry,' I said. 'More sorry than you'll ever know.'

'I mean, it's not as if we haven't had this conversation before.'

'I'll try much harder in the future.'

'Please do, Mr Ridley. Please try much, much harder.'

*

SPIKE IT

I finished my beer, located my Renault on Ladbroke Grove, sent up a small prayer to the parking god that it had remained where I left it, and went to see Detective Inspector Charlie Hobbs.

Chapter Five

He was standing at the bar, two glasses in front of him. One had beer, the other whisky. I ordered the same, just to keep him company.

'Bloody Ridley,' he said. I've never had the heart to tell Charlie my first name isn't Bloody.

'Sorry,' I said.

'Hmph.' Charlie drank deeply from the beer glass. 'Is it bad?'

'Put it this way,' said Charlie. 'I'm so mad I've decided to get back into training, lose a couple a stone just so's I can beat the shit out of you.'

'No need,' I said. 'I'm in no shape. You could probably do it now.'

'The anticipation will be half the fun.'

'I'm sorry,' I said.

'Yeah, course you are. Useless bozo.' His whisky was gone. I ordered another glass by way of a peace offering.

'If it's any consolation, I nixed my career today as well.'

'Whaddya mean?'

I told him what had happened that morning. It brought a smile to his eyes.

'Couldn't have happened to a bloody nicer guy,' he

chortled. 'I'd like a tape of the show. Play it for the lads down at the station. That'll . . .' Charlie looked up, over my right shoulder. I turned.

A tall, sandy-haired man with a neat red moustache stood directly behind me, invading my personal space. Detective Inspector Roger Fitzgerald reached over my shoulder, signalled the barman and a bottle of something foreign was placed on the bar between Charlie and me. Roger Fitzgerald liked to think of himself as one cool dude. No one's told him that having a red moustache means automatic disqualification from the cool stakes.

He elbowed his way through so that he was wedged in between us. Then he turned his back on Charlie. Charlie sighed and stared into his drink.

'Mister Ridley.' Fitzgerald stretched out the syllables in a mocking way.

'Detective Inspector Fitzgerald.' I said it without feeling. Roger Fitzgerald and I go back quite a way, but you wouldn't call us friends.

Charlie sighed some more. 'Leave it, Fitzgerald, you've got your way.'

Roger Fitzgerald ignored him. He smiled at me. I smiled back, although my heart wasn't in it. Roger Fitzgerald is a thug and a bully who's fortunate enough to be able to channel his aggression into service to the public. In his case, the thin blue line houses a seriously mean streak. I don't like him, he doesn't like me. At least we know where we stand with each other. I finished my beer.

'Charlie, I'll catch you later.'

'Don't go, I want a word.' Roger fixed me with that stare.

I shrugged. 'Then call my secretary, we'll do lunch.'
I left.

I'd been able to get a parking space quite near the pub. It was down a narrow street which backed on to a cinema complex. I'd even managed to get a spot under a street light – you can't be too careful when you go drinking with cops – and I was glad of that. But as I walked down that little street I felt as if someone was watching me.

Fitzgerald caught up with me as I was about to put the key in the lock. I hadn't heard the tread of his soft-soled Doc Martens. He surveyed the Renault's ageing lines contemptuously.

'Nice motor, Ridley.'

I unlocked the car door. 'I'd love to stay and chat, but I just don't have the time. You know how it is.'

Fitzgerald smiled some more. 'What I have to say won't take long.'

He was around the car in a trice. He grabbed me by the front of my shirt and slammed me against the wall. Then he punched me twice in the stomach.

Chapter Six

Fitzgerald was a police boxing champion in his younger days, but I didn't need to know that to realize that it hurt like hell. I doubled up, gasping for breath, gasping for anything. He pinched the back of my neck with his huge hands and pushed me down on to the pavement. He had no argument from me. I gagged and retched and tried to persuade my lungs to do the job they were designed for.

Fitzgerald stood over me, thumbs hooked in his belt like the tough guy he thinks he is. 'We've had trouble before, Ridley, you and I. So you know I don't like it when you get in my way. I'm taking over the Elaine York case from Hobbs, so that is your signal to get lost. I don't want to see you. I don't want to hear you. I don't want to hear *about* you. Am I making myself clear?'

'Perfectly,' I croaked.

'Good,' he said. 'You see, I don't see the point of fraternizing with scum.'

He straightened up, took a bunch of keys from his pocket and selected one. He then ran it casually along the passenger side of my car. It sounded like someone scraping their fingernails down a blackboard, and it left a wobbly white scratch.

'You're parked illegally,' he said.

I know that my car is old, but I am attached to it. Call me irrational, but that's how I feel. You mess with a man's car and it gets personal.

I staggered to my feet, wheezing and swaying. I thought I could see bluebirds in my vision.

Fitzgerald straightened up, slid the keys back into his pocket and took a step or two back, arms folded.

'Kiss your career goodbye, arsehole.' I tried to sound convincing, but it wasn't working even for me.

He laughed and pocketed his keys in a jaunty manner. 'I don't think so, Sammy. Your word against mine; a respected officer of the law against an alcoholic hack? I don't think so.'

He walked off.

'My taxes pay your wages,' I yelled after him.

Fitzgerald whistled a merry tune. He didn't look back.

Too late, I looked around for witnesses. The street was quiet.

I inspected the gouge. It was going to be expensive to repair.

'Shit,' I said.

I drove home, dragged myself back up the stairs, sat on my couch and poured a big whisky. My head hurt, my stomach hurt, my feelings hurt.

I decided I would ask the fates if I could trade my life in for another. This one wasn't going that well and, frankly, I didn't have the energy to wrestle with it any more. I thought about something that was more in my line, perhaps a direct swap for the life of a barkeeper in Bermuda. I would wrench Simon away from his mother in a daring undercover raid and we would spend our days fishing and working on our suntans.

While I was fleshing out the details of this little scheme, I fell asleep.

Next morning I woke early, still in the chair. I made to get up and then remembered what had happened to me the night before. My face looked OK – Fitzgerald knew enough about beatings not to mark me where everyone could see – but my stomach felt as if he was still punching it. My palms were stiff and covered in dried blood from when they'd had to break my fall. Showering felt like a new type of sado-masochistic torture; part pleasure, mostly pain. I dried myself gingerly and went into the kitchen, made coffee and lit a cigarette. I switched on the news to hear a person who wasn't me read the whole bulletin without uttering a single profanity. I was impressed.

The Elaine York story played high up, but there wasn't much new to say. The family had offered a reward – twenty thousand pounds – for information. I guessed they weren't exactly hurting for cash. In addition to her psychology practice, Anna had written a couple of books in the how-to-achieve-everything vein. And I'd heard that she was married to a corporate lawyer.

I decided that my day had more or less started, so I finished my coffee and went out for a bracing breakfast. I walked a few blocks to the Blue Skies, my local café. The food's not great, but they know me there.

'Whaddya want?' snarled the skinny middle-aged waitress as I slid on to a seat.

'And a wonderful morning it is too, Pat. Let's see,

I'll have bacon, eggs, toast, mushrooms and – ah – coffee. Got any decaf?'

Pat sniffed in acknowledgement of my little joke. The eating trends that have influenced most of the Western world in the last couple of decades have left the Blue Skies completely unmoved. This is fry-up city. No salads, no white meat. If you even asked for brown bread they'd laugh you out on to the street. I like it a lot. Considering how much I drink and smoke, I figure it won't be bacon that kills me.

Pat wrote my order, snapped the notebook shut and stumped off to the kitchen. She's a kindly soul, but not at her best in the morning. I gazed out of the window. A familiar, shambling figure stood outside in a loose assortment of clothes. He lifted his hand in greeting and I waved him inside. He smiled and came in.

Geoffrey slid into the banquette opposite. His eyes were clear and as always he looked straight at me, without blinking. He had a bushy grey beard, and long grey hair. He wore Oxfam clothes. I've tried to give him some of mine in the past, but oddly he's always turned them down.

We shook hands across the table. Pat reappeared. Geoffrey is one of her favourites. She lifted her eyebrow and he nodded, which in their language means: 'Would you like your usual?' and 'Yes, thanks,' respectively.

Geoffrey Petherton looks and acts like a street person, which in spirit is what he is. He has a place to go to, a little flat in nearby Bayswater, but he spends most of his time on Westbourne Grove, reciting poetry to an uncaring, uncultured public. I've known him for a couple of years. I heard he used to be a functioning member of society way back. That was before a drunken wally behind the wheel of a sportscar struck his wife and daughter down as they stepped out on to a pedestrian crossing on the Fulham Road. Neither of them survived the trip to the hospital. The drunk was out of jail almost as soon as he sobered up.

I had been reading the paper when Geoffrey came in. But now I put it down. I told Geoffrey about the brave new direction my life was taking, leaving out the detail about the profanity. Geoffrey never swears and I sometimes get the feeling that he's shocked when others do.

He reached across the table and grabbed my shoulder, smiling broadly.

'Every new venture is a blessing, Samuel,' he said. He never calls me Sam.

I was mildly irritated. I started to say something like 'You don't know what it's like.' But as soon as I'd thought the words I bit them back. He didn't need a lecture from me on that score. Geoffrey sat there smiling gently, like he was reading my thoughts. I sometimes wonder if he isn't a little on the mad side, but then I think if he'd lived in a primitive society he would have been considered touched by God.

I told him about my swansong assignment, the murder of Elaine York. He doesn't read the papers much, because he doesn't understand man's inhumanity to man.

'Kid's name is Albion,' I said to Geoffrey.

'Visions of the daughters of Albion,' said Geoffrey. 'William Blake. In my opinion one of the great seers of the nineteenth century.'

'What?' said Pat. She snapped my food down in front of me.

'William Blake,' I said.

'Does he eat here? I don't know him.'

Geoffrey smiled. 'He dines in the Kingdom of Glory.'

'So would we all if we had to choose,' I said.

Pat stumped off. 'Just don't expect any free coffee refill,' she said.

Geoffrey picked at his food and read the papers while I wolfed down my meal.

'It's terrible what they'll say about a person once they're dead,' he said. 'They say she was having an affair with her boss. Now, surely, that's her own private business. Why do papers print these terrible things? The only result is grief.'

I paused mid-egg. 'Let me see that?' Geoffrey handed over the tabloid paper that I'd bought in addition to the broadsheet. It said that police were interviewing Mark Matheson, with whom Elaine had been conducting a torrid romance. Judging from the tone of the article, it was a wonder that any campaigning at all got done at Roadblock. Taking the moral high road, the article spoke of lengthy private meetings, long lunches and lovers' tiffs.

'It's probably all lies,' I said. 'These guys will say anything to sell a paper.'

I paid the bill, said goodbye to Geoffrey and caught the number 7 bus outside the café. Notwithstanding the huge mess I'd made of things, I felt pretty good as I made my way to work. Life could have been worse. I had my health, and I had a job. Just. Nothing like a nitrate infusion to set the world to rights.

The portals of City Radio welcomed me as I sprang lightly up the steps. I took the lift to the second floor and strode confidently into the fug of the newsroom. Geoffrey was right. Count your blessings. Look on the bright side. Make the best of a bad situation. I was going to be good. No, not good, exemplary. I was going to be the best goddamned *Female AM* reporter that the world had ever seen. At the end of my probationary month, City Radio would be begging me to stay on.

Lyall was at his desk, buried under paper and holding a phone to each ear. I went to the coffee machine and poured him a cup. Since he gave up the singing syrup, Lyall drinks almost as much coffee as I do. He was still on the phone when I got back to his desk. I couldn't find a spare place to put the coffee down, so I cleared three or four empty cups away. He mimed his thanks. I wanted to tell him about Fitzgerald, but no end to the phone conversation looked likely so I went off to check in with Felicia.

She too was surrounded by papers and tapes and had a phone to each ear. I perched on the corner of her desk. She motioned for me to get off, not very politely, I thought.

'Where have you been? Clock-in time is eight o'clock, which, in case you're interested, does not mean eight thirty or even eight fifteen.'

I was marshalling a feeble excuse when she tossed a file at me. I began to think she liked doing that. She spoke into the phone: 'No, I don't mind holding . . .' She put her hand over the receiver and said, 'We have a guest in at ten to talk about . . .'

Felicia looked up. An expensively dressed middle-aged woman was hovering at my shoulder.

'Guys, guys, can I just say something here?' It was Crosbie Shaw, the presenter of *Female AM*, looking excited. It was a rare event – she had something on her mind.

An exasperated expression crossed Felicia's face. It looked a lot like she wanted to tell her to take a hike. Instead she said, 'What is it, Crosbie?'

Crosbie looked coquettish. She put her hand to her hair. 'I want you to read this letter I got this morning. This guy says he thinks I'm the best woman journalist working in Britain.' She simpered in a self-deprecating manner. 'He tapes the show every day so he can listen to it when he gets home from work at night – to unwind.'

A vision of Crosbie's fan jerking off to *Female AM* sprang unbidden to my mind. I smothered a snort of laughter. Crosbie didn't notice, but Felicia frowned at me.

'So, you think I should send him a photo? He seems like a nice guy, not a weirdo . . . But I don't know . . .'

Felicia pinched two fingers to the bridge of her nose. 'Crosbie, can we talk about this after the show?'

'Oh, er, right.' Crosbie looked genuinely surprised that her issue wasn't at the apex of the morning agenda, but she shrugged, went back to her seat and picked up a magazine.

In that moment I felt sorry for Felicia. She did work hard, and Crosbie Shaw was the journalistic equivalent of a side of dead meat. In the world at large, Crosbie had a reputation for intelligence and hard work. Those who worked with her laughed long and loud when they heard those stories. Crosbie's ideal day consisted of a gruelling hairdresser's appointment before slaving away at lunchtime over smoked salmon and Chablis at the Groucho Club. When she was at work she was usually so exhausted that she simply didn't have the strength to make phone calls or do research. You didn't work with Crosbie, you worked at her.

She'd had her heyday as a thrusting young television current affairs reporter in the seventies. Since then, it was fair to say, her motivation had gone off the boil. She sounded good on air, but that was for the simple reason that a producer who was much better briefed than she was fed her questions through her headphones. Thus, Crosbie's greatest talent – being able to listen to her producer say one thing while she said something else on air – went largely unacknowledged by her fans.

Crosbie sat engrossed in her magazine. Although draped elegantly in off-white Armani, she had her hair plastered into a style that was last fashionable thirty years ago. Maybe she'd never had the courage to tell her hairdresser that she felt like a change.

'Sex and the single parent.' Amazingly, Felicia's train of thought was unbroken. To the phone she said, 'Thanks, I'll call back.' She replaced the receiver.

'A woman's written a book. We're interviewing her at ten. Write some questions out for Crosbie, the usual stuff.'

I went back to my desk, sat down and cleared a space for the file. It seemed straightforward. How do single parents find the time for sex? The problems of paying for a babysitter on a single income, maintaining one's image as a glamour-puss when the kid's thrown up his dinner over the little black dress, that sort of thing. I browsed through the book. My only foray into sex as a single parent had been an abject disaster. Perhaps I could have avoided the obvious pitfalls if I'd read this book.

I made a couple of calls. It's so much easier to track somebody down when they're pushing their book. The whole business couldn't have taken more than ten minutes. I closed the file and went into my computer, searching through the news wires for the latest on the murder of Elaine York. Police were still questioning her nearest and dearest, always the first port of call in any murder inquiry, as well as conducting a door-to-door search of the neighbourhood.

The guest, Rosalie Redmond, arrived ten minutes before her ten o'clock interview. I made her a cup of coffee and got her settled in the green room. She was attractive, about mid-thirties, slim hips, fair hair cut in a bob. She wore a business suit and carried a briefcase, like she was going to meet her bank manager. I tried the chatty approach, set her at her ease.

'Written many books?'

She turned to me with a look of faint distaste, as if I'd tried to pick her up in a bar. The corners of her mouth squeezed up in what could have been a grimace or a smile.

'Yes, I have, actually.'

Saved by the producer's assistant. Andie Turner rushed in, a trail of papers eddying behind her, grasping her clipboard like it was the last plank on the *Titanic*. She introduced herself to the guest and took

charge, leading her off in the direction of the studio. I
watched them as they were sucked through the sound-
proofed doors. Then I went back to my desk. I could
see I was going to have to work on my manner if I
was going to make a go of this job.

I turned up the volume on the speaker on my desk
and listened to the first two minutes of the interview,
just to see whether Crosbie was following my suggested line of questioning. I needn't have worried. She
treated it as if it were a papal bull and Crosbie were
a Third World Catholic peasant. I went back to my
assignments for the next day's programme. A radical
new eating plan based on the diet of African bushmen,
a dating agency run by clairvoyants (no need for you
to contact them; presumably they would take that all-
important first step for you) and a call to a publicist
handling the latest kiss-and-tell involving a captain of
industry, a customized rubber wetsuit and an
ambitious young bottle-blonde. Despite my enthusiastic intentions, I had the distinct feeling it was going
to be a very long month.

But I had a plan. At lunchtime I went out, grabbing
a sandwich from an Italian coffee shop on the way.

Chapter Seven

Mulberry Avenue, where Elaine York had lived and died, looked different in the daytime. A lot scarier, for one thing. The housing estate loomed like some drunken giant over the neighbourhood, some town planner's idea of a joke against poor people. It was about fifteen storeys high, with two lower wings off each end. There were covered corridors connecting the three structures, the better to do drug deals and ambush terrified residents. It was painted an uninterested shade of blue, and was probably not waiting for *Architectural Digest* to call for a five-page photo spread. A handful of kids of about ten years old – Simon's age – played soccer on the scruffy grass.

I passed a newsagent which had roll-down bars on the front and all the alcohol locked away behind thick glass. I went in for a packet of Camels. An elderly man served me quickly and then turned back to his tiny television.

Elaine's flat was surrounded by police tape. There wasn't much to see. A row of about ten mid-Victorian houses divided into flats. Pioneering yuppies, by the looks of the late-model cars parked on the street. The cars had signs in the windows saying 'No Radio'. This was the sort of neighbourhood where you didn't carry too much cash, and didn't advertise to the world that you were popping out of town for the weekend.

I dug out my notebook and checked the name of the neighbour. Magnolia Trevenet. Her flat was right next door to Elaine's and helpfully had her name written on one of the bells. I pushed the button. No reply. I pushed it again. The voice on the other end sounded tinny and suspicious.

'Yes?'

'Magnolia?'

'Yes.'

'Hi, it's Sam Ridley. I'm from City Radio.'

'Who?'

'Sam Ridley. Wondered if I could have a word with you.'

The buzzer sounded, and I pushed the door open. There was a small, narrow hallway with steps at the end. I climbed up to her flat on the second floor and knocked. The door opened almost immediately. She wore flowing black pants, a top encrusted with silver mosaics and about twenty bangles on each arm. Her hair was long and dark, and pulled back with red velvet. Her lips matched the colour of the velvet. I was in love.

I tried out my best smile. She didn't respond.

'Got any cigarettes?' she asked.

Normally I don't subscribe to chequebook journalism, but this once I made an exception. I fished the packet out of my pocket. She took it.

'Great. Come in.'

She led me into a large, light-flooded living room. The floors were scrubbed, the walls dark blue. It looked like a forgotten wing of the Victoria and Albert

Museum. Plunder from Third World nations. African tribal masks, Asian buddhas, Indian bridal chests, Burmese teak elephants. I sat down on a leopardskin-covered couch.

'Want coffee? Just made some.' Magnolia disappeared into the kitchen, and reappeared carrying two large mugs, and a plate of tea biscuits. An old-fashioned girl.

'Nice place.'

'Thanks.'

'Where'd you get all this stuff?'

She shrugged. 'What? Oh, this . . . ?' She looked around as if seeing it for the first time. 'I dunno. Pappa was a rolling stone.'

She sat on the floor and lit up one of my cigarettes. 'Supposed to be giving up. But with the way things have been, you know.'

I nodded. I couldn't help staring at her. She had blue eyes. Normally I never notice the colour of people's eyes, but the effect was startling with her olive skin and black hair.

'So?'

I realized I was staring. She was looking at me as if I were slightly disturbed. Perhaps I was.

'Sorry. I'm doing a background piece, about Elaine.'

She nodded. 'I've already spoken to the police, and the papers.'

'Were you good friends?'

She shrugged. 'Reasonably.'

'I know her sister slightly. Well, we work together. What's she like?'

'Her sister?'

'No, Elaine.'

'Where did you say you were from again?'

'City Radio. You probably know it.'

'Hmm, I don't think so. Look, I really don't think I can help you. I only know what I told the police.'

I took a swig from my coffee and then lit a cigarette. I'm good at getting people to talk. They see my harmless-looking face and think they can trust me.

'I'm looking for more background. What sort of person was she, what were her interests, what was her life like?'

Magnolia looked at me suspiciously.

'It might help the cops to find who killed her.' Journalists use that line all the time, but she didn't act like she'd heard it before. She stubbed out her half-smoked cigarette and reached for another. The packet lay between us. She lit up, hands shaking. 'She did nothing wrong. She worked hard, took care of her kid, gave money to homeless people. A regular Mother Teresa, fat lot of good it did her.'

She waved the cigarette around, bangles jangling on her arm. 'This city is full of fucking crazies. Three weeks ago some guy tried to mug me in a phone box. Everybody around here gets burgled, cars stolen, you name it, and when do we ever see the police? Never. Until something like this happens. They drone on about how drugs are destroying the inner cities and what do we see them doing about it?'

'Did Elaine do drugs?'

Magnolia snorted. 'Are you kidding? Elaine wouldn't take aspirin for a headache. Half a glass of wine and she was as drunk as a coot.' She stubbed out her cigarette, half-smoked, and took a gulp of coffee.

'What about her boyfriend?'

'What boyfriend? She didn't have one.'

'The papers mentioned something about her boss.'

Magnolia lit another cigarette jerkily. 'Well, needn't tell you that you shouldn't believe everything you read.'

'But she had a child. Presumably there's a father somewhere?'

She regarded me through the smoke. 'What an old-fashioned notion,' she said.

I changed tack. 'How did you happen to find the body?'

'I was passing. Went out for cigarettes. Coming back, I saw the door was open and I went in.'

'What time was that about?'

'About eleven. Look, I've already been over this with the police.'

'You stayed in the flat a long time. Why did you do that?'

Magnolia looked at me a long time before replying. 'I couldn't leave her,' she said finally. 'I felt like a bloody watchdog sitting there, but I had to stay with her. Then the cops arrived and everything.'

'And you ran out?'

Magnolia shuddered. 'Elaine . . . The body . . . It twitched, like she was coming back to life or some-thing. It was hideous.'

When I left I gave Magnolia my card, walked back up to Ladbroke Grove and took a taxi to Tottenham Court Road.

I'd been out of the office for an hour and a half. When I got back Felicia was spoiling for a fight.

'Let me explain the situation to you as simply as I

can,' she said, coming over to my desk as I tried to look as though I'd been installed there for some time.

'You may or may not have guessed that my department is not a cosy club with flexible rules of attendance. We do not take long liquid lunches, because if we do, then someone else has to work even harder on our behalf. Does this make sense to you?'

Now, I'm a long-suffering chap, but Felicia was starting to annoy me. I stood up to face her. With her in her three-inch stilettos, we were about eye to eye.

I smiled in what I hoped was a long-suffering and patient manner. 'Felicia, my love, I know I was technically out of the office, but in spirit I was here. Diligently applying myself to the quotidian needs of *Female AM*.' I flicked out my notebook for added emphasis. 'In other words,' I said, 'I was researching a story.'

'What story? We didn't discuss any story. And don't call me your love.'

She was suspicious, I could sense it. Was I making fun of her? Well, yes and no.

I riffled through some pages in my notebook. 'Like the best ideas, it came to me in the proverbial flash. "We should do something on women's attitudes to violent crime. How they feel about going out at night, living alone, that sort of thing. Tie it into Elaine York's murder." That's what I said to myself.' I paused for effect, and also because I couldn't think of anything to add.

We were still faced off against one another. She hesitated, wondering whether to call my bluff, then thought better of it. It was a good idea, and for spur-of-the-moment inspiration even I had to admit I'd done pretty well.

'C'mon,' I said. 'It'll be great. We'll try and get her sister, Anna, on tape. She hasn't spoken to anyone yet. It'll be exclusive.'

She took a step back, relaxing her stance a little. She turned. 'OK,' she said over her shoulder. 'But no more long lunch breaks. I won't fall for this a second time. And get on with the kiss-and-tell woman.'

Round two to me.

The agent for the kiss-and-tell woman called back. Her confessions were no longer on the open market. She'd signed an exclusive deal with a tabloid news-paper for a frank interview and a two-page photo spread. I went over to Felicia's desk and told her the bad news. She seemed unperturbed. She waved a manicured hand at me.

'Look in the ex-mistresses file. There'll be someone there who can talk about it.'

So I began to plough through the list of women who'd forced politicians' wives the length and breadth of the country to insist that they would stand by their man. I made a few calls. Most of the people I spoke to would only talk for money. City Radio prefers not to pay for its news so we find it hard to compete with some of the television talk shows. Eventually I found a woman who was prepared to come on, because she'd just written a book claiming to revive the old-fashioned art of seduction.

Then I rattled off the bushman diet, the clairvoy-ants and their dates, and pushed the loose ends into Andie's hands. Andie was a bright and energetic Sloane who had forsaken the usual career path of those of her ilk. Most of her contemporaries were working in real estate before snaffling an aristocrat with bad teeth and settling in the shires. Andie had other ideas.

I'd tried it on with her a couple of times, seduced by her lovely legs and short tight skirts, but she didn't seem interested. Perhaps my parents weren't closely enough related for her aristocratic taste.

I found Anna York-Baines' number. She was happy to be interviewed. I arranged to go over to her house at six o'clock.

It seemed that Felicia was warming to my idea about violent crime. She appeared at my desk with a piece of paper while I was putting the finishing touches to my day.

'Andie found this woman,' she said, handing me the note. I looked at the name written on it. Margaret Gabor, 643 Summerhill Estate – the incongruously named housing estate in Elaine York's neighbourhood.

'I'm sure I don't need to tell the station's star police reporter that this place has a bad reputation.'

'No, you don't,' I said. 'The station's star police reporter assumes that Mrs Gabor is probably quite familiar with crime in all its permutations.'

'So go and talk to her. Find out what it's like. Bring me back something juicy we can use.'

I felt a surge of optimism. Up till now *Female AM* had sailed serenely forth under the assumption that its audience only ever encountered violence in the crockery department during the Harrods' sale. Some journalists, including myself, were critical of that kind of bubblegum mentality: Leave it to television to treat people like idiots, we said. Radio has a mission – to inform as well as entertain. Unfortunately, Felicia didn't see it that way at all. Give people what they want, she'd say. Give them fad diets, showbiz gossip and colonic irrigation.

If the programme were ever to be introduced to reality, was not I, Sam Ridley, hardened seeker of truth, just the one to get things rolling? Why not?

I took the underground to Holland Park. Anna York-Baines lived not far from me geographically, but a world away in terms of attitude and financial prospects. Lansdowne Road was a place that spoke, though not in a loud or disagreeable manner, of the ease of living that money brings. The trees are fluffy pastel in the spring, green in the summer. The buildings never lack for paint nor the gardens for professional care. The council had passed a by-law stating that one could only park there if one drove a late-model European automobile.

At least that's what it seemed like.

I rang the bell.

She had a face that could launch a thousand cosmetics campaigns. Perfect features, pale skin, wide-set grey eyes. And red hair. Not the carrot shade that kids in the playground are teased about, but dark red; rich chestnut, old oak dresser, dying autumn leaf. It was all the same length, falling to her shoulders in obediently careless waves, framing high cheekbones and straight teeth.

She wore a pink polo shirt and jeans and sneakers. She looked tired and anxious, but when she saw me she smiled.

'Sam. Come in.'

Chapter Eight

I followed her down a wide corridor and into a conservatory on the upper ground floor. It was paved in
slate and stocked with plants and wicker furniture. A
small child sat on a rug, absorbed in a game involving
a kitchen saucepan and a pair of shoes. She looked up
at me as I sat in a chair, but went back to her game.

Anna sat in a chair opposite me. She put her hand
out to touch the child's golden head. Albion had
inherited her mother's hair.

'Hello, Albion,' I said gently.

She looked up again, first at me and then at Anna.

'Darling, this is Sam. Say "Hello, Sam." '

'Dam,' she said and resumed her game.

'That's how I feel most days,' I said.

I looked at the tiny child, engrossed in her game. I
wanted to pick her up and hug her, tell her that things
would be all right, willing them to be all right for her
little sake.

Somewhere in the house a whistle blew.

'Tea?' asked Anna. I nodded.

A few moments later she was back with a pot and
two mugs, which she set on a side table. She poured
two cups and handed me one.

'I begged Elaine to move away from that place.

Robert and I offered her money to get another flat, but she wouldn't listen. She was so stubborn. The only thing I was able to do was convince her to put bars on her windows.' She sighed again, only it was more of a huff. 'The company was supposed to fit them next week.'

'What have the police told you?'

'Nothing, really. It was an opportunistic burglary. There are no witnesses. Doesn't give me much hope.'

'Have the police spoken to Albion's father?'

'She didn't have a father.'

'The papers mentioned a boyfriend.'

She shook her head. 'I don't know who the father is. She never told us. Some casual sexual encounter, I gather. Really, she could be so exasperating, my sister. I . . . well, we had the classic older-sister–younger-sister relationship. I was the responsible one, always running around after her, picking up the pieces. She didn't care about anything.'

'Except her kid.'

'Albion, of course. And sometimes her work, I think. But even that was only a means to an end. She didn't have any career goals, any firm idea about where she'd like to be, what she'd like to get out of life. From what I could see, she didn't have any goals at all.'

'Were you close?'

'Yes. Our father died when we were young. And being the elder I had to help my mother. I felt – I'd always felt – maternal, protective towards Elaine. I think I kidded myself that she couldn't get by without me. Someone to remind her to pay her council taxes, take the baby for her check-up.'

We fell silent. Then Albion, in the process of waving the saucepan over her head, hit herself in the face with it. She burst into tears. Anna picked her up, cradled her gently, walking around the conservatory. 'It's all right, darling. It's all right,' she murmured. Still picking up the pieces of her younger sister's life.

But it wasn't all right. Albion screamed all the more. 'Mummy, I want my mummy.'

The phone rang. I could hear the bell from another part of the house. Anna looked at me, still jiggling the baby.

'Sod it,' she said. 'Can you watch her for a minute?'

She gave Albion to me. The child screamed louder than ever.

'Sshh, it's OK,' I said, casting around frantically for a toy that would divert her. I put her in the chair and waved a cloth doll.

'What do you think of this, eh? What a pretty dolly.'

Albion bent over till her face was almost touching her knees and she screamed some more, just to let me know what she thought of that proposal.

'OK, kid. So the doll wasn't such a good idea. How about the . . . the . . . puzzle? How about we play with that?' I looked about frantically for the puzzle I'd seen earlier; she must have buried it under something else. I got down on my knees, searched under the chairs, sorted through her toy basket. By the time I'd discovered that the puzzle wasn't in either of those places, Albion had stopped crying. I turned back to see what she was up to. She had spotted my tape recorder sitting on the coffee table and was stabbing ineffectually at the buttons.

Saved by technology. I sat down opposite her.

'Here's some valuable career advice,' I said. 'Never become a journalist. It's a mug's game. You'll die poor and people will hate you.'

Albion pointed at the microphone.

'This is a microphone,' I explained.

'Mifone,' said Albion delightedly.

'That's close enough. Right, when someone puts one of these up to your face, you say, "No comment." Can you say that? No comment.'

'Nocomma,' said Albion. 'Nocomma, nocomma, nocomma.' She snatched the microphone from my hand and stabbed at a few of the buttons on the machine, just for the sheer joy of it.

Anna smiled when she came back into the room and saw the two of us.

'I'll have to have you over more often,' she said.

Chapter Nine

The next morning at the Blue Skies I pondered the menu while Pat tapped her sneakered foot. It was a tough choice, death from hypertension or arteriosclerosis. I needed time.

I chose sausages and scrambled eggs. While I waited for my order to arrive I drank coffee and read the papers.

Afterwards I took the number 23 bus and got off at Ladbroke Grove near the overpass. I then walked a few blocks north to the Summerhill housing estate. I'd made an appointment to see Mrs Margaret Gabor and talk about crime.

I looked around for the main entrance and found two rusty metal doors, leading to a set of three lifts. I leaned on the doors hard to get them open and stumbled inside, gasping at the sharp smell of urine. The walls were painted institutional brown, not that that mattered much, since they'd long since been covered in graffiti. Much of it was obscene. There was broken glass and dog shit on the floor, empty soft drink cans and crack vials. I trod carefully over to the lift bay. The first two I tried weren't working. I got into the third and pushed the button for Margaret Gabor's floor, ten storeys up. The lift showed no signs of obeying the instruction. I pushed the button again, and rattled the control panel. Three teenagers got in just before the doors closed, and we began our shaky ascent.

They were about eighteen or so, and dressed identically in baggy jeans and sweatshirts, woollen hats, and trainers the size of space capsules. The shoes looked brand new, like their owners had just returned from buying them.

'What's that?' The tallest boy, with a lank fringe of black hair, pointed at my tape recorder, an obsolete Marantz, with a smirk. It is about the size of a block of A4 paper. Most radio reporters use smaller machines that do roughly the same job, but I've grown attached to mine. I like the weight of it.

'Back when I was a boy, they called them tape recorders.'

The boys crowded around me. Somehow I didn't think it was because they wanted the benefit of my experience and wisdom. I calculated how much money I had in my wallet; about forty pounds, minus the cost of breakfast. Not too much, but enough. I tried a diversionary tactic.

'I work at City Radio. Perhaps you've heard of it?'

The tall boy sniggered.

'Is that pirate?'

The other two, receiving their cue, sniggered as well. The leader looked at me. I looked right back at him. I suppressed the urge to ask them why they weren't at school.

'Wotcha doing here, then?' said Lank Fringe. 'Nobody comes here, not if they've got any brains.'

'I'm working. What are you doing here, then?'

'Hangin' out,' he said. 'No law against it.' He sounded defensive, as if there was a law prohibiting most of the things he liked to do.

They moved in a little closer, and I thought I heard the sound of a flick knife opening. I angled the tape recorder so that it covered a couple of my vital organs. I had to choose between heart and lungs or liver and kidneys. I shifted my weight, assessing the situation. There was, as the song says, nowhere to run to, nowhere to hide. Just them and me, shuddering upwards towards a confrontation which could only end badly for me.

Chapter Ten

The lift bell dinged, and it sounded as sweet as a celestial choir. The doors opened and a heavy-set middle-aged woman stood outside. She looked hard at the boys. They peeled back to a less threatening formation.

'Mr Ridley?'

I nodded and stepped smartly out of the lift.

'Good. I'm Margaret Gabor.' She led me briskly along a dingy corridor and opened the door into her flat. I looked nervously behind me, but the boys had disappeared. I walked into a tiny hall, with a bathroom off one side and a small living room at the end of it. She told me to sit down while she went through the laborious process of locking the doors. I counted three locks and two slide chains.

There was a small alcove with kitchen things in it, off the living room. What estate agents euphemistically refer to as a galley kitchen. Mrs Gabor turned her attention to making tea. The living room couldn't have been more than ten feet by twelve. There were two sofas facing each other, and a coffee table with a miniature television sitting on a stack of TV guides. On a sideboard stood several photo frames, with mostly wedding photos. One was of a young man in RAF uniform standing beside a Second World War bomber.

Mrs Gabor brought a tray with two cups and a pot of tea. She sat down on the sofa opposite me.

'I waited at the lift for you. There've been several incidents, as the police are so fond of describing them. Are you OK?'

'Young kids these days.'

She began to pour. 'A lot of them are real trouble. What the police refer to as persistent re-offenders. What I refer to as right little bastards. They're using crack, amphetamines, ecstasy, anything they can find to stick up their nostrils or shove down their throats. Its fashionable: all their friends are doing it. Most of the time the lifts don't work it's because the kids in this building have vandalized them, which gives you some idea of how bright they are. The people on this floor are scared to go out. Not just at night – at any time. I've gone to the police, the council. Nobody will do anything. Their parents have no control over them.'

She sighed and offered me a cigarette. I took one and we lit up.

'I've lived here since the sixties. My husband Frank and I, we raised three kids. Not much money, but we did all right. It used to be OK. Drugs changed everything. People deal in broad daylight. Last year it was ecstasy – this year it's crack. It's easier to buy round here than eggs now that most of the shops have packed up and left.'

She held her cigarette out and stared at it, as if seeking the answer in the burning tip. 'I lived through the blitz. I won't have some little creeps getting the better of me. The council could clean this place up.

They won't. The police barely come near it. I've been burgled three times this year; they don't give you the time of day when you report it.'

'Is it possible to move?'

She snorted. 'Do you know how hard it is to get a council flat? And how do I know I won't be exchanging one set of problems for another? No, I'm stuck here, for one reason or another. And I think the problems can be solved. It just requires a little thought, and some political will. That's why I've started this residents' committee – we're going to force the police and council to do something, embarrass the buggers into action. They think because we're poor we don't count. Why should they be raking in their fat salaries while we live in terror and squalor? That's what I want to know.'

We drank some more of her strong tea and spent time going over Mrs Gabor's plan. It was cribbed from a similar scheme which had worked successfully in North London. Change the design of the buildings, eliminate those little nooks and crannies where people can hide. Increase the number of beat bobbies. It seemed sensible and not too expensive. As I discussed the details with Mrs Gabor I felt a little happier being closer to my regular work. I had roughed out a script by the time I got back to the office.

'I can see what you were getting at, Sam, but she's very . . . stoical. I was looking for more . . . raw emotion.' Felicia tapped a pencil against the table she and I were sitting at. We listened to Margaret Gabor's interview together in an edit room. 'I wanted more about how she feels about living in constant fear,' she continued.

'Felicia, the woman is pissed off. That's why she's organizing, getting petitions, bugging the local council. She's mad enough to break someone's head. That's how she feels about it. Would you rather have had her whimpering behind the couch?'

I could see from her look that those were exactly the lines she had been thinking along. 'I wanted more of the frustration, the impotence,' she said, stabbing her pencil on the desk.

I got up. 'Yeah, well, I think she's past frustration and impotence and has moved on to something that might change things.'

I left her in there. She followed me out. People generally don't leave Felicia until she has given the OK. She stood in front of my desk, in her usual pose. Hands on hips, hair flicked smartly back over her shoulder. She wanted to scrap. I usually prefer discretion over valour, but a man must sometimes make a stand, and I don't like being told how to write news.

We stood facing each other off for a moment, mentally rolling up our sleeves, loosening our ties.

'Felicia, can I see you for a sec?'

It was Delaney.

He motioned her into his office. Felicia and I gave each other a look that said 'This isn't over yet' and she followed Delaney.

I took advantage of her absence to go back to the edit booth and cut the story exactly as I had planned to.

But my mutiny was not to go unpunished.

'Here's another one for you. We need her for

tomorrow.' It was later when Felicia handed me an assignment sheet about a woman who had invented a new type of aerobic exercise based on those balloons with handles that kids bounce on.

'Is this a joke?' I said.

'Put a Post-it note on your computer. To remind you that you're on probation,' she said before stalking off.

There was no arguing with her logic. I called the woman, whose name was Mitzy. Not surprisingly, she leapt at the opportunity for some free publicity. I arranged for her to come on the show.

Disheartened, I went home.

I snagged a beer from the fridge and turned the radio on as I prepared a simple meal in my kitchen. The pizza packet said it would take at least twenty minutes to heat from frozen, so I turned the radio on while I waited. City Radio is a twenty-four-hour talk station, which means programming gets a little thin at odd hours. I guess it doesn't really matter at night, because most people are watching TV or eating out or otherwise entertaining themselves. For the twenty people in the city who aren't doing that, calling a radio talk-back show is the next best thing to having a social life of their own.

Since I'm one of that twenty, I listen to it a lot. The only reason I don't call in is there's a company law preventing that sort of thing.

The night-time presenter has a voice like old Scotch and patience that would make Gandhi seem like a spoiled adolescent. The world knows him as Lewis Markham. Round the station we call him Four Balls.

He seems genuinely to like dealing with the bigots, drunkards and half-wits who need to have their say on the airwaves. He's been doing a nightly show for about five years. Mostly the shows are to do with the hot issues of the moment. Tonight it was about violence. Everybody seemed to have a story which illustrated how much nastier London was these days.

My phone rang. It was the former Mrs Ridley. She was mad.

'Have you been putting ideas in Simon's head about coming back to London?' Her voice echoed tinnily over the long-distance line. I could hear the echo and her quite clearly. My ex-wife in stereo.

'Hello, Mary, how are you? Weather OK down there?'

'Don't give me that.'

'Don't give you what?'

'I have a right to be angry with you, Sam.' Mary took a course once on her rights. She's been meticulous about them ever since. 'Don't patronize me. You're making Simon unhappy, putting ideas in his head. He won't settle.'

'Maybe it's because he doesn't want to settle. Maybe he misses his father.'

'Oh, be realistic. What child ever wants to move to a new place? They always get used to it.'

'I didn't put ideas in his head. He called me. You can't stop him from doing that. Or perhaps you can. Why don't you do that, Mary? Let him know what a mean-spirited mother he really has.'

'Just leave him alone. Give him a chance.'

'It's not his chance, it's yours. This was your idea – the new life in the colonies.'

'For God's sake, Sam. What sort of a life did he have with you? You're hardly a role model. You're a child yourself. And that stupid job, away all hours of the day and night.'

I suddenly felt very tired. I wanted to explain to her that Simon and I had been happy together, but I couldn't think how to.

'We were happy together,' I finally said. It didn't sound very convincing, even to me.

But it didn't matter. She had hung up.

I sat down. My neck ached. My lungs ached. There was smoke coming from the kitchen. My pizza. I went into the kitchen, opened the oven, binned the pizza and had myself another beer.

Friday morning I awoke and decided to go to Elaine's funeral. I went through my wardrobe to find my one and only suit, a relic from the days when I'd been a court reporter. It was where I'd left it, at the bottom of the closet, but the white shirt that was its sartorial mate was nowhere to be seen. Having to improvise, I snatched a blue denim shirt from the laundry basket. There was no time for ironing, so I buttoned up the jacket and hoped that my body heat would do the trick. A Windsor-knotted woollen tie completed the ensemble. I was ready to face the day.

I grabbed a coffee on the way to work and drank it on the tube. The coffee spilled on my trousers when the driver made a brisk stop at Paddington, so I wasn't able to make my usual dignified entrance at work. I went straight to the toilets and attempted to rectify the damage with a paper towel and a hot-air dryer.

'You're late again.' Felicia didn't look up as I tried to slip past her desk.

'It took longer than usual to complete my toilet.' I stopped at her desk and tweaked my tie to prove I was telling the truth. 'I'm going to a funeral.'

She looked up. She took in the suit, the rumpled shirt and the damp patch on my trousers. If she was amused, she was too well bred to show it.

She plucked a file out from a stack on her desk. She weighed it in one hand, then held it in front of me.

'What time?'

'What time what?'

'The funeral.'

'Three o'clock.'

'Get on with this until then.' I went to take the file from her, but she didn't let go.

'I'd buy a new shirt. You're not going to a food fight.'

At lunchtime I went to Marks and Spencer and bought a white shirt and, just for the hell of it, a new tie to match.

The reception I received from the females in the office upon my return was more than gratifying. I made a mental note to smarten up my act in the hopes of attracting a winsome woman some time in the future.

They dispatched Elaine York not far from where she'd lived. Kensal Rise Cemetery is a historic place that lies to the north of the Grand Union Canal. It's been a fashionable last port of call for hundreds of years.

I got off the bus at the end of Ladbroke Grove and walked up to the cemetery. It was a cool day, overcast and threatening rain. Other soberly dressed people were arriving at the same time, so I followed them. We walked up the main path to the chapel, a single storey in the neoclassical style. Inside it was gloomy and cold. A couple of bar heaters waged an ineffective battle against the chill, and most people still wore their overcoats.

Anna stood at the door shaking hands. Beside her was the man I took to be her husband, Robert. He was slender, of medium height with straight brown hair. He held the golden-haired cherub, who wriggled and played with the lapel on his expensive suit. Albion didn't appear to remember me from the day I visited her house, but I often have that problem with women. Robert's fine olive skin looked well kept, but he had dark circles under his eyes. He looked worn out. He shook my hand nervously and thanked me for coming.

'Sam, you made it. I'm so glad.' Anna squeezed my elbow. Like her husband, she looked tired. There were small lines around her eyes.

'John Marlowe's here already,' she said. 'He's sitting right over there.' She pointed to the front row. 'Do you want to join him?'

I shook my head. John Marlowe was the executive editor of news and current affairs at City Radio. Away from the workplace, we didn't have much in common.

'We're having a few people to the house afterwards.

Please come,' said Anna before moving off to greet others.

The small chapel was filling up. I saw Magnolia take a seat on the other side of the room. Just before the service was to start, Roger Fitzgerald arrived and stood at the back. I kept my head firmly forward, hoping the suit would be an effective disguise.

The service was to the point. The minister spoke briefly, admitting that he'd never actually met Elaine. A woman read a poem and, at the graveside, helped by Robert, Albion laid a single lily on the coffin. It was over pretty smartly. I couldn't wait to get away.

Judging by the rush for the gates, a lot of people felt the same.

I could see Roger Fitzgerald talking to Anna and Robert. I slipped quickly past.

Magnolia's dark curls were in front of me. She wore a crimson overcoat and a long black scarf with bright embroidery. She exchanged a few words with a thin, dark-haired man in a charcoal-grey suit, then he moved on ahead. When I got to the cemetery gates, he was clipping his trouser legs and climbing on to a bicycle.

Magnolia was waiting for me.

The man on the bicycle departed with a brief wave of the hand. Magnolia didn't wave back.

'Who's he?' I asked.

She shrugged. 'Mark Matheson. Elaine's boss. I'm counting on you having a fag.' I excavated my pockets and handed her the packet. She took two and lit them, handing one to me. Fat silver bracelets clanked on her arm. I wondered if she bought them by the yard.

Mourners flowed past us, got into cars, hailed taxis, and walked off down Harrow Road. The rain held off.

'God, I need a drink. Going to the wake?' Magnolia dropped the cigarette into the gravel and ground it with a black-booted foot.

Chapter Eleven

We caught a taxi on the Harrow Road, directing the driver to Holland Park.

At Anna and Robert's house a man in a black uniform stepped forward to relieve us of our overcoats and to direct us through to the drawing room.

I hadn't seen this room on my last visit. It was an impressive space with large French windows leading on to a private garden, and beyond that a larger communal garden. Real art hung on the walls and the furniture looked like the sort I only ever see in BBC costume dramas. The floors were burnished hardwood, covered here and there by extravagantly designed oriental rugs. Waiters circulated with dainty food and wine on trays. A few guests stood about uncomfortably. Anna and Robert hadn't yet arrived.

'I really need that drink,' Magnolia muttered and disappeared in the direction of the wine. I looked out of the windows. The communal garden was calling last orders on autumn. In the centre a solitary leaf clung to a tree. Down below, a gardener raked up the rebel leaf's companions and fed them to a bonfire. I opened the door slightly and the most evocative smell in the world floated into the room.

'I've seen two foxes in the last month.'

I turned to see a frail elderly woman standing at my shoulder. She was tall, with wiry grey hair. She was dressed in the uniform of her generation, a twinset and tweed. She must be Anna and Elaine's mother. The resemblance to Anna, especially, was startling. The same high cheekbones and grey eyes.

'Their numbers are on the increase. That's what I've read. People used to trap them, now they feed them.' Her hand shook slightly as she raised a cup of tea to her mouth. She looked faded, as though the effort of producing two daughters so beautiful had cost her her own looks.

'Mrs York?'

She nodded and took another shaky sip of tea. I introduced myself.

'Did you know Elaine?' she said finally.

'No,' I said. 'But I work with Anna.'

'Grandma!' Albion came hurtling towards Mrs York. She handed her teacup to me, so she could pick her grandchild up.

I stood beside her while she amused the child by pointing things out to her in the garden.

'Look, there's a nice big tree for you to play on. Won't that be fun? And when you get bigger you'll be able to ride your bicycle on the grass. You have a nice big park here, all to yourself. And I bet there's lots of lovely children to play with round here. And you know what? Grandma lives just on the other side of the garden.'

Albion, her attention span exhausted, wriggled to be let down. She dived into the crowd.

I gave Mrs York her cup back.

'A mind of her own and Elaine did spoil her rotten. I saw her falling into the same traps I did after my husband died. Your kids are all you've got so you want them to be everything to you – partner and friend. It makes them old before their time, that's what I learnt with my girls. Still,' she said. 'That's not Albion's problem now, is it? She'll grieve for her mother for the rest of her life because she never knew her.'

Robert had come up beside Mrs York. He put a gentle arm around her. She clutched his hand for a moment, a look of panic in her eyes, then she drew a deep breath.

'OK?'

'I'm OK,' she said. 'We were discussing foxes.'

All of a sudden Albion was back, clamouring for Robert to pick her up. He did so.

'I'm sorry,' he said, turning to me, and clasping Albion's foot to stop her aiming it at his elbow. 'You're from the radio station, aren't you?'

I told him my name again. Then we stood there like a couple of wallies. I'm not much good at small talk at the best of times and I couldn't think of anything even faintly appropriate to say.

'You know what?' he said. 'I can't wait for this to be over. We don't do emotion very well, this family. My side, especially.' He nodded at a stiffly dressed couple across the room. 'Lots of training for the "put up or shut up" side of things, of course. We're experts at that. But when something senseless and stupid and . . . and . . . unfair comes along, we just don't know what to do. Pour another sherry. Shake one's head. Go on about what a tiresome place the world has become. Explain to all who will listen that civilization as we know it has gone to the dogs. That we can do. Care for some wine?' Juggling Albion in one arm, he grabbed a glass from a passing tray. Handed it to me.

'You mustn't be too hard on yourself, dear,' said Mrs York. 'We none of us knows what to do.'

'Maybe we should have hired mourners,' said Robert, who'd put Albion down. 'Women in black whose job it is to weep and wail and express how shitty we all feel.'

Mrs York put a hand on his arm. 'It wouldn't bring her back, dear,' she said soothingly. 'And you know how she hated anyone making a fuss over her.'

They drifted away to talk to other guests. Magnolia came over. I told her about Mrs York.

'Amazing old thing,' she said. 'Her husband died, she raised the kids single handed. Cleaned, took in sewing so they could go to good schools. Worked like a slave all her life. She used to babysit Albion so Elaine could go to work.'

Across the room I spied Mark Matheson telling what looked like an amusing story to the woman who'd read the poem at the service. He gesticulated extravagantly and she laughed, but with one arm across her waist and her hand to her mouth, as though it wasn't an appropriate thing to do at a funeral.

'I read about his organization,' I said to Magnolia. She followed my gaze across the room, looked back at me and her lip curled.

'What's the matter?' I said. 'You don't believe in worthwhile causes?'

'No,' she said. 'Do you?'

'If I did, it's so long ago I've forgotten what they were.'

Mark was still talking, leaning into the woman, and lightly touching her elbow. She didn't look like she was too upset with the situation.

'Was he Elaine's boyfriend?'

Magnolia appeared to be staring off into the middle distance. She brought herself back.

'It was more subtle than that. She played Mary Magdalene to his Jesus.'

'What do you mean?'

'Haven't you ever read the Bible? You should. It's full of great stuff about long-suffering girlies.' She looked across the room to Mark and then back at me, but when she spoke her voice was distracted. 'You've got this guy that's going to save the world. He's good-looking, smart, charismatic and well connected. He could be doing anything he wanted. But he's decided to save the planet. So he gathers his disciples around him, and off they go to do good. And the strange thing is, they succeed. So they love him even more. They worship him.'

'You don't approve?'

'I didn't say that.'

'But you're cynical.'

She raised one eyebrow. 'You don't say?'

'The papers implied Mark was Albion's father. Is that true?'

Magnolia finished her wine. She held the glass delicately by its stem. 'You never stop asking questions, do you?' she said, moving off.

I decided it was time to go. I had to get back to work for an interview with a fashion writer about why hemlines no longer have any direct bearing on the state of the economy. I said my goodbyes and took a taxi to the office.

*

'Ralph called,' said Lyall. I was sitting on his desk. Lyall was editing copy while I told him about the funeral. I'd settled the hemline question and Felicia, for once, was happy.

'He's confessed?' It wasn't really a question. Ralph was City Radio's self-appointed scapegoat. We kept a scoreboard of the crimes he'd owned up to. There were at least a dozen in this lifetime, and a couple of criminal masterminds in history that he believed himself to be reincarnations of. Murders were his favourite, but he also liked to own the odd armed robbery, or kidnapping, just for variety.

Lyall finished marking the sheets and left them in a neat pile on the top-left-hand side of his desk for the newsreader to collect. He started on a stack of wire copy. Shuffling it like the old cardsharp that he is.

'Sam, baby.' Rick Brittan stepped smartly into our line of vision. Teeth and cufflinks flashing. Full of the joy of life.

'Rick. Don't you look good.'

'How was the funeral? I couldn't make it, you know. Something big. A bank heist in Peckham.'

I studied my fingernails, casual-like. 'Yes, I did hear something about that. On the BBC, I think.' I'd actually heard it from Lyall, but the rules of fair play don't apply with Rick.

He avoided answering that. He looked at Lyall. 'I'll have something for seven,' and he hurried off to his desk, a man with a mission.

'Seven?' I said. 'What's his family motto? Better late than never?'

Lyall typed calmly. Sometimes the Dalai Lama calls him for advice on how to control his temper.

'Haircut,' he said. 'He was at Vidal Sassoon. For two hours.'

'Oh well,' I said. 'It's probably one of those expensive cuts that last a long time. You know, keeps its shape as it grows out.'

'Yeah,' he said. 'Probably.'

I looked through the copy that Lyall had edited. Elaine's murder had slipped down the priority scale. The police were planning a reconstruction of her last evening alive, when she'd walked a few blocks to a local restaurant for dinner with Mark, to see if it jogged any memories. But so far it seemed that the interviews, public appeals and house-to-house searches had produced a big fat nothing. There was a soundbite with Detective Inspector Roger Fitzgerald saying as much.

I collected my things and got ready to go home. The evening yawned ahead of me. I would forgo my usual range of exciting social options of either drinking at the pub or alone at my flat, I decided. Instead I would force my presence on someone who didn't want to see me.

Chapter Twelve

I found Detective Inspector Charlie Hobbs at his local.

'Bloody Ridley,' he said. 'Do I have to die to be rid of you?'

'Good to see you too, Charlie.' I brought two pints over to the corner table where he sat. And I produced a pack of cards. Nothing like some light recreation to take a chap's mind off his troubles.

'Gin rummy?' I enquired as I shuffled. It's the only card game I can ever remember the rules to, mainly because it's one of Simon's favourites.

'Fuck off,' he said. 'I play poker.'

'Gin rummy's more restful.'

'I'm quite rested,' he said.

I took no notice.

Resigned, he reached for the cards I handed him. I told Charlie about Fitzgerald roughing me up.

'He's a mad bugger,' Charlie said.

'Thank you for your kind expression of sympathy. What should I do to get even with the bastard?'

Charlie deftly rearranged his cards. He had an evil gleam in his eye.

'It's your own fault. Keep out of his way,' he said.

'I was thinking more along the lines of a Stinger missile attack,' I said.

'Pretend it never happened,' said Charlie. 'He's mean. The reason he can afford to be mean is because he's politically astute. He's mates with the big bosses, gives them the secret handshake that gets them so excited. Their wives have tea together, their kids go to each other's birthday parties. Trust me on this. If you go after him you won't win. And even if you did he'd make you pretty fucking sorry. Gin.'

He laid out the cards on the sticky table in front of us. 'Besides, Ridley, you started it. Can you blame him that he's pissed off? I'd be pissed off if you—'

'Yeah, yeah,' I said. I knew which direction the conversation was heading, and I didn't want to go with it.

'It's your own bloody fault,' Charlie went on. He liked saying those words, I could tell.

I put my cards down. I sighed. 'I didn't start it, Charlie. How many times do I have to tell you?'

'Well, if you didn't start it, then who was the stupid fuck who slept with his wife?' Charlie smirked.

'His ex-wife, Charlie. When I met her she was his ex-wife.'

Charlie snickered while he arranged his cards.

'She didn't even let on who she was married to. Who she *used* to be married to,' I said. 'I didn't know.'

Charlie laughed some more. 'Just your bad luck they decided to get back together. A regular Burton and Taylor, Fitzgerald and his missus.'

I didn't want to talk about it. I still felt a shameful wrench in my gut whenever I thought about me and

Mrs Fitzgerald. We met at a party given by mutual friends. She was a ditzy blonde with a loud laugh and great legs. I was blinded by lust and loneliness. The Fitzgeralds were divorced by that stage, but none of my so-called friends told me who she was divorced from, and neither did she. I don't know, maybe it slipped her mind.

You couldn't have called it a romance, really. We went out a couple of times, we stayed in a few more times than that. Then, for no particular reason that I could see, she got all nostalgic for married life. She went back to her husband and told him what a naughty girl she'd been. Detective Inspector Fitzgerald didn't find it the slightest bit funny. He even came around to my flat to explain to me how unamusing it was, from his point of view. He was sure I understood his position. I told him that I did understand, I was an understanding sort of chap, and he could be reliably assured that I would never make the same mistake again. Not my finest hour.

I changed the subject. 'So what's the story with Elaine York?'

'I'm off the case,' he said.

'So am I. What have you heard?'

'Big pressure to bag someone. Big pressure.' Charlie frowned over his cards.

'Robert Baines – the brother-in-law – is a lawyer, works for his father. His father plays golf with the commissioner. His father's on the phone to the commissioner every bloody day. So far, nothing. No witnesses, that's the problem. Nobody saw a bloody thing. And no weapon.'

He laid down another winning hand. Then a few more.

'Call again,' Charlie said as I left.

I went home. It was too early to call Australia, so I poured myself a stiff Scotch and found a paper and pen. I would write to my son.

After that, it was the weekend. I did the usual chores, visited my usual pub and watched the usual amount of television. Just for old times' sake I went to a shoot-'em-up movie, the sort that Simon and I used to go to with fifty other screaming ten-year-olds. The plot was ridiculous and instantly forgettable, but I imagined that he would have liked it. When I got home I called Australia, but the answer machine message said they had gone away for the weekend.

Monday was a good day for *Female AM*. The day when a royal scandal breaks is always a good day for the media. I know there are people who say we should get rid of the royal family. It's not healthy, this obsession with people who're only in the job because of institutionalized nepotism. But hell, I say as long as they're providing entertainment for our taxes, we should keep 'em. Sure, it's not quite as cheap as a ticket to the movies, but I'd say in sheer humour-value for money we do pretty well.

I was more or less usefully employed, what with lining up Royal Marriage experts, Royal Marital Discord experts, Royal Divorce experts and the like. The day was over before I knew it.

On the way home I bought another frozen pizza. As soon as I got in I heated it up and ate it in front of the evening news. There was a story about Elaine, which reminded me that *Crimewatch* was planning a re-enactment of her last hours tonight.

I was curious and idle, so I went along.

Chapter Thirteen

It was a cold night but death is a big crowd puller. Police officers, television crews and rubber-necking locals gathered around the brasserie where Elaine had eaten her last meal with Mark. The television lights made it as bright as day. We watched a couple sitting at a table in the window; the people they had chosen to stand in for Mark and Elaine. They chatted casually and sipped wine, apparently not noticing the crowd that stared at them from outside.

A blonde policewoman stood in for Elaine. She wore the same clothes; black dress, black high heels. Her overcoat was dark grey. She was about the same age and build, but not nearly as attractive, judging from the photos of Elaine published in the newspapers. The restaurant was at Notting Hill. It had floor-to-ceiling glass windows fronting on to a busy street. Dining à la fishbowl. The cop who was Mark's stand-in arrived late, just as he had done that night. Elaine had sat for ten minutes on her own, toying with a glass of wine.

Dinner took maybe an hour. Short, really. They ate spaghetti and clams and afterwards said a brief goodbye on the street. She walked down Portobello Road. He turned in the opposite direction and unchained his bicycle from a nearby stand.

The policewoman walked steadily down Portobello Road, turning left towards Ladbroke Grove. On Ladbroke, she walked a few blocks and turned left again. Here the trees and pretty houses give way to no trees and concrete public housing. She took a couple more turns and wound up on Mulberry Avenue. Outside Elaine's flat more television people fussed over expensive equipment. They'd erected barriers so that locals didn't inadvertently get into the shot.

A crew filmed from the wide bay windowsill while Elaine's stand-in fumbled with the combination lock on her front gate. It opened with a rusty screech and she went down about three steps and along the path to her front door. She let herself into the flat.

Then she had to come out and do exactly the same thing so the camera could capture her from a different angle. I watched for a bit, but I was cold and ready for a good malt. I wasn't learning anything so there didn't seem any point in putting that drink off. I headed home.

I saw her as I turned. She was standing on the same side of the road as I was, staring at the police officer who was standing in for Elaine. She wore a well-made wool coat and had wrapped a scarf around her head to guard against the cold. Her face was curiously expressionless, as though she'd just passed by coincidentally.

'Mrs York?'

She didn't move. Her cheeks were bright red with the cold. I said her name again, louder. She turned in the direction of my voice. Her eyes were lost in their own depths, then she focused and saw me.

'I'm Sam Ridley. We met at Anna's house the day of the funeral.'

In an instant she collected herself. 'I remember you, Mr Ridley. It's rather brisk out this evening, isn't it?'

'Perhaps you'd like to walk with me for a while.' I offered her my arm and she took it.

'They're going to put this on the television, aren't they?' she asked.

'The more people who see it, the more chance that someone will come forward to help.'

I offered to walk her all the way home, and she seemed relieved. 'It's not safe these days,' she said, taking my arm. 'Not safe at all. Elaine didn't walk out on her own. She didn't like the dark. She'd been that way since she was a little girl. Her imagination was always too vivid.'

'Why do you think she walked home alone that night, then?'

She didn't answer me for such a long time that I thought she hadn't heard. Then, just as I was about to repeat the question, she said, 'I don't know. Perhaps she didn't have the money for a taxi. She didn't have a great deal of money, ever. I tried my best, you know. I worked hard to educate my girls so they wouldn't ever be in the same situation I was placed in when my husband died. Financial independence, I drummed it into them. I wanted their lives to be easier than mine. But what child ever listens to its parents? Elaine didn't care about money or security.'

Our breath hung in front of us as we walked up

Ladbroke Grove. The pubs were closing and the take-away bars were doing a brisk trade. People, mostly men, stood in small groups eating smelly kebabs and fish and chips.

Mrs York walked slowly. At one stage I offered to get her a taxi, but she refused.

'She never gave me a moment's trouble, you know,' she said.

'Elaine?'

'She was a good girl. They both were. I was very lucky with my two girls. Elaine was bright. She could have done anything she wanted. A natural academic. She went to a very good school as a scholarship student. She even skipped a year, she was that clever. Maths, physics, English, she was good at everything. I had scraped the money together for Anna, but Elaine got in on a scholarship – flew in – and came top of her class every year. I was so proud. I gave her a brooch which belonged to my mother. Elaine was so thrilled. She took after my mother. They were both gifted.'

As suddenly as she began, Mrs York lapsed into silence. I couldn't think of any words of comfort. I don't believe there are any for a parent who has lost a child.

We crested Notting Hill and she indicated a driveway. The house was tall, and painted in white stucco. There were five names on the entry buzzers; hers was second from the bottom. The tall, stuccoed building looked solid and reassuring. And there were geraniums in the windowboxes.

'You have a lovely home,' I said as she searched for her keys.

'Yes, isn't it? Anna and Robert bought it for me, so I could be near them. We live on the same garden, on opposite sides. I've been lucky, Mr Ridley. My family hasn't forgotten me. I know that often happens to old people.'

She fumbled with the lock, the cold making her hands unco-operative.

'Won't you stay for tea?' she asked when the bolt slid back.

'Frances, hi.'

Behind us, Robert lumbered up the steps with a brick of water bottles in one hand, his briefcase in the other.

'Brought your water,' he said, puffing. 'Sorry I'm a bit late. Work, as always. It never lets up.'

'Robert brings me my mineral water,' Mrs York explained as we trooped inside. 'It's a terrible extravagance but I can't bear the tap stuff. The smell puts me off. Care for tea?' she asked Robert.

'Thanks,' he said. 'I'll ring Anna and let her know I'm here.'

Mrs York brought tea while he spoke to Anna on the phone.

We chatted for half an hour or so about the weather, Mrs York's cut lilies (another of Robert's delivery services), property prices on the communal garden and the timetable for spring planting. Elaine wasn't mentioned once, but she lingered in the air like the fragrance from the lilies.

After my third cup of tea I made my excuses and left. Robert wasn't far behind me.

'She went to the police thing, didn't she?'

I nodded. 'That's where I saw her.'

'Her doctor didn't think it was wise. But then she's never exactly been any good at following orders. It's a trait that runs in the family.' He pushed his hair back nervously and laughed. 'I'm surrounded by women who're used to getting their own way.'

'Maybe it helped her to try and make sense of things.'

'Maybe,' he said.

I got to work early the next day. Felicia wanted me to follow up on a survey which had been commissioned by a women's magazine. It had found that, given a choice of women, men tend to prefer blondes with big breasts. For once, she had my complete attention.

'Someone paid money to find this out?' Lyall asked, when I told him my enviable task for the day. We were drinking our morning cups of heart-starter at his desk.

The phone rang. Lyall picked it up. He handed me the receiver.

'That Ripley?'

'Ridley,' I corrected automatically.

The voice on the other end was male. It sounded purposefully gruff.

'I wanna talk to you.'

'And so you are, my friend.' I was in an expansive mood. 'Who's speaking?' I made a face at Lyall.

'I got information.'

'And what is the nature of your expertise?'

''Bout the girl who got killed the other night. I know sumfing about it.'

Chapter Fourteen

I scrabbled around in the clutter on Lyall's desk for a pen.

'You mean Elaine York.'

'Yeah.'

'What's your story?' I said as Lyall handed me a biro.

'I seen sumfing. That night. I were there. Then I heard there's a reward. They said on the radio there's a reward.'

'Well, if you were a witness, then you should call the police. I have the phone number here, if you need it.'

'No!' The voice became sharp and went up a couple of octaves. 'I wanna talk to you and no one else. Don't bring anyone with you.'

He told me to wait for him at Boxley Green at eight o'clock. I said I'd be there.

'How did you get my name?' I asked.

'I seen you around,' he said.

The line went dead. I filled Lyall in on the mystery caller.

'Don't go,' he said, inspecting the bottom of his coffee cup.

'Why not?' I was forming a plan.

Lyall leaned forward on his desk. He looked very patient, like he was explaining something to one of his kids. 'He won't show up. He's a very sad bloke who needs attention that only a trained professional can administer. Besides,' he said, with a gleam in his eye, 'if he's truly dangerous why not send Rick?'

But I've had lots of practice at ignoring Lyall's good advice. And a plan was taking shape. It involved a scoop. A sensational, enviable investigative piece of journalism that would expel me from *Female AM* faster than you could mumble 'washed-up old hack'. I'd had a lucky break – a source with a hot tip – and now it was up to me to make the most of it. Reinstatement in my previous position, the keys to the city and an OBE were probably on the cards as well.

At home I showered and considered my wardrobe. It's fair to say that I'm not exactly cruising the cutting edge of fashion. I own too many things that are brown and corduroy. I had even owned a corduroy suit once, but it disappeared under mysterious circumstances. I suspect that Mary donated it to Oxfam, but we were having so many other problems at the time it seemed churlish to bring it up. Now I'm just happy if I've got something to put on that's clean and has the correct number of buttons. As it happened, there were a couple of things that fitted those requirements. I put them on, and shoved a load of dirty stuff in the washing machine for good measure.

I had an hour to kill, so I went to a restaurant on All Saints Road for an expensive hamburger and a designer beer. The place was full to overflowing with young things talking about their documentary proposals. At 7.55 I left and walked down to Boxley Green.

During the day the green is a funky place. It's surrounded by shops selling crystals and incense and healthy bread. In the middle of the green, which is mostly covered with concrete, there are stalls selling a lot of second-hand junk that tourists seem to really go for. At night it takes on a more businesslike air, when smaller packages are exchanged for larger amounts of money.

There were a couple of chaps hanging around, hands in pockets, casual-like. And me. They looked lazily at me, but didn't catch my eye. A young couple walked briskly through, eyes front, on their way to a dinner party by the looks of things. He carried a bottle of wine in a plastic bag. I looked out of place. I felt out of place. I sat down on a bench and checked my watch. Exactly eight o'clock. There didn't seem to be anyone there who wanted to meet me unless the transaction involved chemicals and money. I smoked a cigarette, and then another. People stared at me, but not for the right reason. I practised my air of nonchalance.

At eight twenty my putative informant still hadn't arrived. At eight thirty, cursing my gullibility, I gave up. I went to my local for a couple of beers and went home. Back in the days when I had real news stories to deal with, I would have been more discriminating. The guy hadn't even told me his name.

I checked the answer machine but Simon hadn't called. I remembered that I hadn't posted the letter I'd written him. It stared accusingly at me from the mantelpiece. Then I opened another beer, sat on the couch and watched the local TV news, which is kind of a hobby of mine. The lead item this night was traffic chaos in London – a big surprise, that one. We looked at a shaky grey and white photo of the traffic going nowhere, which is the usual state of affairs in this town. Then a pert blonde popped up to tell that exact same information all over again. I didn't mind; she was cute. Good teeth, just the right amount of cleavage.

I hoped Simon wasn't watching too much television in Australia. He'd need his brain for later on in life.

I sat through a couple of other stories, one of them involving a 'major disaster' and the other a fire in which a building was 'razed to the ground' and I fondly recalled the days when sub-editors didn't stand for that sort of thing. Frank Spring, an old editor I used to work with back in the days before indoor plumbing, when I was just a stripling in the news business, was rather prickly about abuse of the English language. 'Ever heard of a murder that wasn't brutal?' he would shriek as he ripped some poor sod's copy to shreds, usually mine. He loved words and it genuinely grieved him to hear reporters using expressions like 'at this moment in time', and 'emergency situation'. I learned a thing or two from Frank, including how to drink.

The next story on the evening bulletin was more interesting. Several members of Roadblock were in jail following a small misunderstanding with some drivers from the Solomon Construction company. TV crews had been on hand to record the event, which involved protesters lying in front of bulldozers and chaining themselves to trees. The construction workers, who were in line for fat bonuses if they got the work done quickly, were upset at the disruption to their working day, and got down out of their machines to kick a few kidneys. The protesters' avowed commitment to non-violent means of demonstration became a bit strained at that point, and a pitched battle was in swing when the police arrived. I watched Home County grannies and Rastafarians alike being loaded into paddy wagons. Say what you like about Roadblock; it has a broad socio-economic catchment. Then the newsreader popped back up to say that the government was soon to release a white paper which would outline its roads policy for the next few years. All the indications were that lots more roads were about to be built. A nice clean-cut Roadblock spokesman said they would fight them on the footpaths, or some such thing.

He looked familiar. The font told me that his name was Mark Matheson. And I remembered that I'd seen him at Elaine's funeral.

'He didn't show up. I'm stunned.' Lyall's fingers moved swiftly over the keyboard. He didn't take his eyes off the computer screen.

It was the next day and I was filling him in on my evening: the one where I didn't meet an informant with a scoop that would jet-propel my career back into its rightful orbit.

'You were right,' I said at the end of my sad tale.

'I'm seldom if ever wrong,' he said, typing busily.

'I'll let you know when God's job falls vacant,' I said, picking up my coffee and my *Female AM* assignment.

Chapter Fifteen

'When did you first realize that you had a serious caffeine addiction?'

Jenny Lionels pretended to consider the question. She paused, she pondered. She'd answered it a thousand times before.

'I guess a couple of years after I was first married. One day my neighbour came over for a drink and a chat, and it was two o'clock and I realized I'd already had five cups that day.'

It was afternoon, we were in one of the smaller studios and Ms Lionels was flogging her book *Caffeine – How to Beat It*. I was bored. I needed a cup of coffee. I wanted my real job back. Real stories to write, real issues to wrestle with. Back in the newsroom, I collapsed next to Lyall.

'How was it?' he asked.

'She had a problem.'

'Of course she had a problem. That's the only way to get on *Female AM*.'

'She drank more than five cups of coffee a day,' I continued.

'She what?' Lyall stopped typing.

'Sometimes drank six cups a day. On a bad day she could suck down seven.'

Lyall was silent for a bit. Then: 'Did you tell her we drink that much by mid-morning?'

'No,' I said. 'I didn't want to upset her.'

Back at my desk, and in a melancholy mood, I leafed through the pile of assignments that Felicia had lined up for me. I toyed with the idea of dropping them all in the bin. I held them all up together and wondered if they'd fall at the same speed.

I thought about making calls. I didn't have anyone to call. I leafed through a pile of papers on my desk. Again.

Felicia waved me over. She seemed calmer than usual. I smiled in my winsome way. She waved at me to sit down while she finished a conversation with the telephone receiver.

'Yeah, it is a good idea. No, it wasn't mine. Sam's. Sam Ridley. Yeah, I'll keep you posted.' She put the phone down.

'Marlowe,' she said by way of explanation.

John Marlowe was the executive editor in charge of news and current affairs programming, which made him boss of both Felicia and me.

'Thanks for the good word,' I said.

'I didn't do it for you. I did it for me, Ridley. The sooner you're redeemed in the eyes of management, the sooner you move back to news, the happier we'll all be.'

There are days when I think having a thick skin is the most blessed of traits.

Felicia rubbed her eyes, then carefully ran the side of her little finger under her lower lids to remove any smudges of mascara. She looked done in. There was a coffee stain on the sleeve of her shirt.

'We're going to do a whole show based on your idea. It's topical and the guys upstairs like it. We'll have precut packages, studio interviews and a phone-in.'

A whole show based on my idea. I nodded. Made sure she saw me looking unassuming and modest.

'Anna Baines has agreed to take part. Marlowe called her. She wants to do something, so we're giving her the phone-in.'

'That's crazy.'

'That's what I said. But she thinks it'll mean more publicity, and the more publicity the better chance the police will have of finding whoever did her sister in. And it's probably better for her than sitting around at home.'

I looked unconvinced.

'That's what she said.' Felicia gathered some papers together and sorted them into a neat pile. 'The guys upstairs loved the idea.'

Anna came into the office the next day. She had Albion in tow. A woolly-hatted cherub with a backpack instead of wings. Felicia and Andie went all gooey. They oohed and aahed and spoke to the child as if she were some kind of moron.

I waved to her from across the newsroom.

Today she remembered me. 'Dam!' she said, and came tottering over to show me her latest toy. I put her on my knee while she bashed away on my computer keyboard, gabbling in her own language.

The *Female AM* staff packed into Delaney's office for a planning meeting. The special programme would generate quite a lot of publicity for the station, so that meant the marketing department as well as the editorial people needed to be involved. As everyone knew, the station was up for franchise renewal. We had to be seen to be doing our bit to serve the community.

I didn't want to be involved in the middle-management posturing. I told Felicia I would look after Albion and man the phones, and she could brief me afterwards. She agreed. Albion discovered my telephone. She was delighted when it rang. She put out her chubby hand to answer it. I gently disengaged the receiver from her, which she didn't like at all. She scrambled down off my knee and went in search of some other sucker.

'That Ridley?'

'That's Mr Ridley to you.'

'Yeah, I called before. We talked about the girl.'

Chapter Sixteen

I have a clever little device which allows me to record phone conversations. I switched it on.

'Right, the man who doesn't keep his appointments.'

'Yeah, got tied up. Got called away on business. Heh heh.'

'Well, it must be wonderful to be in such demand. Why are you bothering me if your commitments are so pressing?'

There was a brief silence.

'There's a reward, innit? I seen sumfing, so I want the money.'

'But you can't have the money if you don't give the police the information. That's the way rewards work.'

There was another silence. It was apparent that Einstein's reputation was secure in the face of any assault from my informant.

'I need the money.'

'What is it that you saw?'

The sound of heavy thinking. Then the sound of a pay phone running out of change and the frantic search for another coin to feed it with.

'So, Mr er . . .'

'Shark.'

Shark? Oh, Jesus. The levers began to fall into place. There are times when I'm not the brightest light on the block. I think it's the alcohol. But finally I was up to speed on this one. The explanation was simple. My anonymous informant was one of my esteemed colleagues having a jolly wheeze at my expense. It didn't take too much imagination to put the face of Rick Brittan to the voice. The enthusiasm for hoax calls waxes and wanes in our office, but there's no doubt that if it ever became a competition sport we could field an Olympic-strength team.

'Yeah, right,' I said.

'So meet me tonight.'

'Sure,' I said. 'A little dinner, a little dancing. And then, well, who knows what might happen?'

'What?'

'Pick you up at eight,' I said, and put the phone down.

A wave of power perfume overwhelmed me from behind. It was Crosbie Shaw. She carried bags which bore the names of Bond Street shops, and her hair was standing up in such an improbable way that it looked like she'd been styled by a hairdresser who bore her a deep and long-standing grudge. She stood in front of my desk.

'My God,' she said. 'Has the meeting started without me?' It was a rhetorical question. There's no early or even on-time on Planet Crosbie, just varying degrees of lateness.

I looked at my watch. 'You're a little late, but only fashionably so.'

She groaned, dumped the bags at her desk and dashed off.

I was sitting on Rick's desk when he came back. It's the neatest desk in the whole newsroom. Some would say obsessively neat, but I'm not one of them.

I flicked the tape down. I sighed.

'Rick, Rick. What shall we do with you?'

He looked up in a puzzled manner, then he smiled like a weasel. 'Why, Sam, whatever do you mean?'

'Being a police reporter is supposed to keep you busy.'

'Oh, but it does, old thing.'

'So why, Rick?'

'Why what?'

'This.' I indicated the tape.

He looked at the tape, looked back at me, then he smiled like he was trying for the Clark Gable look. 'My dear chap, do make your meaning clear.'

That guy. Should have been on stage. I sighed once more for effect and shook my head a couple of times. Then I went to rescue Albion from one of the sub-editors, from whom I feared she must have been gleaning bad habits.

The 'Women and Violence' special, scheduled for the following Monday, was gathering the momentum of a speeding Royal Mail delivery van. After Anna had collected Albion and left, I went over to Felicia's desk to offer assistance. She was, as usual, on the phone. I waited till she got off.

'Set up the studio discussion – Margaret Gabor takes on the council and the police. What are they going to do about Summerhill? How many more people have to die before they tackle the problem? Et cetera. I want you to get the bums on seats, and do background for Crosbie, who'll chair it.' Felicia moved yet more piles of paper off her desk and into my hands.

I made calls all afternoon. The police offered to send their community liaison officer. I held out for someone of a higher rank. The council volunteered their deputy mayor, an energetic young thing most anxious for re-election on his law and order plank. I accepted. Then I called Margaret to see if she wanted to bite some official legs.

'God bless you,' she said. 'At last someone is taking some notice.'

On Friday night I went to the pub and surveyed the wreckage of my week. On Saturday I did my laundry. It didn't take up as much time as I'd planned. I was devising another way to camouflage the emptiness of my weekend when the phone rang.

'Sam?'

'The same.'

'Hi, it's Anna.'

In the background I could hear a small voice squeaking, 'Dam, Dam, wanna talk to Dam.' Then Anna: 'You're flavour of the month here. Can you talk to her for a minute? Otherwise she won't shut up.'

'Sure.'

I heard the sound of childish breathing. 'Hi, Albion, how's it going?'

There was a small silence, then a giggle. I tried again. 'Albion, it's Sam.'

'Dam!' she squealed. She launched into a detailed account of her day, with me interjecting words like 'Really?' at suitable moments. Then suddenly she lost interest and gave the phone back to her aunt.

'Sorry about that. She insisted.'

'No problem,' I said.

'Fine. Look – well, I hope this isn't too much of an imposition, but I was wondering if we might have a chat?'

We arranged to meet at a café on Kensington Park Road at six thirty.

She wore a gun-metal grey overcoat with a fur collar. Her hair was neatly encased in an Angora beret, her hands in smoky-grey kid gloves.

'Nice coat,' I said as she divested herself of it before we sat down. 'What sort of fur is it?'

She laughed delightedly. 'A hundred per cent fake. I never wear the real thing.'

An unctuous young waiter took our coats. He didn't actually say out loud, What's a slob like you doing with the flame-haired Scythian goddess? but his expression conveyed the general meaning. The café wasn't full. We took a table in the window.

'I didn't tell Albion I was going to see you, or I would never have got out of the house without her,' said Anna. 'You've made a pal.'

'What can I say? The kid's got taste.'

'I'm only just beginning to understand the scope of our new responsibilities. Even having her for a whole day today has left me exhausted. Robert had to take her to the park to torture squirrels just so I could have a rest. I don't know if I'm cut out for mothering.'

'Kids have a way of getting under your skin.'

She laughed. 'Well, that's certainly true, especially after they've emptied your kitchen cupboards on to the floor. I swear there are times when I catch myself wondering when her mother's coming to take her home.'

She changed the subject abruptly. 'Anyway, I'm so glad you can help talk me through the show,' Anna said. 'I'm a bit nervous and Felicia is so, well . . .'

'Bolshy?' I offered.

She smiled. 'I was going to say busy.'

Our wine arrived, a honey-coloured Californian Chardonnay that she had chosen. The glasses were as big as brandy goblets. Anna clasped the stem of hers with both hands. Her fingers were slender and white. She had pale pink polish on her nails, a single gold wedding band and a large, old-fashioned brooch of red and blue stones. It set off her dark grey dress perfectly. I found myself wondering what she looked like underneath it. Then I found myself reminding myself that she was a married woman.

Anna brought me back to the world of the fully dressed. 'Felicia is a bit off-putting, but I think it's because she feels insecure,' she said. 'There's a lot of politics in a job like hers. And Marlowe, well, I get the feeling he doesn't like her.'

'Marlowe hired her.'

She shrugged. 'Just a feeling.'

Like Delaney, Felicia hadn't been with City Radio that long, and she hadn't had any background in news.

But she'd sent Marlowe a clever application letter for the job when it was advertised and he'd hired her, he said, on his instincts. As a veteran newshound, Marlowe put a lot of store by his instincts. In Felicia's case, it had paid off. Whatever one thought of the quality of her product, in ratings terms (which are the only terms in commercial radio), it was a success.

'Look, Sam. There's something else . . . I . . . Rick told me that someone rang you with information. He thought it was to do with Elaine. Is that right?'

'Yes. Someone rang and arranged to meet me. I went, but he didn't show up. And then he called again the next day. I figured that it was Rick Brittan having a joke at my expense.'

'Why would he do that?'

'You don't know Rick.'

'I mean, why would he then tell me about it, if he was having you on? It's not in very good taste.'

She had a point.

'What did he say? What did he tell you?' she asked.

'Nothing. He said he had information and that he wanted to meet.'

'Why did he ring you? Why didn't he call the police?'

'He said he didn't want to. As to why he contacted me, I have no idea. Maybe he heard me on the radio.'

'This is most frustrating,' Anna said. 'You know the police don't have any witnesses? This guy could be important.'

'I'm sure that if he really did know something, he'd come forward. Twenty thousand pounds reward is a pretty strong incentive.'

'That was the general idea,' she said, finishing off

her wine. 'God. I'm sorry if I was a bit abrupt, it's just that nothing seems to be happening. It's dreadful to get up each day hoping that there'll be some news – anything at all. And there's nothing.'

We said goodbye and I went home and communed with a Scotch bottle while I mentally reviewed the conversations I'd had with Shark. I had a choice between beating myself up or taking the philosophical approach. I decided on philosophical. If the mysterious Shark really had seen something and he was serious about the reward, he would go to the police. There was nothing more I could do.

Monday morning. Margaret Gabor arrived half an hour early and was clearly very nervous. It was my job to settle her. I gave her a cup of City Radio coffee, which I figured would at least take her mind off her troubles. She downed it in two gulps and sat twisting the strap of her handbag around her knuckles. I patted her arm. 'You'll be fine,' I said in my most soothing tone. 'Just tell them what you told me.'

'Right.' She sounded unconvinced.

'And remember, you're mad enough to bite someone's head off,' I said as I steered her to the studio.

'Right,' she said. She looked around at the unfamiliar territory: the bare room with a round felt-topped table, the microphones hanging from the ceiling, the thick glass window which separated her from the control room.

'Forget that people are listening,' I said. 'It's just you and them.' I turned to go.

'Sam, what if I dry up?'

CHRIS NILES

'You won't. Think about the dog shit in the hallways.'

I went through to the control room.

She performed like a professional. The deputy mayor was evasive, the cop spouted facts about funding and detection success ratios. Crosbie was clearly out of her depth in a situation that required her to think on her feet, but Margaret took up the slack. She chipped away at the two men with a persistence born of desperation. The switchboard jammed with calls.

'How was I?' she asked, when her turn was over. I handed her another cup of coffee.

'You were a pain in the arse.'

'Good,' she said. 'That's what I was hoping.' She sipped the coffee. 'The deputy mayor was a joke, wasn't he? Perhaps I should think about standing for office.'

I seated her at my desk and turned up the monitor so that she could hear the rest of the programme. I went back to the studio; we were in an ad break. Felicia sat at a large console next to Gary, the engineer. She was completely absorbed in the job.

'Let's keep the deputy mayor on a bit,' she said through the intercom to Crosbie. 'The voting public want to have a word.'

He couldn't very well refuse, so we ran a few callers by him. None were what you would call sympathetic.

'This wasn't what I was told when I agreed to come on,' he blustered when we finally let him out of the studio.

Felicia smiled sweetly. 'It's good practice for the hustings.'

'This is City Radio's *Female AM*, and we've come to the part of the show where we take a closer look at the effects of crime,' Crosbie read dutifully from her cue cards. 'There's much debate about what constitutes suitable punishment for criminals. Is the death penalty a deterrent? Do prisons reform or simply encourage recidivism? The people that are often left out when these issues are discussed are those who are most affected – the victims. Here in the studio to discuss this is City Radio's Dr Anna York-Baines, who has suffered her own personal tragedy recently . . .'

I watched Anna through the glass. She seemed composed as she spoke briefly about Elaine's death. Crosbie asked her a couple of other questions, and then said they'd be taking calls after a word from our sponsors.

Andie began answering the phones, which started ringing almost immediately. Through the intercom to Crosbie, she said, 'Georgina from Hammersmith. Her flat's been broken into three times in the last six months,' and she transferred the call to Crosbie in the studio.

'Hello, Georgina . . .'

Anna was, by turns, sympathetic and practical. She listened carefully to each caller and gave good advice, never cutting them off before a decent amount of time had passed. It was good stuff. I got carried away listening to it, which was why I didn't hear about Shark until it was too late.

Chapter Seventeen

'Our next caller is . . .' Crosbie had her left hand up to her headphones, as if she was having trouble hearing what Andie was telling her, '. . . Shark, have I got that right?'

'Let me have him,' I hissed to Andie, but it was too late. He was already on the air.

'Yeah,' said the low, gruff voice that I'd spoken to not days ago. If I needed any further proof that it wasn't Rick, this was it. I had the feeling I was about to get a shit load of trouble.

'What did you want to discuss?' It was Crosbie.

'I wanna, to ah, talk to the other woman.'

'You're speaking to her,' Anna said. 'How can I help you?'

There was another silence. Crosbie made a 'Shall-we-cut-him-off?' gesture, but Anna shook her head.

I held my breath. If he was a hoaxer, then he had balls of steel.

'It's about your sister's killing,' said Shark. 'I was there that night. I seen something. I talked to one of your reporters.'

Anna started.

'What do you—' she started to say, but Crosbie cut in.

'You saw who killed Elaine York?'

'Din' I just say that?'

'Ask him what he saw,' Felicia said into Crosbie's earpiece. But Crosbie, for once, was in control.

'What happened that night?' Cool and sharp, an echo of her old self.

In the control room there was pandemonium. 'Jesus Christ, someone call the cops,' wailed Felicia. I was already on the line.

'Try and get some details,' said Felicia into Crosbie's earphone. 'Times, anything, keep at him.'

'I wanna talk about the money,' said Shark.

Anna had recovered herself. She took a sip of water before replying. 'There is a reward, but since it's my money, you have to tell me what you know.'

I got through to the incident room and spoke to the detective on duty. Fortunately it wasn't Roger Fitzgerald. I told him where to tune his radio.

'You have to prove to me, and to the police, that what you're saying is true,' Anna continued.

'It's true,' said Shark.

'Why haven't you been to the police before now?' asked Crosbie. Anna frowned at her, warning her away.

'I don' like the police, they don' like me,' said Shark.

'But you'll tell me what you know, in exchange for the money?' Anna was in professional therapist mode, trying to draw him out, make him connect with her, make the transaction a personal one. Shark was playing it cool.

'Yeah,' he said.

'Ask him what time he was there,' Felicia hissed into Crosbie's earphone. 'Get him to say something, for God's sake.' I walked across the studio control room so I was standing next to Felicia's shoulder.

'Leave Crosbie out of this. Let Anna handle him,' I said quietly.

But Crosbie had already put the question to Shark.

'Look,' said Shark. There was a rattle of coins; he was calling from a phone box. 'This ain't a quiz. I don' have to answer no questions.'

'What would you suggest we do, then, Shark?' asked Anna, her voice soft and soothing, but she was glaring at Crosbie for her unwelcome interference.

Shark paused. 'I'll be in touch,' he said, and he hung up. The place fell to pieces. In the control room people were shouting. Crosbie threw to an ad break. Anna leaned forward, her head in her hands.

'Are you OK?' said Felicia through the intercom to the studio. Anna didn't look up, but she nodded.

After the show finished, the police arrived. They took a copy of the tape, questioned Anna, then left. I didn't tell them that the reporter Shark mentioned was me. I saw Margaret Gabor to her taxi.

I went in search of Rick. He wasn't at his desk. The tape that I had so rashly given him wasn't there.

'Are we trashing Rick's desk? If so, I can help.' It was Lyall.

'Where is he?'

'Editing. And looking well pleased with himself.'

I found him in one of the edit suites.

'Sam, old timer,' he said. He was making a copy of the tape I had given him. 'Good job you gave me this. It'll make a great follow-up to the call-in. I'm working on my intro now. Perhaps you can help me with it:

"Veteran crime reporter misses scoop." How does that sound to you?'

'Sounds like your usual sensational approach, Rick.'

He laughed at that. The tape had finished copying by then, so I reached out to get it. He got to it first, but he handed it to me anyway. Just letting me know who was in control.

'I have the original,' he said. 'But you can't get into much trouble with this.'

On the lunchtime bulletin City Radio was the news. Prospective witness calls in on talk show, it made good headlines. Despite Rick's protestations, Lyall smoothed over the part where Shark had called me. But word of it had got about, and several people wanted to judge me using the benefit of hindsight. It didn't look good. The police wanted to see me. They sent an officer to collect me. Delaney and Marlowe wanted to see me too, but they had to wait.

I got into the back of the police car. There wasn't enough room for my legs, but my polite request to have the front seat moved forward met with official denial. The officer didn't speak as we crawled through the lunchtime traffic. Fitzgerald kept me waiting for forty-five minutes. I hadn't eaten lunch. My stomach snarled as I sat in an empty room.

'You're a tosser, Ridley,' he said when I was eventually admitted. 'How do you manage it?'

'Practice.'

'Why did this guy phone you?'

'No idea.'

'Ever heard from him before?'

'No.'

'Know who he is?'

I could have told the truth, that I had the dawning of a suspicion, but the fact is, I just don't like Fitzgerald. 'No.'

'Any ideas at all about this?'

I shrugged. 'Maybe he listens to the radio.'

Fitzgerald looked at me narrowly. He knew he wasn't going to get co-operation from me, but he had to ask for my help and it galled him.

'He may contact you again. If he does, get in touch.'

I got up to go. 'Of course, Roger. Always a privilege, nay, a pleasure, to help Her Majesty's Constabulary.' And I left. There was no police car to take me back to the office, so I bought some lunch at a café and then caught the tube back to Tottenham Court Road. I wasn't in any particular hurry because I knew John Marlowe wanted to see me in his office. And that was a very bad sign indeed.

Chapter Eighteen

Marlowe sat behind his desk, feet up. He wears bespoke suits in dark blue pinstripe. His shirts are in clashing colours like pink and yellow. His ties are in bold checks and tartan. Marlowe dresses as if to say 'I don't give a damn,' and for all I know, he probably doesn't. Pushing fifty-five, his face is fleshy now and he has the beginnings of a drinker's nose, but he was probably quite a turn-on about fifteen years ago. He's married to a minor member of the aristocracy, a woman with a double-barrelled name who's so thin it looks like she diets for a living.

Marlowe and I have one thing in common; he is a smoker. His office has the faintly rancid smell of a man who's given two fingers to the anti-smoking rules. But he didn't invite me to light up. He didn't want me at my ease.

'You don't know where to put yourself these days, Ridley, do you?' His voice was gruff and not that strong, the child of many late, whisky-sodden nights.

He didn't expect an answer. I didn't offer one.

'Your personal life is tough, I hear. Your wife and kid left.'

'Yes.'

'You're on your own, then,' he said.

'Yes.'

He took his feet off the desk and leaned forward to face me. 'Listen to me, Ridley. Delaney may give you all that caring bullshit, but I don't give a fuck. Your personal life is in the toilet, I don't give a fuck about your personal life. I'd prefer it if you didn't fucking have one. Sleep in a box under Waterloo Bridge if you like, drink turps from bottles wrapped in paper bags. I don't give a rat's arse. All I care about is how you spend your time under my roof. I want you to turn up at work sober every day, work your nuts off for City. Breaking stories, covering news, that's what you're supposed to do. Pull your shitty life together. Because if you don't stop being a big fucking albatross around my neck I'm gonna cut your balls off and feed them to the fucking birds in Trafalgar Square. Don't make me do that to you, Ridley, because, by Christ, I will if I have to.'

I suppose I should have been listening to what he said. He was serious. Marlowe didn't kid around about stuff like that. But sitting there trying not to take it all too personally, my mind started to wander. And when it does that, sometimes the gods give me answers to questions I haven't been able to think of the answers to because I've been trying too hard. But it was there now all right.

I knew why Shark had chosen me to call. It was because we had met before. The voice had been teasingly familiar, but up till that moment I hadn't been able to place it.

I got up, pulled my shoulders back, put my chest out. 'Mr Marlowe, you're right. Quite right. Pull myself together. Try harder. Stiff upper lip, jolly good show, there'll always be an England, eh what?' I said. 'I'll start right now,' and I ran out of his office.

I knew who Shark was, and I was going to find him before anyone else did.

I was going to find him and throttle the living daylights out of the little prick.

Chapter Nineteen

I called Margaret Gabor. 'The kids, that day in the lift when I came to your flat,' I said. 'Who were they?'

'Well, I see them around, but I don't know their names,' she said.

'Do you know anybody who would?'

'I'll phone some people and get back to you.'

Anna cornered me by the coffee machine. 'Crosbie, I could kill her,' she said. 'I had him, you know? And she bloody barged in like a bull elephant.'

I thought of sharing my suspicions about Shark's identity with her, but discarded the idea. I was going to present Shark on a platter, with flourish and fanfare and a side order of chips.

'The police will find him,' I said.

'They think he'll try to contact the station again. I'm staying here in case he does.'

'He'll call back,' I said. 'He has to.'

Margaret rang back to say that a bloke called Terry Wigan might be able to help me. She told me that he was a window cleaner whom Shark had once worked for. She gave me his mobile number. I called Terry and arranged to meet at his house on St Mark's Road.

It was a fine evening. I eschewed the Renault in favour of a walk.

Terry's was the ground floor flat of a smallish thirties house that had been divided in two. It was easy to find because a van outside had his name written on it, advertising his services as a professional window cleaner. I rang the bell. I was buzzed straight in.

The sound of squabbling children filled the house; taunting banter, a thump and a young girl began to wail. She ran out of a room to my right and down the corridor to the other end of the house. 'Shawn, I'm gonna get you for that!' she yelled as she ran. 'Bastard!'

'Alison, how many times have I told you not to use that language?' A young blonde woman in jeans came out of another room. She looked frazzled. Alison curled her lip and muttered: 'He started it.'

'Do I look like I care?' said her mother. She pointed to another room, presumably Alison's. 'Get in there and *do your homework*.' To me she grimaced. 'Kids,' she said. 'Can't live with 'em, can't cut them up into tiny pieces and feed them to the crows.' She produced an elastic band from her pocket and pulled her hair into a ponytail. 'I'm Rachel. You're here to see Terry. He's in the bath, but he'll be out any second. Take a seat in the kitchen.' She indicated a third door on my right. I went through, pulled up a chair to the table and waited. I heard 'Aw, Mum,' as another child was forcibly shepherded towards his homework.

'Sorry about all that,' she said, back in the kitchen. 'Beer?'

'Love one.'

Terry arrived moments later, sweet-smelling and clean.

He was thick-set with the beginnings of a paunch. It flopped against the top of his belt buckle and looked like it had plans for further expansion. Terry had a wide, friendly face, framed by thinning black hair. He wore jeans and a checked flannel shirt with the sleeves rolled up. We shook hands and introduced ourselves and he grabbed another beer from the fridge.

'Rache?' he asked his wife, holding up the bottle.

'Thanks, later.' She turned on the taps and filled the sink with water.

'Leave those, hon. I'll do them,' he said, taking a seat.

She shook her head. 'After fighting with those damn kids for two hours, I need to work off some aggression,' she said and began vigorously soaping dinner plates. 'Besides, this way I get to listen in on some adult conversation.'

This was obviously one of those happy families that you hear so much about. I felt jealous of Terry, drinking beer in his kitchen, smiling stupidly at his wife, his kids a mere two rooms away. So what if the little darlings spent all their free time trying to dismember each other? At least he got to watch them grow up while they did it.

'Margaret said you wanted to know about Shark,' said Terry. 'I know Shark. He worked for me a few months ago.'

There was a snort of derision from Rachel. 'He was employed by you. There is a difference.'

'Yeah, well, whatever you call it. He showed up for about two weeks. Unreliable little bugger. Never turned up on time. Window cleaning business, you gotta be reliable. I woulda sacked him in the end, except he just stopped coming.'

'Tell him about the money,' said Rachel. She'd started on the cutlery.

'It wasn't anything,' said Terry.

'It *was*.' Knives and forks jangled.

'What happened?' I prompted.

Terry took a great gulp of beer, and the level in the bottle sank to half.

'He said I owed him money. Said I should have paid him even though he walked out on me. I refused, and he showed up at the house. Little prick produced a knife and started threatening me.'

'What did you do?'

'Nearly broke the fucker's arm. He wasn't expecting me to go for him. Thinks a knife gives him respect. He threatens my family, I'll shove his respect up his arse and take his appendix out with it.'

'Did you tell the police?'

'Yeah.'

'What happened?'

'Nothing.'

'Have you seen him lately?'

'Seen him around, not to talk to. He gave me a wide berth. Very wise, 'cos I got a long memory.'

'What about his mates?'

'Hangs about with a guy called Max Adams. He wanted to get Max a job with me, but I said no. They were the same kinda lazy bastards. Found out later that Max was multi-talented. Robbery, fencing, mugging, turn his hand to anything. No wonder they wanted jobs as window cleaners. Ideal for ripping off the clients. Would have been a disaster for my business.'

'Where does Shark live?'

Terry shrugged. 'Not sure. He was living on the estate with his mum, but they had a fight and she kicked him out. Who knows what he's been up to.'

'What about girlfriends? Did he mention anybody else that he hung about with?'

Terry took a swig from his beer. 'No. Shark was real gallant like that. He didn't kiss and tell. I think there was someone, but I don't know who it was.'

'What about work? Is it possible that he got another job?'

Terry just laughed at that.

'What's his full name?'

'Sonny Harkness was what he told me. Who knows, though? The guy couldn't lie straight in bed.'

'What about Max? Do you know anybody who knows Max?'

'From what I've heard, everybody tries to avoid Max. You'd be hard pressed to find anyone with a good word to say about him.'

'I know Max,' said Rachel. She'd finished the dishes and had collected a beer. 'Well, not him exactly – his sister. She's in my step class down at the leisure centre. She's nice, not like him at all. Her name's Stephanie, Stephanie Adams. She lives in that block off Bishop's Bridge Road.'

While we finished our drinks we chatted about football, or rather Terry chatted and I listened. I'm not a sports fan myself, but I never let it stand in the way of a convivial conversation.

As I left, he said, 'You might try the Rover, off Golborne Road. I heard they drink there.' He gave me his business card. I put it in my wallet.

I walked to the Rover via Summerhill Estate. It was

dark and I didn't see much sense in going inside. So I just hung around for a bit outside the monstrous building. I got chilled to the bone, and I didn't see anyone I recognized.

The Rover was a misnomer for sure. It should have been called the Dealer. The clientele didn't exactly stop and stare when I walked in – they were much too polite for that – but my arrival didn't go unnoticed. The walls were black, the lighting dim. Music from a band with a name like 'Kill the Cops' vibrated in my chest. I made for the bar and ordered a beer. The barman was a woman. She wore black Lycra shorts and a black halter top. They didn't meet in the middle by a long way and the effect was bracing. She looked like she spent a lot of time at the gym. I wondered how she managed to keep her belly button ring and the chain attached to it from getting tangled in the stairmaster.

'I'm looking for someone,' I shouted across the bar to her.

She stared back at me in a 'So what?' kind of way, then turned away. I saw her take a sip from a glass full of a green slimy liquid. It was the same healthy junk that Delaney drank.

I slipped a ten-pound note on to the bar. 'I said, I'm looking for someone.'

She eyed the note. She eyed me.

'I'm not that kind of girl,' she said.

I decided to ignore that. 'Two blokes – Shark and Max Adams. I was told they drink here.'

'And who might they be?' she said in a way that

123

showed she didn't really care. She took a wad of chewing gum out of her mouth, inspected it and put it back in her mouth.

'I was hoping you'd know them. Do you?'

She shrugged. She looked at the note. 'Sometimes they come here, yeah.'

'Well, when's a good time to catch them?'

She leaned over the bar. I could see down her top; the view was breathtaking, but I'm a gentleman. I forced myself to look up.

'What if they don't want to be caught?'

'Look, I'm not a cop.'

She started polishing a glass. It seemed like a waste of effort; the customers didn't look that choosy.

'I just want to talk to them.' I smiled, but it cut no ice. She shrugged and turned away.

I ordered another beer and left the ten quid on the bar. She hadn't strictly earned it, but I'm a soft touch when it comes to trim bodies in black Lycra.

Shark didn't show that night, but I had a very interesting conversation with the resident drunk about breaking and entering. He was also able to tell me about the specialities of most of the other drinkers. They were indeed a talented bunch. The Rover appeared to be the crook's Eton – make good contacts here and they stand you in valuable stead for the rest of your professional life.

Closing time lurched around, and I decided to call it quits. I said goodbye to my new friend, promising to call him when I planned my next burglary, and stepped out into the chilly night. The Rover wasn't too far from my flat so I decided to walk. As it turned out, that was a mistake.

Chapter Twenty

I left the pub and turned on to Golborne Road. It's a convivial place where street stalls, second-hand furniture shops and cafés attract a lively crowd. When Mary and I were together we would often go down there and buy junk we didn't need, promising ourselves that we would restore it to a glory it had never possessed.

That night the shops were shuttered and the street was quiet. I walked quickly in an effort to keep warm. I could hear footsteps behind me, also moving quickly. I didn't think too much about it until I was grabbed by both arms and bundled off down a side alley.

There were two of them. I didn't get a good look at their faces, but I could tell they were younger, meaner and bigger than me. Once in the alley, they got my attention by wrapping their hands around my larynx and dragging me along on my heels. I couldn't breathe, my head felt as though it were about to be ripped off. I struggled to get my balance but they moved at a snappy pace. Once they'd found a more suitable location, they propped me upright. The first one held me while the second one punched me in the stomach. I felt a serious need to double up, but they held me tightly. They punched me again and again. I lost count. At last I fell forward. It felt good to be lying down. I needed a nice rest. Although I could feel my face bleeding from where it had struck the pavement, it didn't bother me too much. Deft hands removed my wallet from my back pocket, and a foot connected a couple of times with my kidneys. I passed out.

When I came to, they were still trying to kill me. I attempted to open my eyes. It required much more concentration than usual, but eventually I was able to see as much as was possible in the dim lighting. I realized that the men had gone, but someone else was trying to dislocate my shoulder. The woman from the bar.

'You OK?' she said, which seemed like a pretty stupid question under the circumstances. She took her hand off my shoulder, for which I was thankful.

I nodded.

I struggled to get up. She put her hand under my arm to help me. I felt sore. I felt sick. I was freezing.

'You poor bugger, you're a sorry sight,' she said as we got me more or less vertical. 'And don't give me any of that shit about the other guy looking worse.'

We stood there, swaying. I tried to say something, but no sound came out.

'Shall we try and walk, then?' She wedged her shoulder under my arm for ballast, and we set off at an uneven pace back to Golborne Road.

A black cab came by and my rescuer hailed it. The driver slowed down, took one look at me and sped off into the distance.

'Fucking arsehole,' she shouted at his disappearing tail-lights.

We waited another three years, or so it seemed, for

the next one. The driver watched curiously as the woman from the bar helped me into the back seat.

'St Mary's Hospital, is it?' he said when we got settled.

I shook my head and managed to croak out my address.

He drove us there without ado, but became quite upset when he discovered I didn't have any money to pay him. My rescuer tried to shame him into waiving his fee, and some rather harsh words were exchanged. He drove off shouting, 'I'm not a bleeding charity!' or words to that effect.

'Poxy scum,' she said.

The journey up the stairs to my flat seemed endless. My legs didn't want to move or bend; my head swam. I wanted to lie down on the landing and take a small nap, but as I started to do that my Sherpa prodded me on. Eventually we reached my front door. I still had my keys. She unlocked the door and I stepped through and collapsed on the couch. I needed a cigarette desperately. So, it turned out, did she.

'Fags are on the bookcase,' I croaked.

As she fetched the cigarettes I was gratified to note that her rear view was just as pleasing as her front. 'Lucky me. I managed to get you back to my flat on our very first date.'

'I see they didn't break your funny bone, then.' She lit me a cigarette. I wanted to marry her.

I took the cigarette from her. 'What's your name?'

'Dean.'

'I'm Sam. Will you marry me?'

She studied my wrecked face. 'Depends. Have you got life insurance?'

I shook my head. She shook hers. Regretfully, I like to think.

The cigarette tasted good. All my important little places still hurt like hell, but somehow it didn't matter so much. I took off my shoes and studied the one part of my body that didn't appear to be damaged. Accentuate the positive.

Dean flipped through my record collection while she smoked. It was clear she approved of Jimi Hendrix, although she probably hadn't even been born when he was at his peak.

'I'd tell you that hanging around the Rover is a health hazard, but you've probably figured that out for yourself,' she said.

I nodded.

'Why do you want Shark, anyway? I mean, it's fairly apparent that you didn't run into each other on the cocktail circuit.'

'His aunt died and left him a vast fortune. I've got to deliver the money to him.'

'I see. Well, why don't I pass the message on when I see him? It'll probably be safer than you coming over our way.'

'When will you see him?'

'Dunno, he's a creature of uncertain habits. But he's generally around and about.'

I sighed. The effect of the cigarette was starting to wear off. 'OK. I'd appreciate that.'

She stubbed out her cigarette and stood up. 'I'll be off now. Sure you're OK?'

I wasn't that sure, but I said I was. Dean picked up her bag and coat. I wrote my name and number down on a notepad and gave it to her. Before she shut the door behind her, she turned.

'You know, you really shouldn't get involved with those guys,' she said.

'What guys?'

But she had already shut the door.

I went into the bathroom. The face that stared back at me from the medicine cabinet mirror was a study in colour. My forehead was bruised and starting to affect a delicate dirty shade of yellow. I had a cut over one purple eye and dried blood ran down my cheek and neck. I cleaned it off. I ran the bath. The only emollient I could find was a bottle of bubble bath in the shape of an American footballer, which Simon had left behind. I unscrewed the footballer's head and tipped some of his insides into the water. The strong smell of commercial cleaning agents struck me almost immediately. It wasn't your classic soothing ungent, but it would have to do. After the bath I poured myself a glass of whisky, then I took a bunch of painkillers and went to bed.

I woke cautiously the next day. It was a bit like the morning after a particularly rigorous drinking session: the slightest movement was going to involve a disproportionate amount of pain. I eased myself out of bed and into the shower. Then I dressed and went into the kitchen. I ground beans and made coffee, all at the speed of an arthritic eighty-nine-year-old. What with Roger Fitzgerald and last night's chaps, getting roughed about was starting to become a bad habit. And I had enough of those already.

*

It hurt to swallow, but the coffee was good and it cleared my head. I found enough change for my bus fare to work and left to face the day.

I made an impressive entrance as I shuffled, half bent, into the office. My colleagues clustered round. Some offered to fetch me coffee. All wanted to hear my story. So I told them, with a few minor modifications for a general audience. They oohed, they aahed, they lost interest and wandered off. I shuffled over to Felicia's desk.

'My God,' she said. 'What hit you?'

'A fool and his money are soon parted.'

'Doesn't look like it was that soon to me.'

I shrugged modestly. She stood up and walked around me. Finally she stopped in front of me, hands on hips, and said, 'Go home, Sam. You don't work in news any more, and we don't give prizes for heroics in this department.'

I nodded. I felt tired, so very tired. I turned and headed towards the door.

She shouted after me, 'Don't forget to call the bank and cancel all your credit cards.'

I nodded, and continued on my way. Felicia was still shouting at me. My head hurt. I wanted her to be quiet.

'Sam, wait.' I stopped, turned round. She was approaching at speed, with her huge black handbag swinging. She stopped in front of me and started rummaging around in the bag. She pulled out a small purse.

'Have you got any money?'

I shook my head.

Felicia waved a note in front of me. 'Take this

twenty. No, wait a minute.' She dived back into her purse. 'And here's a couple of fives.'

Pride ordered me to refuse, but I couldn't afford to. I had less than one pound to my name and no immediate means of getting any more. I took the money.

'Thanks.'

We stood there, looking slightly embarrassed. She turned away first.

'And for God's sake, go and see a doctor,' she said over her shoulder.

'OK,' I said. A doctor. A good idea.

'And call me and tell me what he says. I need to know if you're going to be around this week.'

I took a taxi to my doctor and waited some time before he could fit me in. The others at the surgery regarded me with undisguised interest. I buried my head in a twelve-month-old magazine.

My doctor inspected me thoroughly. He's a brusque, bulky guy who used to play rugby for Scotland, so my colourful injuries didn't impress him in the slightest. He took X-rays and checked me over for concussion.

'Will I live?' I said at the end of it.

'Not if you have any say in it.' He leaned back in his chair, ticking points off on his fingers. 'Let me see, there's the smoking – twenty a day, is it? And there's the drinking – I'm not even going to begin to guess how much whisky you sock away in a week. Take any exercise, do we? Don't make me laugh. Eat a well-balanced diet? I can't imagine it. Factor all that together and I'd say a fruit fly has a better chance of living to a serene old age than you do, Ridley.'

I didn't take too much notice. I know he disapproves of my lifestyle; he's told me so before.

At home I took Felicia's advice and cancelled my plastic cards, and had the bank send out new ones. Then I took another handful of painkillers and passed out on the couch.

It was six o'clock when I woke to an alarm going off. I raised my head from the pillow. The room swung. I put my head back where it belonged. The bell kept ringing. I listened hard. It was the telephone. No, it was the doorbell. The alarm clock. I'd played this game before but I wasn't getting any better at it. Taking pot luck, I pressed the release button on the entryphone, not particularly caring who, if anyone, I was letting in.

Felicia stood outside, holding a ceramic dish covered in tin foil. She wore jeans and a sweatshirt with the name of an American university on the front. She seemed different. Shorter, that was it. It was the first time I'd seen her in flat shoes.

Without waiting to be asked, she swept in, made straight for the kitchen and turned on the oven.

'You didn't call,' she said.

'What are you doing?' I asked as she turned the dial.

'It's my lasagne. It's very, very good, and you are going to eat it.'

I'd had enough of being ordered around by her. I took a stand. 'I'll have it later.'

I might as well not've spoken. She put the dish in the oven, closed the door briskly and began rummaging in my cupboards. 'It's an old family recipe, my mother's. You'll eat it, or I finish up where they left off.' She gestured at my injuries. 'You choose.'

I ate it while she watched. She was right. Her mother knew a thing or two about lasagne.

When I'd finished, she emerged from the kitchen with a bottle of wine.

'Where did you find that?' I asked.

'In the cleaning cupboard, but it's perfectly OK.' She proceeded to uncork it. I looked at the label.

'It's Australian,' I said.

'So?'

'I don't use anything from Australia. I'm boycotting the whole country. It's personal. Don't ask me to explain.'

Felicia looked bemused. She handed me a glass of wine. 'It's red wine. Good for you. Drink it or die. And then tell me what's going on.'

I drank. And then I told.

'I got mugged. It could happen to anyone.'

'Oh, please.' She swiped the wine bottle and pointed it at me accusingly. 'I wasn't born yesterday. When you work for me, I have a right to know what you're up to. And you are up to something, I can tell.'

So I told her about my attempts to find Shark. She listened carefully.

'Surely if he's after the reward then he'll get in touch again.'

'He's been jerking me around. If I can find him,

133

then we can deal on my terms. We don't even know if he's telling the truth. It could still be a hoax.'

Felicia looked doubtful. 'But won't the cops find him?'

'I want to find him first. It's a guy thing.'

Felicia rolled her eyes. 'What if he doesn't want to be found?'

I told her I had a lead – Max's sister, Stephanie Adams. As it turned out, she was easy to find. She was listed in the phone book.

'Let's go and see her,' said Felicia, grabbing her bag.

'You're coming too?'

'Sure. Besides,' she said, casting an eye over my injuries, 'you need me. There's no way she's gonna let you into her flat looking like that.'

Chapter Twenty-one

The building that Stephanie Adams lived in was a
post-war block of flats. Judging by the care that had
obviously been taken over the complex, a great
number of the flats were now privately owned. The
block was surrounded by well-kept lawns and shrub-
bery. There were windowboxes containing healthy
plants, and the paint on the buildings was fresh. Felicia
found a parking space in a well-lit street and we
walked over to the building's main entrance. Helpfully,
the flats were numbered with the names of the occu-
pants alongside. Stephanie Adams was in Flat 4H.

Felicia pressed a buzzer at random. When someone
answered she said, 'Hi, it's me,' and we were let in.

'You'd think people would take more care,' she said,
as we climbed the stairway to the fourth floor. When
I had to rest on the second- and third-floor landings
she frowned but said nothing.

She knocked briskly on Stephanie Adams' door and
stood squarely in front of it, so that when she looked
through the peephole Stephanie couldn't see my dis-
coloured face.

'Miss Adams, my name is Felicia Randall. I'm a
reporter. I'd like to have a word with you, please. It's
about your brother.'

There was a pause. Then the door opened a fraction on a safety chain. In the background I could hear a child crying.

'I don't have anything to do with my brother.' The door started to close, but Felicia put her foot in the jamb.

'May I come in, please? It's quite important.'

There was another pause. Then we heard the safety chain being released and the door opened. A plain woman of about twenty-five stood on the other side. Everything about her was thin; her brown hair, her face, her figure. She wore stone-washed jeans and a cotton sweater. She frowned when she saw my face, but ushered us into a small, underfurnished room. There was a sofa with a sheet over it, a writing desk that doubled as a dining table. Stephanie switched the television off and directed us towards the sofa.

'What's he done now?' she said flatly.

'Nothing,' I replied. 'We need some information about his friend, Shark. I heard they hang out together.' I smiled reassuringly, hoping it would help her see past my battered appearance.

Stephanie sat down on the only other chair in the room. She lit a cigarette and inhaled like a woman with too few pleasures in life. Taking her cue, I lit up as well. There was a full ashtray on the coffee table in front of me. Felicia pointedly waved the smoke away from her face.

'I haven't seen Max for weeks. The last time he came here he wanted money. Like I can afford it, living on benefit.'

'Did he say what the money was for?' I asked.

'No, and I didn't ask.'

'So you didn't give him any?' Felicia asked.

Stephanie snorted. 'I wouldn't give him a penny if I won the lottery. My brother is a waste of space. I don't think you'll find too many people who disagree with me.'

'Yet you keep in touch?'

'No, we don't "keep in touch". He calls me from time to time, usually when he wants something. I say no. Then I don't hear from him again until the next time.'

A small, whimpering child, wearing only a T-shirt, wandered into the room. Tears had dried on her chubby cheeks. Distractedly, Stephanie ran her finger round the little girl's gums. The child stared at me and Felicia, and I waggled my fingers at her, pulled a funny face. She looked away.

'Do you know Max's friend Shark?'

'Shark? What about him?'

'We need to speak to him. Do you know where he's living?'

She blew smoke. 'What do I look like? Directory Inquiries?'

'It's quite important that we find him.' Felicia fanned her hand in front of her face again.

'He was living at the Summerhill Estate, but I was told he moved out.'

Stephanie sighed. 'Look, I really can't help you. I don't know why you came here. I have nothing to do with my brother. I don't see him or any of his friends. I'm trying to make a go of it on my own here and it's not easy. The sooner I can put distance between me and people like him, the better off me and my kid will be. Jeez, it's tough enough raising a kid with bugger-all money without having to deal with all the shit my dear little brother dredges up.'

'When was the last time you saw your brother?' Felicia persisted.

'As I thought I had already explained, I really couldn't say,' said Stephanie firmly. She stood up, gestured to the door. 'If you don't mind, I've got things to do.'

I left my card and asked her to call if she thought of anything.

'So much for that,' I said to Felicia as she unlocked her car with a small automatic device.

'She was lying,' she said.

'What about?'

'How do I know what about, Ridley? All I know is that she was. I've done enough of it in my time to be able to spot it. And besides, did you notice her feet?'

'What about them?'

'They were tiny – she's a size four at most – and yet there was a pair of trainers behind the couch that were at least a ten. All that crap about being a single mother, I don't buy it.'

'She probably thought we were spies from the social services.'

'Maybe,' she said. We drove the rest of the way in silence.

'Get some sleep,' she said as she dropped me outside my place.

I waited until she'd gone, then caught a taxi to the Rover.

Dean wasn't working that night. But otherwise the pub appeared to be pretty much as I had left it. The music was uncongenially loud, and a spirited game of darts was taking place in one corner. I approached the barman with my best imitation of a swagger, and ordered a Scotch.

'Shark been in tonight?' I asked the barman, a hefty black man who must have been at least six foot five.

'Why?' he said.

'I'm looking for him.' I took a sip of my Scotch. The cheapskates had watered it down.

'Well, he ain't here, and I ain't his muvvah.'

'What about Max Adams – seen him tonight?'

'Nah,' he said, before turning away.

I switched to beer and settled down for a wait. Nothing much happened till around ten thirty, when the place went silent.

It was like one of those scenes from a wild west movie, where the gunman walks into the last chance saloon and everybody from the card sharp to the hooker stops what they're doing. Although it was coincidence that the juke box stopped at that very moment, it did give Detective Inspector Roger Fitzgerald's entrance an air of drama that he probably hadn't intended. I don't suppose it's Fitzgerald's fault, really; he was in civvies, but you could dress him up like Coco the Clown and he'd still look like a cop.

He went up to the bar, ordered a beer and turned around to take in the place.

And his eye fell on me.

'What are you doing here?'

'Hoping to get lucky.'

'Piss off, Ridley.'

'Free country, Roger, although I know you'd like to change all that.' I drained my beer. I'd pretty well figured it out that since the world and his wife knew that Shark drank at the Rover, then chances were he was giving the venue a miss for a bit.

Feeling lucky, I walked home. I reckoned the odds on being beaten up three times in as many weeks were low.

'Dad, it's me.'

'Hey, how's it going, kid?' I forced myself to sound cheerful. I didn't feel cheerful.

'Mum says I can only talk for ten minutes.'

'That's OK, it's expensive. Get my letter?'

'No.'

'It'll be there soon.' I could see it sitting on the benchtop, where I'd moved it from the mantelpiece. A stab of guilt. 'How's things?'

'Grant's kids call me a pommy bastard.' Mary's new husband had two children from a previous marriage, who lived in Sydney. 'They make fun of my accent. I don't have an accent, do I, Dad?'

'That's an outrageous slur,' I said. 'Tell them your English is as good as the Queen's.'

'They don't like the Queen much here.'

'Ah. What about school?'

'It's OK.' There was a short silence. I could hear his breathing on the line and the grief hit me so hard that I thought it would be too much to bear.

'Dad?'

'Yeah?'

'They have Marmite here, but it's not the same. Everything's different.'

I knew the feeling. I lit a cigarette. It helps when

you need to keep it together. I took a deep lungful of soothing nicotine.

'Want me to send you some Marmite?'

'It's OK. I expect I'll get used to it.'

The ten minutes passed like two and I could hear Mary telling him to hang up.

'Well. 'Bye, then.' He sounded near to tears.

Fortunately I'd thought to stock up on Black Label.

The first glass was a toast to Marlowe. The rest, I don't really remember.

My hangover hit me as surely as morning follows drinking. I avoided breakfast and rode the number 7 bus to work on the lower deck, where I was less likely to further aggrieve my already delicate stomach.

'Looks like the cops found your mate – Shark,' said Lyall while I massaged my temples. He gave me coffee.

'Oh? Where?'

'Stuffed in a skip in Queens Park.'

Chapter Twenty-two

It took my alcohol-abused brain a moment to process the information.

'He's dead?'

'Unless he's Jesus Christ.' Lyall handed over a hard copy of the wire story. It didn't say much more than what he'd told me. They'd found the body, and Sonny Harkness – Shark to his mates – had Elaine's wallet. He was seventeen years old.

I called Charlie.

'What's the connection, Charlie?'

'Bloody Ridley,' he sighed. 'Don't you have a home to go to?'

'There has to be one. He saw whoever killed Elaine York.'

'Yeah,' said Charlie, 'and the Pope and the bloody Queen Mother were in it together.'

'It makes sense.'

Charlie sighed again. 'On the Ellery Queen show. Look, this guy, Shark. He owes money to a loan shark – no pun intended – guy called Rufus. He owes a lot of money, and let's say Rufus's repayment terms are less flexible than the bank which likes to say yes. He misses a coupla deadlines, and guess what? He's history. They found his fingerprints at her flat. He probably went there to rob her, but it didn't pan out and so he hears about the reward and tries to extort some money by going directly to the sister. But he's a useless fuck, and Rufus eventually catches up with him.'

'So what's up with Rufus?'

'Guy's a paid-up member of dial-an-alibi. Probably arranging character references from the Archbishop of Canterbury for all I know.'

'So that's it? All neatly tied up?'

'No, it isn't bloody it, Ridley. We lean on the guy, hope that he cracks. If he doesn't, we wait for him to commit another indiscretion. The next time he refuses to help a little old lady across the road, he finds himself detained at Her Majesty's pleasure. That's jail to you.'

I hung up. I had lots to think about, but Felicia didn't intend to give me time for any of it.

'Tomorrow's national Aromatherapy Awareness day,' she said, handing me a piece of paper with a name written on it.

'I've been marking the days on my calendar,' I said.

'Just get me the interview, Ridley,' she said, stalking away. 'And spare me the witticisms.'

When Felicia wasn't looking, I went out to the Post Office to mail my letter to Simon. Then I set off for Maida Vale to interview Deborah McGuinness, aromatherapist to the stars.

The news at the tail end of the day was that the police were investigating Shark's death. They weren't saying whether it was connected to Elaine or not. And what they were saying didn't answer any of my questions. I needed to speak to Rufus the loan shark. See what he had to say about Shark's death. I decided to consult the oracle.

'Believe me, Sam, you don't want to talk to Rufus.'

'Dean, how long have we known each other? Think of it as a favour for an old mate.'

She looked at me with narrowed eyes. Music blared at the Rover. I sipped my Scotch.

'He won't see you. I'm telling you that for nothing.'

'You know him?'

'He's a popular guy,' she said dryly.

'Just tell me where he lives. I'll ask him myself.'

She reached under the bar and brought out a mobile phone.

'All right, I'll call him. See what I can do.'

She turned away so I couldn't hear what she said. I was surprised that she could hear, the music was so loud. A minute later she turned back.

'So I was wrong,' she said. 'He says to come over.' She gave me an address in Hereford Road.

Chapter Twenty-three

Rufus's building was in the process of being divided into flats by a property developer. It was half painted and a load of builder's debris sat in a skip on the paving out in front. Some of the fixtures were in place, though; the front-door knocker was an oversized dolphin. I grasped it by the snout. A large, well-muscled gentleman in a checked suit opened the door. He was obviously new to the job and had not yet read the manual on being polite to visitors.

'Yeah?' he said, keeping his foot behind the door so I couldn't just barge in.

'I'm here to see Rufus.'

'Name?'

'Ridley. He's expecting me.'

Butch the butler led me down a short hallway. The house smelt of new paint and varnish, and there was no furniture in any of the rooms I could see into. The carpet was so thick it made my calf muscles ache from walking on it. I was ushered into a small room looking out on to a floodlit garden.

'Mr Ridley, delighted to meet you.' A slim man in his early forties stood up, arm outstretched.

'Mr Rufus, how do you do.'

'Just Rufus,' he said. 'Like Madonna.' He smiled.

He had a diamond in his left canine tooth. Class, I thought.

'Whisky?'

'Twist my arm.'

'I don't twist arms,' said Rufus, turning to an extravagantly stocked bar. 'I have staff for that.' He carefully poured two generous shots of whisky.

'Sit down, please,' he said, directing me to a leather Chesterfield. He wore jeans and cowboy boots and, incongruously, striped dress shirt with a cravat. He spoke with the exaggerated 'gor-blimey-guv' accent that often indicates that its owner wishes to disguise years of expensive public schooling.

Rufus settled down in a deep buttoned-leather chair, behind a large mahogany desk that was the room's only other significant piece of furniture. He put his feet up on the desk. The heels of his boots needed re-soling.

'What was it you wanted to see me about?' he asked, idly swirling his drink.

'I spoke to a chap called Shark last week,' I said. 'He mentioned your name.' That was a lie, but Rufus didn't need to know it.

'Did he? How interesting.'

'It was in connection with some money he owed you.'

Rufus made no reply, waiting for me to go on.

'When I spoke to him he appeared to have come up with a way to pay back that money.'

'Which way was that?'

'I believe it was because he was witness to a murder.'

Rufus drained his drink.

'How would that help him pay his debts? Assuming, for the sake of argument, that he had any?'

'The family of the murdered woman offered a substantial reward for information – twenty thousand pounds.'

'Ah. This is extremely interesting, Mr Ridley, but, er, what exactly does it have to do with me?'

'I was told that Shark was in debt to you. And as you are probably aware, the police think he was killed because of that debt. I was supposed to meet Shark on Friday night, but he didn't show. I thought it was because he was a casual hoaxer. But having thought about it a bit more carefully, I came up with another explanation.'

'Oh, really?'

'I started to think about the priorities of a young man with no job and a large debt. Probably a desperate young man with a desperate plan. Now, what could have been more important for a desperate young man than meeting the person who can possibly help him get his hands on twenty thousand pounds?'

Rufus flashed his rock. Some would have called it a smile. 'I give in, what?'

'A meeting with his creditor is what I'm thinking, Rufus. I think he had to beg for more time. And I'm thinking that at that meeting he may have explained what it was he saw that was worth so much. As a kind of surety. Correct me if I'm wrong.'

Rufus took his feet off the desk.

'Mr Ridley, are you saying I wouldn't co-operate with the police in a murder inquiry? I'm hurt.'

'Why should you help the police? They might not believe you. They might say to themselves, "Here is a

147

man who'll say anything to save his own skin."
Especially when Shark's death ties up so many incon-
venient loose ends. It suits the police not to believe
you, Rufus. The truth is harsh, but there it is. I, on
the other hand, will listen with an open mind.'

Rufus twirled the ice in his glass. An indolent smile
played on his face.

'Well, Mr Ridley, I'm sure I should be thankful that
you have my best interests at heart, but I'm afraid I
can't help you. I haven't seen Shark for weeks.'

'The police said he owed you.'

'Then killing him would considerably reduce my
chances of getting any return on my investment,
would it not?' He set the heavy cut-glass tumbler down
on a leather coaster. 'I told the police that too, but I
think you're right. They didn't believe me.'

He rose, indicating the interview was over. 'The
burden of proof, Mr Ridley, is a wonderful thing,' he
said as he showed me to the door.

When I got home there was a message from Terry
Wigan, the window cleaner who had employed Shark.

'Sam. It's Terry – I hate these blasted machines.
OK . . . was thinking about our talk, and remembered
a bloke called Mitchell, John Mitchell. Don't know that
it's any use to you now that the little blighter is dead,
but anyway, I have his number. Shark used him as a
reference when he came to me about work.' He recited
the number. I copied it down.

I looked at my watch. The night was young. I
called John Mitchell.

I got lucky. He answered on the first ring. I told him that I was looking for information about Shark.

'I don't want to be quoted,' he said.

'It's just for background.'

'Well, I'm off to the gym now, but I'll be free in about an hour and a half.'

He told me where I could find him. The trusty Renault was in need of a run, so I excavated it and drove out to Acton.

Mitchell's gym was located in an old warehouse. It was the sporting equivalent of a supermarket own-brand label. There were no bulletin boards advertising aqua-aerobics or re-birthing classes, no lithe young things in spandex. Just a large room with a boxing ring, and, off to the side, a smaller room with free weights.

I stood at the door and looked around. John Mitchell was easy to spot because he wore a shirt with his name stitched across the shoulders. He was doing curls with a barbell the size of a small car. I stood well back, watching him huff and heave, his face straining till it was a shade of purple. He was shorter than me, but probably weighed twice what I do. Every muscle in his body seemed to be accentuated by the strain of the load he was lifting. Impressed, I waited and watched.

A few minutes later, Mitchell noticed I was there. He wiped his hands and face on a towel and came over to shake my hand.

'I'm done for the night. Fancy a beer?'

After he'd showered and changed we stepped across the road to a pub.

He ordered two pints. I paid for them.

'Suppose we should drink to Shark, wherever he is,' he said quietly. 'Stupid bastard. It was just a matter of time before he ended up on a marble slab.'

'How come?'

'The people he hung out with. The things he got up to. Riding for a fall, that kid. Been the same ever since his father shot through. His mother didn't know how to handle him; the kid's been wild since he was twelve years old.'

'I spoke to Shark before he died. I met him when I was at Summerhill on a story, and he called me later to tell me he had some information about the girl Elaine York, who was murdered. He wanted the reward money.'

'Sounds like him.' John took a swig of beer and wiped the moustache off with the back of his hand. 'Shark was working the angles, always figuring out a way to make money. It never occurred to him to get a bloody job.'

'The police said he owed money to a loan shark.'

John shrugged. 'Wouldn't surprise me.'

'Do you think he was capable of murder?'

'Dunno. Premeditated, probably not. But if he panicked and got carried away, who knows? He was a mixed-up kid.'

'How did you know him?'

'I stepped out with his mother once.'

'How long ago?'

'Let's just say I knew her before she was blonde.'

'Terry Wigan said that she'd moved away from Summerhill.'

'Yeah, snared husband number three, bloke called Trevor Spandal, and left for pastures new.'

'Know where?'

'Somewhere around here, I think.'

Behind us someone paid the jukebox. The opening bars of James Brown's 'Sex Machine' filled the room. Two girls in short skirts began dancing. John Mitchell looked them over appreciatively. He wasn't the only one.

'Do you know where I can find his mate Max?'

'I don't know Max. Met his girlfriend once. She works at that supermarket on Queensway. Name's Jenny. Can't remember her last name, something Irish, I think.'

I imbibed some more when I got home and awoke the next day in the same clothes and with a pain above my neck where my head should have been. The Blue Skies beckoned.

As I sat down to a plate of bacon and eggs, I realized I hadn't seen the wandering poet of Westbourne Grove lately.

Pat had evidently been thinking the same thing. 'I haven't seen Geoffrey for four days. It's not like him. I worry that he's not eating decent meals. He doesn't eat, you know, unless you remind him.' She slopped more coffee into my mug. 'He's not on the phone, so I can't ring.'

I took the hint. 'I'll go over tonight to check on him.'

'We need a couple of stories on the shelf for next week,' said Felicia. 'Self-explanatory. Have a read through.' I took the file from her hand and made off back to my own desk.

I looked in the file. My mission was to set up a studio interview on pornography for women.

Some guys have all the luck.

I phoned Damien Jay, a director who had made a pornographic film called *Blue Satin*.

'So,' I said. 'A lot of guys would be downright jealous of your job.'

He just laughed. He told me he had recently graduated from a prestigious film school, but had been unable to find work. The proceeds from *Blue Satin* were to subsidize a less raunchy film that he had written and couldn't get backing to produce. He agreed to come on the show and talk about the importance of sensitive pornography for women, if he could think of something meaningful to say between now and then.

I typed out a few questions for Crosbie into the computer and then printed them out. I took them over to her.

'Dar-ling,' she said when she looked at them. 'This is good. Your idea?'

I shook my head.

'Still, you're fitting in well here, I think.' She leaned back in her chair and tipped her glasses off the end of her nose. 'How are you finding it?' Crosbie has the gift of professional insincerity most often found in news presenters and politicians.

I considered my answer. The people who work with her think Crosbie is a joke, but the bosses take her very seriously indeed.

'Well, Crosbie, I'm still finding my feet. You know,

there's a lot to learn, but I feel I'm learning . . . a lot,'
I said, which was probably true.

Crosbie seemed satisfied. She leaned back, put her
glasses back on. 'Good, good,' she said. After the
second 'good' she picked up the paper again. My audience was over.

When my shift ended I went to the supermarket
on Queensway where Max's girlfriend worked.

'May I help you?' asked an officious young man
when I enquired at the office for Jenny. His laminated
name tag advised me that he, Leonard Anderson, was
the assistant duty manager for the evening.

'I hope so, to be sure,' I said, affecting a rough but
likable Irish brogue. 'I'm looking for my cousin Jenny.
Oonagh gave me her address before I left Cavan but
she wrote it on a small piece of paper, and I'm
ashamed to say, well, I lost it is the honest truth. Now
I don't know how to get in touch, and it's a bit of a
problem. Y'see I've brought a pound cake from Granny
O'Dowd – she bakes cousin Jenny one every year and
whichever of the family is going to be in London at
this time delivers it to her – so I have to get it to her
soon. Now I know what you'll be saying: why not just
call Oonagh back in Cavan and get her to give you the
address again? But, y'see, the trouble is she's as deaf
as a post. Never hears the phone ring, Lord in heaven
knows why she has one, and does she complain when
the bill comes in! But will she get rid of it? She'd rather
die!'

The assistant duty manager did not look convinced. He had a strange expression on his face; half-
sneer, half-frown. He didn't know what to make of the

situation, so he gave in to a time-honoured impulse and palmed me off on to someone else.

'Liz, when is Jen on next?'

'Tomorrow morning at eight,' said the woman behind the till.

'If you had her home address, I could be dropping off Granny's cake. It would break her heart if it was stale before . . .'

'Come back tomorrow, mate,' said the assistant duty manager. 'And don't try anything funny, or I'll call the police.'

I remembered that I'd promised Pat I'd look in on Geoffrey. His flat was walking distance from Queensway, in Queen's Gardens. It's a smart street except for Geoffrey's building, which the freeholder hasn't made any improvements to in the last twenty-odd years. The neglect was useful to me, though. It made the front lock easy to manipulate with a plastic card. I was forced to take this route after there was no reply to my ring. I climbed three flights of stairs and knocked on Geoffrey's door.

'Geoffrey, it's me, Sam.'

I knocked louder. 'Geoffrey, are you in there?'

I knocked again. I tried the door, it pushed open. The flat was as cold as a crypt. Geoffrey's bedroom was straight off the tiny foyer. It was empty. Geoffrey wasn't in the living room either. I tried the kitchen, and then went through to the back where the bathroom was. I walked in slowly, dreading what I might find.

Chapter Twenty-four

He was lying half naked in the bath, facing a large window which was open. A slight humming sound came from deep within his frail body. He appeared to be in a deep trance. I stopped in the middle of the room, not wanting to approach him too suddenly. I said his name softly. There was no reply.

I went over to him and put my hand lightly on his shoulder. He let out a great bellow, like the sound of an animal in pain. Then he started gabbling, nonsensical sentences which sounded like the last words of an aged prophet before he meets his God. I watched in horror as he got up on his knees and began rocking back and forth. He still took no notice of me. I went in search of the phone, and then remembered he didn't have one. I went downstairs, hammered on the neighbour's door. A young man answered.

'My friend who lives upstairs is very sick. May I borrow your phone?'

He nodded mutely, and led me through to his living room. A bottle of champagne sat on the floor, along with two empty glasses and plates with scraps of food.

'Phone's in the study,' he said. He pointed the way. The study had enough high technology to launch a manned space flight. Computers, printers, a fax machine, an electronic keyboard, an expensive Scandinavian stereo.

'Phone's there,' said my host.

'Jerry? What's happening?' came a voice from another room.

The man called Jerry disappeared, and emerged a few moments later with another young man. Both wore Levis and white T-shirts.

I called my doctor. He was in the middle of a dinner party.

'Ridley, the days when I did house calls are well gone.' It was a formal dinner party with many important people saying nice things about his wife's goat's cheese gratin and sundried tomato coulis.

'Well, just tell me what to do, for Christ's sake. He's freezing, he probably hasn't eaten for days, and it looks to me like he's had some sort of a nervous breakdown.'

'Get him to a hospital,' he said and hung up.

'Remind me, when this is over, to change my GP,' I said to Jerry. He introduced Mike.

'We'll take my car,' said Mike, hopping on one foot as he pulled on his boots. Jerry and I went back upstairs to Geoffrey. He was lying silently now, exhausted and frozen. We picked him up as gently as we could and carried him downstairs. Outside, Mike was waiting at the wheel of a Japanese space wagon, the type that can seat fourteen and still have room for a pool table. He'd rolled down the back seat and we slid Geoffrey in. The van was so big he could lie out straight. Jerry ran back upstairs to fetch a blanket and a pillow.

We took him to Accident and Emergency at St

Mary's Hospital, where the gods were with us. A harassed young doctor took one look at him and loaded him on to a gurney.

'We'll run some tests,' he said, as Geoffrey was wheeled away. I went over to the reception to take care of the bureaucratic details, and Mike and Jerry went off in search of coffee. I told the receptionist as much as I could about Geoffrey, which wasn't that much. Then I called the Blue Skies to pass a message on to Pat. Mike and Jerry came back with three polystyrene cups filled with coffee and some hermetically sealed biscuits.

'I hadn't seen him for a few days,' said Jerry, 'but I had no idea that anything was wrong.'

'He'll be OK,' I said. 'Tough as old boots.'

About half an hour later the young doctor came back.

'Your friend is lucky he didn't catch pneumonia. He needs to rest now, so no point in hanging around. I suggest you come back tomorrow.'

Mike and Jerry drove off. I looked about for a cab, but there wasn't one so I began to walk home. It was a warm night and the pavements were wet although the air was dry; my favourite weather conditions in London. I walked slowly through the streets, thinking about what it was like to lose people you love.

On Saturday morning I fired up the trusty Renault. It may look a little shabby, but it starts first time, every time. It was twenty past eight when I pulled up outside the supermarket where Max's girlfriend Jenny worked. I parked illegally (there's very few other ways to do it in this city) and went in. There was only one woman working the tills. She had glossy black, curly hair and glossy black skin to match. No wonder the management had been so patently unimpressed by my performance yesterday.

'Jenny?'

She had the slightly puzzled look that people wear when someone they don't know addresses them by name. 'Yeah?'

I introduced myself.

'Ah, you're the nutter who called yesterday.'

'I need to speak to you. Can you spare a few minutes?'

''Fraid not. You don't sound very Irish.'

'Well, you know, been away from the old country for a while. It's about Max.'

'Max has done nothing wrong,' she said defensively.

'Did I say he had? I need to speak to him about his friend Shark, who was killed this week. It's very important.'

Jenny looked over my shoulder. A queue had formed behind me. Tight-faced customers were clutching breakfast supplies and willing me to drop dead or move on. I moved on.

A quick stroll around the supermarket and I was back, this time with a pint of milk and a loaf of bread.

'That'll be a pound ten,' she said. I dug in my pocket for the money. 'And I don't think I can help you.'

'It won't take a moment,' I said.

'Miss Oden, please. There are other customers.' Another officious young man with a laminated name tag had approached us. Jenny looked at him sullenly. There was a murmur of assent from the queue gathering behind me.

'Open another till,' I suggested brightly. 'There's lots to choose from.'

'Bugger off,' said another disgruntled shopper.

'Whatever happened to old-fashioned service?' I asked as I was directed to the door. I stood outside on the pavement, looking in. Jenny had begun serving the person behind me. She looked up and I was still there. She sighed, wrote something down and gave it to the customer, a burly-looking chap in bikers' leathers.

'This is for you,' he said as he emerged with his purchases.

The card read 'The Bottle, 68 Roman Road, Vauxhall. Underneath it Jenny had written, 'I'll be there from eleven tonight.'

I rescued the Renault from a traffic warden and drove up Westbourne Grove to the Blue Skies, parked illegally again, and went in.

'I called the hospital this morning. They wouldn't tell me anything,' said Pat as she delivered a mug of coffee to my table.

I told her what had happened.

'Stupid old fool,' she said.

'Nothing to worry about,' I said. 'Doc says he's gonna be fine.'

'They'll say he's crazy. They'll take him away and put him in a loony hospital and he really will go loony.'

'No, they won't. Firstly because we won't let them, and secondly because every single public hospital in this country has a waiting list of at least eighteen months, and we'll have got his false papers and new identity arranged by then.'

Pat wasn't amused. She went off to fetch my breakfast.

I took the milk and bread I had bought from Jenny home and put them in my fridge. Then I stood for a few minutes simply admiring them. They looked good. Gave the place a homey feel.

At two o'clock I picked Pat up from the Blue Skies and we drove to the hospital. It was the first time I had seen Pat in civvies. It was slightly disconcerting, like meeting the twin of someone you've known for some time. She looked fragile and thinner than ever in jeans and a woolly jumper. She held a light grey vinyl handbag and a bunch of flowers.

'Perhaps we should buy him a book,' she suggested. 'He likes to read.'

We stopped in at a book shop and wandered round for a few minutes before admitting that we didn't have the first clue what to get him.

'Probably the last thing he needs,' said Pat, getting back into the car. 'If he didn't have so many ideas stuffed in his head, this would never have happened.'

Mike and Jerry had been in before us, bringing flowers and supplies from Geoffrey's flat. A pile of poetry books sat on the floor, next to the bedpan.

The patient was pale. A drip was attached to his left arm. He saw us and struggled into a more upright position.

A nurse came over. 'Ten minutes, no more,' she said.

'They're treating me like an invalid or something,' Geoffrey said apologetically. 'There's really no need. I'm as healthy as I've ever been. I'm going to be out of here tomorrow.'

The nurse smiled and touched his shoulder lightly. She was sweet and young.

'Now, you know that's not true,' she said. 'You have to stay with us for a little bit longer than that.'

'Stay a bit longer?' said Geoffrey. 'Why on earth? I've never been in hospital in my life. It's not that I don't like you, dear, it's just that, well, I have business to attend to.' He plucked at the drip that connected his arm to a plastic bag filled with fluid. The nurse went to stop him but he waved her away. Confused, she took a step back. Geoffrey peeled the plaster back.

'Geoffrey!' snapped Pat. 'You do what you're told, you hear me?'

Stunned, Geoffrey looked at Pat, who had retrieved the plaster from the bedside table where he had placed it.

'Now look,' she said in the same stern tone. 'You're going to obey the nice nurse because she knows what's good for you. Now let's keep this drip where it is. Sam's come to see you. Why don't we have a nice conversation? Or maybe Sam can read you some of your books. Would you like that?'

For a minute I thought Geoffrey was going to sulk, but he couldn't bring himself to. He lay back in the bed while the nurse re-fixed the drip.

I sorted through the pile of books by his bed. Second from the bottom was a volume of William Blake's verse. I leafed through it until I found 'Visions of the Daughters of Albion'.

I read it aloud to Geoffrey. The poem is not very long and it is a little obtuse in places, but it has a haunting quality. I got carried away. I was the lovely maid Oothoon, wailing to the gods, kicking herself for having slept with the wrong guy, Bromion, especially after her real love, Theotormon, found out and refused to forgive her. When I'd finished I was so involved in the poem that I hadn't noticed Geoffrey had fallen asleep.

Driving across to South London and the Bottle that evening, I wondered why Elaine York had chosen to name her child Albion. Had the poem been a favourite of hers? Or had she just liked the name?

I was expecting the Bottle to be a pub. It was a dance club, tucked away under railway arches. It had just gone eleven when I stepped up to the door.

'We're not open,' said a burly man in black leather.

'I'm here to see Jenny Oden.'

His expression indicated that he thought it a feeble excuse but he let me in anyway. The room was bigger than the outside suggested. There was a bar, a dance floor and, on a low stage, a DJ checking sound equipment. The DJ was Jenny. She waved to me and came down off the stage. We sat at the bar with two beer bottles in front of us.

'Sorry about creating trouble for you at work,' I said.

'This is my work,' she said. 'The other is what I do to earn money.'

'How'd you get started?'

'A mate used to do it. He got sick one night – too

many brightly coloured tablets – and I took over. Been doin' it ever since.'

'How does Max fit into this?'

'Explain to me again why you want to see him?'

So I told her about Elaine York and Shark's phone calls, and Rufus and Mitchell, which led me neatly back to her.

'But you're not a cop?' she asked.

'No, I'm a reporter. I'm hoping you'll be able to tell me where he is.'

'He doesn't need any aggro.'

'Neither do I. I just want to ask him about Shark.'

Jenny sipped from her bottle and put it slowly on the bar. 'He comes here most Saturdays. You'll just have to wait and see.'

'How will I recognize him to speak to?'

'Easy. He'll be the only white geezer 'sides you in the room.'

At eleven thirty exactly, the music started.

Chapter Twenty-five

The music was fast and loud, like the beat of a thousand drums on an endless loop. Sometimes when Jenny put a track on I thought I recognized a song from my era, but they'd been whisked away from their origins and re-mixed, whipped up into a frenzy of rhythm. It was so loud I could feel my ribs vibrating. My ears hurt. I could hardly breathe. Using sign language, I asked the barman to serve me another beer and I looked around for Max. So far, mine was still the only white face in the room. The only face over twenty-five. The only body not clad in a rainbow of Lycra.

They danced as one, like people possessed. They danced erotically and energetically in turns. They danced with partners and by themselves. They danced as if there was no other thing in the world that they'd rather be doing.

'What sort of music is this?' I said to the barman during a lull when Jenny jumped down off the podium to take a quick break.

'Jungle,' he said.

I nodded. I'd never heard of it.

Dancers who came to the bar for drinks before

plunging back into the maelstrom looked at me suspiciously.

'They think you're a cop,' said the barman. 'Are you a cop?'

'I take that as an insult,' I said.

I sat there for about an hour. The music was rather enjoyable once you got used to the punishing rhythm and volume. Periodically, I scanned the room for Max.

At twelve thirty I saw him on the stage: a skinny kid with lank black hair talking to Jenny. I recognized him from that day in the elevator. She was yelling in his ear and gesticulating towards me. The kid looked up, saw me. You didn't need to be a body language expert to figure out what he was thinking. His face filled with panic. He jumped down off the stage and merged with the crowd.

I went after him, pushing my way through legs and arms. A flying limb caught me on the cheekbone as I tried to forge a path. I could see Max's head. He reached a fire door, yanked it open, went out. I followed.

The coldness and silence hit me. My ears were buzzing, but that was blessed relief compared with the aural torture I'd just been through.

Then I remembered what I was doing out here. The fire exit led out on to a small cobbled alleyway. I looked up and down, no Max.

'Max!' I yelled. 'I just want to talk to you.'

Silence.

I turned right, walking quietly. There was a shadow in a doorway up ahead. As I approached it ran off. I went after it. We ran to the end of the alley and turned right again. Another street, this one a little wider, but still deserted. The street was a dead end, as it turned out, although you couldn't see that until you were almost upon it. Max took a flying leap at the six-foot-high brick wall, and disappeared nimbly over the other side. I attempted to follow, but he had more than twenty years on me. My fingers grabbed the top, but my grip wasn't secure. I slid back, grazing both hands. I tried again, taking a longer run. This time I got a grip and was able to scrabble up despite banging my right knee on the wall. Not without suffering, I got my right leg hooked over the top and after a bit of heaving the left followed. I fell in a heap the other side.

I landed in a pile of rubbish in what appeared to be a car wrecker's yard. Max was nowhere to be seen.

'Max! There's no need to go through this. I'm not going to hurt you. I don't want to get you into trouble.' I walked gingerly around the various dark shapes, my eyes becoming more and more accustomed to the dark.

Apart from the distant rumble of traffic, the car yard was about as quiet as this city ever gets. I heard a cracking sound. It appeared to come from behind a small prefabricated building just ahead. I crept around the side wall.

'Max, come and talk to me, for God's. This is about Shark, it's not about you.' Round the back of the building, I tripped on a stray bumper and went headlong. When I started to get up he was stand-ing over me, with a gun. I couldn't see it that well, because he was trying to make a secondary connection to my windpipe with the barrel. It's true what North Londoners say. You should never go south of the river.

'Don' get up,' he said. 'Or I might hurt *you*.'

Chapter Twenty-six

'I'm going nowhere,' I croaked. 'But let me stand up at least. The ground is wet here.'

' "The ground is wet here," ' he mimicked. 'Stay where you are.'

'Hey, kid. You get to my age, these things start to matter.'

'You wan' to talk, here's your big chance.' He took the gun away from my neck. But it was still too close for my comfort. A thought occurred to me. Maybe Shark had been offed by his mate Max. It probably wasn't a politic time to ask. I remembered what his sister had said about Max and wondered why I'd ever thought it was a good idea to seek him out.

'No,' said Max, interrupting my reverie to change his mind. 'I got the gun, I do the talking. Are you working for Rufus?'

'No, do you owe him money?'

'Everybody owes Rufus,' he said.

'Did Shark?'

'Yeah, I guess.'

'Did he talk to you about getting reward money?'

'Why you interested in me?'

'I want to know what Shark told you. About the

reward money. He told me he'd seen something. But he didn't say what.'

Max shrugged. 'Shark always had ideas, yeah? Always gonna do this, gonna do that. Gonna make a million. I din' take much notice ur what he told me.'

'Try and remember. It's important.'

'Why? He's dead now. Ain't gonna bring him back.'

'Police think Rufus killed Shark because he didn't pay back a debt.'

Max shrugged. 'Suits everybody then, don' it? Rufus gets put away.'

'But he won't, though. People like that never do. It's only poor mugs like Shark who take the rap.'

Max shrugged. 'Shark's dead. He don't care what the pigs think.'

'He must have told you something, Max. Did you see him the night Elaine York was killed?'

'Yeah.'

'What time?'

'At the Rover, 'bout one thirty.'

'Did he have anything with him?'

'No.'

'A bag, a woman's wallet?'

'No.'

'Have any extra money, any more than usual?'

Max snorted. 'If he did, he din' tell me.'

'Did he say anything at all about where he'd been, or what he'd done that night?'

Max rubbed the bridge of his nose with one hand, as if that would facilitate thought. 'I dunno,' he said eventually. 'I was pretty far gone, y'know.'

'Think hard.'

'I can't remember.'

I was suddenly tired and cold.

'Max?'

'Yeah?'

'Can I get up now?'

Fortunately Max seemed to have lost interest in me as an adversary once he'd learned that I wasn't in Rufus's employ. He waved the gun in a gesture which probably meant 'yes'. I decided to risk it. I got up slowly. My knees were stiff and sore from kneeling and from when I'd grazed them getting over the wall. He put the gun away, tucking it into the back of his baggy jeans. I took out my cigarette pack and wrote my number on it. No sense in letting him know where I lived.

'Call me if you remember,' I said.

'Yeah, right,' he said.

We climbed back over the wall and I limped back to the club and my car which was parked outside. I smoked as I walked. It took some of the pain away. I unlocked the car as Max went back into the club. Then he turned around and came out again.

'Hey, will I get the reward money if I remember what Shark told me?'

'Yeah,' I said.

'I'll think about it, then.'

'You do that, my friend.' I put the car in gear and drove off. I got lost a couple of times before finally finding a main road. When I drove over the Thames and got back on the right side of the river I felt much better.

The next day was Sunday and it seemed as good a day as any to reflect on the week's events, and to slowly drink myself into a stupor. I got up, made coffee then smoked a cigarette while I inspected the bruises from last night's jaunt. Max's gun had left a large mark on the side of my neck that looked suspiciously like a love bite. That'd silence those wagging tongues in the office who said I had no social life.

But then I remembered I had responsibilities these days. Instead of staying at home, I called in at the hospital to see Geoffrey. He was asleep when I arrived, so I sat with him for a little while. He woke, but wasn't lucid. I read him a couple of poems, which seemed to calm him, and he went back to sleep. Later I went in search of the ward supervisor. She said that he was improving, but that he needed rest. The hospital's diagnosis, from the little they had spoken to him about it, was post-traumatic stress.

'He talks about an accident,' she said.

'His wife and child died five years ago – hit by a car.'

'Something's triggered it off. I'd say he's been sitting on five years of grief.'

At home I lunched well from one of the Krispy Krust range of frozen pizzas. I decided to use the rest of the day to find out what I could about Shark's mother. I looked her new husband's name up in the phone book. I got in the car and drove to Willesden.

I like to think of Ladbroke Grove, the part of London where I live, as being cheerful, working-class rough. But in my heart of hearts I know that it's not that at all. It's trendy inner-city rough, which is quite a different thing. To get real working-class rough you have to go to somewhere like Willesden, in the north-western suburbs of London. It's grim enough to satisfy the grittiest working-class requirements. It looked even grimmer on a cold Sunday afternoon: rows of desperate pebble-dashed terraces interspersed with off-licences, shabby mini-cab offices and pubs with darkened windows. None looked enticing. Mrs Spandal's house presented a facade indistinguishable from the others on her street. I pressed the doorbell and heard a small dog bark. A woman in leopardskin leggings and a gold lamé jumper came to the door. She had a terrier lodged under one arm, like a handbag.

'Mrs Spandal?'

'Yes.'

'My name's Sam Ridley. I'm a reporter from City Radio.'

'We only listen to Capital,' she said, and began to shut the door. I put my foot in it.

'I wanted to speak to you about your son.'

She looked suspicious. 'What about him?'

'Well, I spoke to him before he died and I wondered if I could talk to you about him?'

She looked behind me, as if to somehow confirm that I was telling the truth.

'You might as well come in, then.' She opened the door to let me pass through.

'Down the hallway, first on your right,' she said, letting the dog down to scamper in front of me. I followed her directions. The room was small, with low ceilings. There was a three-piece lounge suite in white leather, a small bureau covered in knick-knacks, and a large flat-screen television. I sat in the chair, which was so soft I knew that getting out again was going to be a challenge. The dog came up to sniff my knees. I scratched his head. I wriggled forward, to try and sit at a more dignified angle. Mrs Spandal sat on the sofa and lit up a cigarette from a packet that had a name like 'Satin-Puff'. She offered me one. I shook my head and reached into my pocket for the full-strength coffin nails I knew to be there.

'I'm sorry about your son,' I said. 'This must be an awful time for you, and I'll try not to make it any harder than it already is.'

'What's your story, then?' She looked at me steadily through the smoke she exhaled. She was mid-forties but holding up pretty well, notwithstanding her debt to Max Factor.

'Your son called me. We spoke on the phone twice just before he died.'

'What about?'

'I met him once, at Summerhill Estate. The reason he rang me was that he said he'd been witness to a murder. He wanted to get the reward money, but he didn't want to go to the police.'

Mrs Spandal snorted and briskly stubbed out her cigarette. 'Now there's a surprise,' she said.

'I went to the first meeting that he arranged, but he didn't show. By the time the second call came I thought it was a crank call, so I didn't go. That was the weekend before he died.'

Mrs Spandal delicately lit another cigarette. Her long pink fingernails made the job more cumbersome than it need have been. She said nothing.

'I wondered if he'd spoken to you about what he saw. He may have mentioned something in passing. You see, the police think he may have killed Elaine York, but I don't entirely buy that.'

She paused before she replied, and she took a long draw on her cigarette.

'I told the police. I told them my son was nothing but trouble,' she finally said. 'He moved out – I kicked him out – when he started bringing home drugs and stuff he'd stolen. I argued with him, threatened him with everything. Didn't make a blind bit of difference. He left school, wouldn't get a job. I tried to get him work as a window cleaner. That lasted about two weeks. Then I heard he was dealing drugs. Am I supposed to be surprised that he winds up dead in a skip? I've been expecting it for as long as I can remember.' There was a tear in her eye, which she wiped away with the back of her hand. 'I wanted him to move away with me when I married Trev. Come out here, away from the Estate. We'd try again. But he wouldn't leave his mates, he said. His mates? Never mind about his bloody family.'

'When was that?'

'About six months ago.'

'When did he leave home?'

'About two months before that.'

'Do you know where he went, where he was living?'

'No. He'd call me sometimes, said he was crashing with mates.'

'What about Max Adams? Did he ever talk about him?'

'They used to hang out together. He lived on the Estate. Sonny knew I didn't like him hanging about with Max.'

'Do you have any other children, Mrs Spandal?'

'One older, she's married and living in Dagenham.'

'Would Shark have been in contact with her?'

She snorted again. 'Not likely.'

'Do you really think he was capable of murder?'

She seemed to crumple. 'I don't know what he got mixed up in.'

I decided there was nothing further to be gained from Mrs Spandal. I gave her my card and told her to call if she thought of anything. Then I drove back to civilization as fast as I legally could.

Back home, I opened a can of beer and settled down to watch whatever the telly was offering. The phone rang.

'It's Max,' he said.

'Hello, Max.'

'I remembered sumfing Shark said to me that night.'

'Great. What was it?'

'I'm not tellin' you over the phone. Come and see me.'

'Well, you may be surprised to hear this, but I don't fancy a repeat of last night's escapade. Tell me over the phone.'

'You come here. I'm at the Rover.'

As cats everywhere know, curiosity is a dreadful thing. Swearing, I left the comfort and warmth of my flat and took a taxi to the Rover.

'Wot you wanna go there for?' said the cabbie as he dropped me off.

'Mind your own business,' I snapped.

*

'I'll have a pint,' said Max, who was waiting at the bar.

'You're too young to drink,' I said. 'Hi, Dean.'

'Hi, Sam. You're looking better.'

'The air in here agrees with me.'

'You know each other?' said Max.

'It's a small world, Maxie my son. You'll realize this when you get older.'

'I brought something for you to sign.' He handed over a grubby sheet of A4 paper. It read:

I herby declar that Max Adams told me what Shark Harkness told him the nite that ——— was kiled. And that Max Adams is dew the money from the reword.

'Remind me to get the name of your lawyer,' I said.

'You can fill in the name of the girl,' he said. 'I left it blank.'

'What did Shark tell you?'

'I remembered after I saw you,' said Max. 'Was goin' home and I nearly run into a geezer on a bike. I nearly din' see him, he had no lights. Then I remembered. Shark, he was waitin' to do some business that night, y'know, near her flat, an' he said he'd nearly been run over by a geezer on a bike. No lights and goin' like the clappers. Wonder he wasn' killed, he said.'

'Outside Elaine's flat?'

'Din' I just say that's where he was?'

'OK,' I said. 'Thanks, Max.'

Max sniffed. 'Think I'll get the money?'

*

176

I went home for another beer and a think. I thought about geezers on bikes and I thought about Mark Matheson. The night of the re-construction it had occurred to me to wonder why he hadn't walked her home, or at least seen her to a cab. Elaine was the nervous type, she lived in a dodgy area. Why, then, had she gone off on her own? Did he have another engagement? Did they have a fight? Or maybe I was being quaint and old fashioned. Maybe men don't see women to their doors any more. Either way, I had to see Mark. If he had changed his mind and come back, he may have seen Shark.

'Campaigning grannies.'

'Campaigning what?' Felicia asked. Her phone rang. She answered it, waving me to sit down. I did so, balancing a cup of coffee on my knee. Felicia spoke in French for a few minutes, then put the receiver down, her face set and angry.

'So?'

'So what?'

'You think I don't like working at *Female AM*, you think I spurn the programme and all that it stands for. Well,' I gestured theatrically, 'you're quite wrong. You want me to come up with stories, I've got one: women with a cause. Women with a cause and a bus pass. Geriatrics fighting to save the planet. It's great. You're gonna love it.'

Felicia sighed and pressed her thumbs to her eye-sockets. 'All right, then, go. Get out of my way. But don't think I don't know what you're up to.'

I picked up my tape recorder. That woman was so hard to please.

'This is no substitute for a life, you pathetic bastard,' she said to my departing back.

Roadblock's offices were in Camden, in a converted gin warehouse. It had been well restored and adapted for office use. I read a plaque explaining about the building's former life as I waited for Mark to see me. An arctic blonde with blood-red lips sat behind the reception. She'd obviously not listened when her mother told her it was rude to stare.

'Nice place,' I said to Mark as he led me through to his office, which sat on a mezzanine floor looking over the workers. The space was large and light, even on this overcast day. About seven or eight people sat in front of computer screens.

'Isn't it? We get it rent-free from a benefactor. The surplus of office space in London has been a boon for us.' We walked to a small alcove, where a machine extravagantly described as a coffee dispenser poured chemically scented liquid into thin plastic cups. Those guys, what kidders.

'You know about Roadblock, presumably?' said Mark as we walked back to his office and got seated.

'A little.'

'Well, you'll know then that we're an umbrella group for lots of small environmental groups who specialize in fighting road development. Most of them have no organizational skills at all, so we do all that. We plan and co-ordinate campaigns, find sponsors, stuff like that. There are more than a hundred anti-roads groups in London alone, to give you some idea.'

'Do the other groups pay you for this?'

'No. We rely entirely on donations. That's another part of our work, lobbying for funds.'

'Sounds exciting.'

'It is. We're on the edge here. The first years were hard, but now – now I feel like the tide is about to turn.'

There was a knock at the door and a young man entered nervously.

'Sorry to disturb you, but you did say you wanted this as soon as possible,' he said to Mark.

Mark took the folder he held out, looked briefly at it and put it down.

'Thanks, Eddy.'

The young man backed out of the room.

'How did you get into this line of work?'

Mark grinned. I could see why women would find him attractive.

'Escaping my destiny. When your father, uncle and grandmother are politicians, the pressure to continue the line is immense. This way I get to take pot shots at my father's party in public. For a rebellious younger son, I can't tell you how satisfying that is.'

'But that's not the only reason?'

'Of course not. Roadblock is not that popular now, but someone will thank us one day. Maybe even my family. Call me an optimist, but I don't believe it's too late to change things for the better.'

'Did Elaine feel the same way?'

'Elaine? Yes. Yes, she did. She was one of the most enthusiastic members of the team. We miss her professionally, on top of everything else.'

'What sort of work did she do?'

'She ran the office, did the accounts, made sure we

were good stewards with the money that was given to us.'

The coffee was too awful, even for me. I put the cup down half drunk.

'That kid, Shark, that they found dead,' I said. 'The police think he might have killed Elaine.'

'I know,' he said. 'I heard that.'

'What's your theory?'

He shook his head. 'I really don't know. If the police think this Shark character did it, then that's good enough for me.' He took a quick swig of his coffee.

'Those stories in the papers,' I said. 'About you and Elaine being lovers.'

An expression of disgust crossed Mark's face. 'I'm furious about that. I don't know where the reporter got that from. It wasn't true.'

'Where do you think it started, then?'

'We had a thing for each other a few years back, but no. I took her out that night because we had a few work things to discuss and she had virtually no social life, what with the kid and all. I thought it would do her good; get out, have a nice meal. So you see, Mr Ridley, I'm responsible for her death in a way.'

'How does that make you feel?' I could have gone soothing and sympathetic on him, but I had the impression that that was what he expected of me.

'What do you think?' he said simply.

'Someone I spoke to said they saw a cyclist outside Elaine's flat that night. Did you go that way? See anyone?'

He looked annoyed momentarily. 'No, of course

not. I got on the canal up at Great Western Road and went in the opposite direction.'

'So it wasn't you outside Elaine's flat, then?'

Mark smiled. 'There are a great number of cyclists in London, Mr Ridley, and if Roadblock has its way there'll be even more.' He became suddenly brisk and businesslike. 'Now,' he said. 'Didn't you want to speak to one of Roadblock's senior members?'

He'd arranged for me to interview Esther Andrews, an energetic woman who'd taken up campaigning at the age of seventy-five when an aggressive roads pro-gramme had threatened the home she had been born and raised in. She won the campaign – and the hearts of the public – by chaining herself to the tree-house she had played in as a child. Supporters winched up her food supplies. She was now a key member of Roadblock, advising on protest strategy. Her grey hair was pulled back in a loose bun, and she was dressed modishly in palazzo pants and a loose tunic with bold ethnic jewellery wound round her neck and wrists.

'People often ask me what my philosophy on life is, Mr Ridley. They say to me, "Esther, you can't have lived seventy-odd years on this planet without having picked up some nugget of truth that would be helpful to us, the generation that will succeed you." And you know what I say to them?'

Receiving my cue, I said, 'What do you say, Mrs Andrews?'

'Common sense, Mr Ridley. It's what we've all lost sight of. Common sense is a greatly undervalued com-modity. My generation placed a much higher premium on it, and we had a more mature society because of it. Wouldn't you agree?'

She was, as we say in the business, great talent.

I needed a cigarette very badly after I'd been in the pure air of Roadblock's offices. I began plucking at my pockets as soon as I got out of the building.

'Got a light?' The young man I'd seen in Mark's office was standing on the steps.

'Sure,' I said. I handed him my plastic disposable. 'Eddy, isn't it?'

'You have a good memory.' He inhaled deeply on his cigarette. 'Nicotine. There's nothing quite like it.'

'What do you know about jungle music?' I asked Lyall in the pub later that day.

'Been around a few years. Combination of hip-hop, techno, dub and Jamaican dance-hall. The English answer to rap. Played mostly on pirate stations.'

'How do you know all this stuff?'

'Teenagers,' he said. 'Come to my house, you'll hear jungle.'

We were silent for a bit.

'I've heard it said,' I said, just for the sake of conversation, 'that I don't have a life.'

'Who said that?' said Lyall, putting his hand to his chest in mock outrage.

'It's written on the wall in the women's loo.'

'The depths to which some people will sink.'

'Perhaps if I had a hobby?'

Lyall considered me. 'Hobbies.' He took a deep draft from his tomato juice. 'Hobbies are good. I don't see you with hobbies.'

He had a point. I didn't see myself with hobbies.

'Perhaps if you were to ask a woman out. On a date,' Lyall suggested.

'Which woman?'

'Any woman. The place is crawling with them. A great guy like you.' He looked at me. 'On second thoughts, you should get a life first.'

On the way home I called in at the hospital to check up on Geoffrey. Mike and Jerry were there as well. We sat around his bed in the awkward way you do in hospital and chatted about nothing in particular. On the way out, I told Jerry about what the nurse had told me last time I was there about Geoffrey suffering from post-traumatic stress.

'That would make sense,' he said. 'A little girl was run down and killed outside our building last week. A hit-and-run driver.'

'And who said chivalry was dead?'

'Yeah,' said Jerry. 'Guy did everything but reverse back over her to make sure he'd finished the job. Geoffrey could well have seen it. It was right outside our place.'

When I got home I opened a beer and trawled through my stack of newspapers. It didn't take me long to find it – a big story in the local rag from last week. Emily Stevenson, aged six, had been killed crossing the road. Locals reported hearing squealing tyres as the driver made his or her stout-hearted getaway, but nobody had seen anything. The police were appealing for witnesses. I studied the photo of the pretty little girl, who looked as though she had expected a sun-filled life. Her eyes were bright and intelligent; her wide smile didn't hide a mouthful of crooked teeth. The telephone rang.

'Hello?'

'It's Magnolia, Elaine York's neighbour. You, ah, you interviewed me.'

'I remember it well. Hello,' I said.

'Hi. Wondered if you were free for a drink?'

'When?'

'Was thinking tonight.'

'Sure, why not?'

'Meet me at work at ten. I'll give you the address.'

I wrote it down. It was an address in Soho. Anyone who said I didn't have a life was dead wrong.

The club where Magnolia worked was called the Kit Kat. Not terribly original, but that didn't preclude them from possibly having a dress code. I decided to wear my suit, just in case. She hadn't told me what she did there, but as her occupation had been described as 'artiste' in the newspapers, I assumed she was waiting tables between acting jobs.

At nine thirty I took a taxi into the West End.

The Kit Kat, as one might have expected, had a neon sign with its name and, underneath, a Martini glass. There appeared to be a faulty connection because it blinked in a headache-inducing way. It was hidden down a side street between a sex bar and an adult book shop. I wondered why Magnolia had to work in a place like this when she could have as easily chosen a place not frequented by sad men in dirty raincoats. I went in, checking in my raincoat at the door.

The place was done out in red plush. Small tables were gathered around a low stage. Each table had a candle stuck in a wine bottle. Velvet curtains framed the stage and the tables were covered in a jaunty checked material. There were about fifty people there, women as well as men. I was surprised to see that they were young and modishly dressed. I selected a table about halfway back from the stage and looked around for Magnolia. She wasn't about. I concluded that she must have finished her shift and be changing into her civvies. Half of me was hoping she wouldn't – the waitresses' uniform was a tight black number. Very short. A real treat. Just then, one came by and took my order. I beamed a few lustful thoughts in her direction, lit a cigarette and settled down to wait.

There was a drum roll and an MC came out from behind the stage curtain. He wore a fifties-style dinner jacket in pink with stovepipe trousers. His tie was a leopardskin print. I suddenly felt as if I hadn't taken enough care when dressing.

'Ladies and gentlemen. Please welcome Magnolia Trevenet.'

There was a smattering of applause and some wolf whistles as the curtain rose to reveal Magnolia as I had not expected to see her.

Chapter Twenty-seven

She was dressed to cater to a middle-aged man's fantasy of Arabian nights. Baggy satin pants, bra studded with rhinestones. Hair piled on top of her head, dressed with silver and gold trinkets. She wore gold at her bare waist and gold around her ankles and a jewel in her navel. Her eyes were heavily made up and lined in black.

The music started like the wailing from a minaret at prayer time and with studious concentration Magnolia began to dance, her body following her hands.

I leant back and enjoyed the show. I hadn't had such a good time since I can't remember when.

'How'd you like it?'

'Terrific.'

'Good,' she said.

'Of course it didn't give me the belly laughs I was hoping for.'

'Har-deh-har.'

'Sorry, you've probably heard that one a thousand times.'

'Thousand and one. Got a fag?'

It was about an hour later and Magnolia had

changed into her usual clothes. We'd left the Kit Kat and gone to a small drinking establishment round the corner that she was a member of. Magnolia had ordered a bottle of throaty red wine and we were giving it the attention it fully deserved.

'How did you get into this?' I asked.

She lit a cigarette. 'Finished university, couldn't find a job, started waitressing in clubs and one night I saw someone dancing. I was hooked. Of course, it's not the professional achievement my folks were hoping for. But, hell. I tell 'em, you can't have everything.'

'What were your folks expecting?'

'Something worthy. Dad's a mining engineer, mother is a mathematician. Funny, huh? I can't balance my chequebook.'

'Or prospect for oil, presumably.'

'Yeah,' she said. 'That either.'

She wore the same black wool dress she'd had on at the funeral, this time with a purple velvet scarf around her neck. Large silver earrings of ornate oriental design hung from her neck. All I wanted to do was look at her. But she was in the mood for conversation.

'I listened to your programme,' she said. 'Pretty exciting, that guy calling up and everything.'

'Yeah.'

'They said on the news that you'd spoken to him twice.'

'Yeah.'

'What did he say?'

'Nothing much. He didn't want to talk over the phone, he wanted to meet.'

'But you didn't meet him?'

'No.'

'Why not?'

I was getting sick of answering this question. 'Because he didn't show up.'

'He must have given you a hint, though. He must have said something.'

'He patently didn't have my best interests at heart.'

She looked like she didn't believe me, but she let it pass. 'Don't know why Elaine wasn't more careful,' she mused. 'She had a combination lock on her front gate that took ages to unlock. A very tempting option for a scumbag who just happens to be passing and who's not used to wrestling with moral dilemmas. I told her it was dangerous, but she never got round to doing anything about it. She was funny like that. Paranoid about some things, didn't care about others. Like, she was scared of the dark. Yet she lived on her own down that spooky little passage.'

'Maybe she didn't have a choice.'

'But she did. Her sister wanted her to move. Her mother wanted her to move. They said it wasn't safe for Albion. They offered her money. She turned it down. A bit sniffy about other people's money, got quite offended by any suggestion that she couldn't cope.'

We finished the bottle and called for the waiter to bring another.

'The police have been back and forth to see me, of course,' said Magnolia. 'You find the body and you're number one suspect.'

188

The wine was going down at a rapid rate. Magnolia refilled both our glasses. 'I don't even know how much of what I remember from that evening was real or made up. I sat there for what seemed like years until the police turned up. Then suddenly the body did that twitchy thing. I had to get out of that place.'

'I know, I was there too.'

'You were?'

'Yeah, when you fell over Charlie.'

'I didn't notice you.'

'You were tied up.'

'Don't remind me. Talk about embarrassing.'

'Don't be embarrassed. You made Charlie's year.'

'Jesus,' she said. 'Was he hurt? Perhaps I should ring him and apologize or something.'

'No need. You've already done more than he deserves.'

We finished our wine and talked about other things. When they started putting chairs up on the tables at the club, we took it that they meant us to leave. We tottered unsteadily out on to Beak Street. By some freak planetary confluence there happened to be a free taxi passing. We got in. Magnolia sat close to me and I could smell her perfume. It was sweet. We drove through the rainy streets of the West End, sliding closer and closer together.

When the taxi drew up outside her flat, she grabbed my hand.

'Come in?'

I've faced tougher decisions. I paid the driver and followed her upstairs.

Inside, her flat was warm and dark, lit only by the

sulphurous glow of the street light through the bay windows.

'Sit there,' she said. She pushed me gently on to the sofa. 'I'll be back.'

She came back with glasses and a bottle of champagne and we sat on the couch. We drank some of the bubbly, then we lay on the couch, then the carpet, fumbling around like two teenagers behind the school bike sheds.

She undid my shirt, noticing my bruises as she did so.

'My God, what happened to you?'

'I ignored my mother's advice and fell in with the wrong crowd.'

I have a friend who says that if you do without sex for long enough when the time rolls around again you feel like a virgin. I wouldn't go quite that far, but I did feel like the class jerk who has suddenly and unexpectedly scored with the girl everyone's been lusting after for months.

'I should warn you,' she said, as she undid the buttons on her dress to reveal the perfect navel I'd seen earlier. 'I'm broken-hearted.'

'So am I.'

Despite this, or perhaps because of it, we gave those Persian carpets a fair old workout.

When I awoke it was six o'clock and I'd been asleep for two hours. I was still on the floor, although covered with a duvet. She was asleep on the couch, wrapped in a blanket. I was lightheaded from the booze and lack of sleep. My mouth was parched and my back stiff. I felt fantastic. I searched as quietly as I could for my scattered clothes, wrote her the wittiest note my scrambled brain could manage and left.

Next door, Elaine's flat looked ghostly in the grey light. The windows had been covered up and the wrought iron gate double-locked with an industrial-sized padlock. There was no sign of the combination lock she had used to secure it. Presumably that had been taken away by the cops. I stood there for a little while, thought about Elaine and realized there wasn't much I could do now to help her. 'Life is for the living, my son,' I said as I walked briskly home for a shower and change of clothes.

My colleagues are a droll and suspicious lot.

'You're still drunk,' said Lyall as I entered the news-room, breezily greeting the assembled staff.

'How come I have a hangover, then, if I'm still drunk?'

'You act like you're still drunk. And you look like you've been hit by a bus,' said Lyall.

'I resent that,' I said.

'What's up?'

I plonked myself down on the chair in front of Lyall's desk, arms folded.

'Smug bastard,' he said. 'Who was it?'

I said nothing.

Lyall leaned forward. 'Animal, vegetable or mineral?'

I whistled nonchalantly.

'Anyone here?'

I smiled.

'Ridley, if you're shagging Andie, you have to buy a drink for every man in the place. No, make that two.'

I inspected my nails. 'Coffee?' I said and got up to get some. Lyall followed me over to the machine.

'Ridley, come on. I can keep a secret.'

'So, my old pal, can I.'

That afternoon I sat at my desk struggling with the eternal question: to phone Magnolia or not to phone her. In the end my good breeding won out and I decided to call. It was only fair. The polite and proper thing to do. But the polite and proper thing to do presented another moral dilemma: to make another date or not? How was she feeling? Embarrassed at getting drunk and getting laid? Hoping that I had been struck down by a Reliant Robin that very morning so she'd never have to see me again? Lusting after my body and panting in expectation of our next meeting? After forty minutes with this one, I decided the last option was the most likely, and that I would at least make the call and see how the land lay. I felt nervous and foolish as I reached for the handset.

I had definitely got out of practice with the gentle art of relating to the opposite sex. Apart from my brief acquaintance with the police officer's wife – which by no stretch of the imagination could have been called dating – I had not had anything even remotely approaching a relationship since Mary left more than a year ago.

The phone rang five times before her answer machine picked up. Her recorded voice sounded distant and cold. I plunged in.

'Hi. Hi, Magnolia, it's Sam. Just calling to say, ah, hi. Hope you're well and everything's fine. Just wanted to say, ah, that I had a great time, and, ah, if you like hanging about with broken-down police reporters you should give me a call.'

I put the phone down.

It rang again almost immediately, making me jump.

'Sam Ridley? It's Eddy Cooper. We met yesterday at the Roadblock offices.'

I remembered the nervous young man who'd brought the file into Mark's office.

'Are you free this evening? I wondered if we could get together. I heard you asking Mark about Elaine. And something strange has happened in the office since she died.'

Chapter Twenty-eight

The pub that Eddy had chosen was in Soho. It was smoky and crowded with cool people. Eddy had carved out a niche at the bar and had a pint of Guinness in front of him when I arrived. Feeling like some real nourishment, I ordered the same. He seemed as nervous as when I'd seen him the day before. Although he couldn't have been more than twenty-five, his blond hair was thinning and he had the look of a middle-aged man.

'I'm the new kid on the block,' he said. 'Most of the people at Roadblock have been there since day one – about three years now. Let me tell you it's not easy. I came in on a salary, whereas they had worked as volunteers. It wasn't anything anyone actually said, just a feeling I got that I was the spoilt younger brother who had it easy. I've tried very hard to be accepted – worked longer hours, generated more enthusiasm, more ideas. It finally seemed to be paying off. Elaine was training me to take over some of her responsibilities. She handled a lot of the administration and accounts and stuff like that. I think she wanted to scale down her involvement, ease herself out – I met her kid, who could blame her – and I wanted to learn all I could. That's one of the reasons I started in a small operation, to learn how to do everything.'

He took a swig of his Guinness, then wiped his mouth with the back of his hand. I felt like a careers counsellor.

'It's a tough business, you know. You have to keep a step ahead of the government, the media. You have to come up with plans that are not only effective but grab the television news by the balls. The more publicity, the more money. The more money, the more you can do.'

I was peckish and still hung over. I ordered a packet of crisps.

'I'm an accountant. Well, that's what I studied at college. I don't want to make a career of it. Anyway, Elaine was pretty good with figures too. She did all the book-keeping, kept it all on computer. There's some charity commission which gives prizes for the best sets of accounts, and she was going to enter ours this year. It's quite important; we're starting to get lots more donations, especially after Esther's stunt. The thing is that I'm supposed to be taking them over. I was going to do that anyway, but since she died there's been nothing. I haven't been allowed near any of her work. I dunno, it just seems kind of strange.'

'Did you tell the police?'

'Well, no, I didn't, because when they came round to interview us all in the first few days after her death, everything was in such a state in the office that nobody really knew what was going on. I'm not sure what to do now. I thought, you know, you might have some ideas, being a reporter and everything.'

'Why do you think this has anything to do with Elaine? Do you think she was cooking the books?'

'I don't know. I don't think so. It just doesn't sound like the sort of thing she would do. She was idealistic, and even if she weren't I don't think she would have had the guts for it, frankly.'

He leaned forward, his head in his hands.

'I don't think this is happening because they're unhappy with my work. It just doesn't feel right.'

'Were you given any explanation?'

'That's the strange thing. A few weeks ago Mark called me into his office and said that Elaine had too much on her plate and that he thought I would be suitable to take over some of her duties. He wanted me to start training with her right away, which I was more than happy to do. It's not as if she put me up for it and when she died he didn't have to have me there.'

'Did you see anything that made you suspicious?'

'Nothing, only that the computer records are off limits to me now.'

'Are you saying you think Elaine's death had something to do with her work?'

'I don't know. I just don't know. There are some times when I think I must be flipping out, imagining intrigue. Maybe the stress of this is too much for me. People get killed senselessly all the time. Why not her? Why can't I just come to terms with the fact that she got offed by some crackhead?'

A thought struck me. 'Were you in love with her?'

He flushed a deep red and took a nervous swig of beer. 'I . . . she was nice to me, right from the very beginning. She helped me to figure out the ropes. I .

196

didn't know anything. I was fresh from university. She was a good person.'

He looked at me in an imploring way and he suddenly seemed much younger. 'Sorry, I've been wasting your time. It's nothing to do with you. I don't even know why I asked you here, except that when we spoke the other day you seemed, well, approachable. Now that I've told you you probably think I'm a total dickhead.'

There was a message from Magnolia on my machine when I got home. It turned out that she was interested in hanging out with a beaten-up journalist. She was working tonight, but would I meet her outside her flat at midnight?

'Hallelujah,' I said to no god in particular. I made a few calls, then set my alarm for eleven and lay down to take a nap.

At ten to twelve I was waiting outside her front gate with a bottle of champagne and a flower stolen from a garden further along the street. Her taxi pulled up, and she waved to me before paying the driver.

'Hey there,' she said. 'Ready to play?'

Her kiss was gentle. Some minutes later, we went inside. For two nights in a row I counted myself the luckiest son of a bitch in London.

'Did Elaine ever talk to you about her work?' It was later and we were lying on the bed, finishing off the champagne.

'You can't stop thinking about her, can you?' She

pulled the covers more tightly around herself. 'Is that what you're into? Some form of necrophilia-by-proxy?'

'Just curious. A fatal flaw in old hacks.'

But she would not be placated. 'We've just spent an hour in bed having pretty damn good sex, in my opinion, and you're still banging on about her. For God's sake, she's dead. Let her alone.'

I leaned over to take her hand. 'It's my job, that's all.'

She snatched her hand away.

'Leave your bloody job outside the door in future. I'm not interested in it.'

I apologized and we lay in silence for a few minutes, before both reaching for the cigarette pack.

'Perhaps I'd better go,' I said.

'Perhaps you had.'

During my lunch hour the next day I went down to the office library to get the file on Roadblock. It was a fat one, and I had barely grazed the surface of it before I was called off to do a package on bizarre uses for baby alarms. The good thing was that it took me down near Westminster, and I was able to catch City Radio's political editor before he rushed off to something important.

John Baker has been doing the job for even longer than I have. He's weary and overweight and a chronic workaholic. His wife hates it that he's never home in the evenings. She's left him a couple of times, but always comes back.

'Thanks, old chap,' he said as I brought him a packet of cigarettes. Delaney's anti-smoking influence does not extend as far as the Westminster office, which operates as a self-declared republic.

'Why do you want to know about Matheson? There's no more to him than meets the eye.'

'I met his son.'

'Ah yes, the famously irritating son. Not exactly playing the happy families game.'

'Daddy must be thrilled.'

Baker shrugged. 'It's a cheap way for the tabloids to take a dig at him. He's dry. Takes the edge off all his talk about family values when his son says his party is "driving the country to destruction". Still, Matheson senior can't be all that worried. His son's activities give him a higher media profile than most backbenchers of middling ability.'

'Does Roadblock have any real influence?'

'Not directly, no. But it is starting to represent a sea change in public opinion, something that the clever people who run this glorious country haven't cottoned on to. The roads lobby is powerful and wealthy and the government is in thrall to it. I'm sure that doesn't surprise you. But things might change. Environmentalists have high hopes for a transport white paper that's coming out next week.'

'What's that going to say?'

Baker finished his cigarette, stubbed it out in an already full ashtray. 'They'll fudge it like they always do. The mighty automobile reigns supreme in this administration. Why do you want to know all this? Hardly your beat.'

'I'm just fishing. Trying to come up with a story which may herald my reinstatement.'

Baker grimaced. 'Rough business. Could have happened to anyone. Did happen to me once. Fortunately we were on delay. Some quick-thinking producer bleeped the word out. Guy saved my life. I was so grateful I sent him a case of whisky.' He looked at his watch. 'Gotta run. Call me if you need me. If you have anything more specific I could make a few enquiries – suck it and see.'

He walked me to the door of his office and then trotted off in the opposite direction, shrugging on his suit jacket and a tape recorder.

I couldn't face going home, so I took my stack of files to my local on Lancaster Road and settled in for the evening.

Roadblock had packed a lot into its short life. Formed by Mark Matheson about three years before in response to some half-arsed plan to put a road through the middle of a breeding ground for rare birds, it had earned kudos for its witty campaigns and its results. Its confrontational style recalled the early days of the big environmental organizations that had now grown a bit staid. Its colourful and energetic protests were always staged to best monopolize the television news, and had made a star out of Mark. He was oft-quoted in the magazine supplements of Sunday papers. He was young and good looking and had abandoned a career in banking to save the planet. The clippings showed that his opinion was sought on issues ranging from where he ate out to cruelty-free make-up. It took me a while before I'd made any significant progress through the pile. There were several more stories to read, but I decided it could just as easily be done at home with a glass of whisky. I gathered up my belongings, paid my bill and left. The night was warm and drizzly. I was covered in a film of damp and smelled like a wet sheep by the time I got home.

Outside my flat there was a black-coated figure with a bag full of groceries.

'This is by way of an apology,' she said. 'I'm assuming you haven't eaten.' The bag had a bottle of wine poking out the top, and the name of an expensive delicatessen on the side.

Her red lips were cold. 'You must be freezing,' I said.

The bag contained snacks, dips, salads and bread. Magnolia rustled it up expertly in the kitchen while I set the table and opened the wine.

'Domesticity,' I said as I stepped back to admire the final effort. I had created the indoor picnic effect, with an old sheet spread on the living room floor. Covered with food, wine and glasses it looked quite presentable. It reminded me that my flat had once been a place where I had enjoyed living.

'Not bad,' said Magnolia, coming out of the kitchen with laden plates.

We fell on the food, then we fell on each other.

'I can't stay the night,' she said later. 'The lock man's coming tomorrow. Getting a new door and locks. With what happened to Elaine I can't afford to take chances.'

Soon after she'd left, Eddy rang. He'd done a little surreptitious overtime going through Roadblock's computer records that day and ended up no wiser.

'I haven't been much help,' he said. 'I just can't get the information I need. It seems to have disappeared from the system.' I told him I hadn't made any progress either.

'Maybe we're approaching it from the wrong angle,' I said. 'Tell me what we know so far.'

'Well, what I think we know – what I think is that Elaine was possibly killed because of something she knew.'

'OK, given her position in the organization, what would be the things she knew?'

'Finances – that's the obvious one. Hmm, staff histories, what they earned, et cetera. She knew the agenda for our protest campaign. Mind you, she wasn't the only one.'

'Had she had any arguments with anyone?'

He laughed. 'If you knew her you wouldn't even ask that. She was the sort of person who'd apologize if you stood on her foot.'

'What about all the protests Roadblock have staged? That must have made some enemies.' I thought about the thuggish building contractors I'd seen slugging it out with Roadblock members on television.

'Well, yes. But that would be the organization, not any specific individuals. Besides, Elaine didn't have that much to do with the front-line stuff. She didn't have the stomach for it.'

'We need to find those records,' I said. 'And I think I know someone who can help.'

The Rover was becoming like a second home for me. I could tell this by the way the patrons took no notice of me when I came through the door. Strictly speaking, it was past closing time, but after-hours drinking was just one of the services the Rover provides its discerning clientele. Dean was behind the bar. She wore the usual assemblage of revealing Lycra. If anyone ever troubles to ask me, I'm going to tell them that foxy wonder fabric has made the greatest contribution to my quality of life in this, the late twentieth century.

'Dean.'

'Sam. Bruises fading fast.'

'Thanks. What's happening?'

'Oh, quiet. Cops been around, asking about Shark. A fat guy.'

'That'd be Charlie. The old bastard is as good as his word.'

'What do you mean?'

'Nothing. Who owns this pub, by the way?'

'Me.'

'A nice girl like you in a place like this?'

Dean pulled a pint. 'My boyfriend got into some trouble, signed over all his assets, then got nicked. He died in prison.'

'Too bad.'

'Yeah,' she said. 'He got food poisoning on a day trip outside. Still, it's an ill wind.'

She poured me a whisky which wasn't watered down. My stock was definitely rising at the Rover.

'Tell me,' I said. 'The first evening I was here, I spoke to a chap about housebreaking. Short guy, Sonny Bono moustache, jeans rolled up at the bottom.'

'That'll be Stumpy.'

'Cute name.'

'He had polio as a kid. You probably didn't notice, but he walks with a bit of a limp.'

'Then he's had to work hard to overcome the disability, what with his line of work.'

'He's very determined,' she said.

Dean took me over to Stumpy, who was hidden away in a back corner playing darts, and we were formally introduced. He apologized for not remembering me, but said that he'd probably had rather a lot to drink that night. We had a friendly chat, the result of which was that he agreed to supply me with a small piece of equipment at a minimal charge. It turned out he had one on him, so the whole transaction, including pleasantries and a free introductory lesson, took less than ten minutes.

'See you inside, me old china,' he said, patting me on the back as I left. Oh, the wacky charm of the English working class.

I arose in a sprightly fashion the next day and went straight to the Blue Skies for sarcasm and sustenance.

'You haven't been to see Geoffrey for several days,' said Pat even before I'd had time to give her my order. 'He wants to know where you've been.'

'I've been busy,' I said guiltily. 'Busy with work.'

'Well, some people think friends come before work, and I happen to be one of them.' She stomped off to the kitchen.

*

Eddy called me at the office while I was wrestling with a story about the problems of lesbian parenthood. He was warming to the cloak and dagger routine.

'Can you talk?' he said.

I said I could.

'Good. Me too. I'm in a phone booth. Can't take any chances, you know, In There.'

'Prudence is advisable.'

'Have you got it?'

I said I had.

'Great. I've done my bit too. This is a half-baked idea, Sam. But I can't think of a better one!'

Chapter Twenty-nine

Friday afternoon passed slowly. It's a relaxed time for a week-day show, and for once Felicia didn't have a list of assignments for me to prepare for the coming week. I made a couple of calls to set up a studio interview concerning a cellulite cream that had just been launched with great fanfare.

'We need both sides,' Felicia said, handing me a shiny brochure showing the thighs of a model who looked about fourteen. 'Get a doctor as well, some old bloke who'll say it's all bollocks. And don't sneer,' she said as I flicked through the brochure.

'That was no sneer. It was a leer.'

Felicia snorted. 'Cut the crap, just do the story.'

'Nobody is more interested in the state of women's thighs than me,' I said, hand on heart as she stalked back to her desk. Just for a moment she stopped, turned back to give me the full benefit of her disapproval.

The look would have sent the world's glaciers into retreat.

I finished the job and did some thinking about Felicia and me. For the sake of my employment prospects it was time to begin a diplomatic offensive.

I sauntered over to her desk. 'Fancy a drink after work?' I said.

She stared at me through narrowed eyes. Trying to figure out what my agenda was. I pasted a silly, I'm-a-harmless-sort-of-chap grin on my face. She didn't appear to notice it.

'No thanks,' she said and turned away to her filing cabinet.

I'd taken the plunge all right, but the water was icy, and shallow enough to break your neck.

I could see Lyall looking in our direction. Both eyebrows were raised. When I got back to my desk my computer screen beeped and the word 'message' blinked in the top right-hand corner. I pressed the button to recall the message.

'Was it her?' was written on the top line of the screen.

I typed in 'No'.

'Too bad,' came the reply. 'All that aggression. It can only be good.'

Companionless drinking didn't seem like such a good idea that night. I'm a gregarious person, and although I've learned to put up with my solitary state, running into Magnolia, however briefly, had spoiled me for my old ways. I decided instead to see Geoffrey. When I arrived at the hospital he was sitting up in bed, staring at a blank television screen. When he saw me he pressed the remote control, although it had no perceivable effect on the screen.

'Television is so much more peaceful without the picture,' he said and smiled. 'When I watch it the normal way I do find it difficult to concentrate. So many distractions, and the advertisements.'

He looked much better. There was colour in his face and he was washed, shaven and had had his hair brushed neatly. His hands didn't shake or pluck at the bedclothes.

A few minutes later Geoffrey's neighbour Jerry arrived. He had brought a child's board game, which we played noisily until a nurse threatened to kick us out. After about an hour Jerry and I left together.

'I checked on the hit and run,' I said as our Doc Martens squeaked in unison down the corridor. 'The police say they've got no witnesses. I wonder if we should raise it with him outright.'

'I'm coming again tomorrow,' he said. 'I'll have a word with the doctor.'

We said goodbye on the front steps of the hospital. I walked down Praed Street in the direction of the tube, then changed my mind and decided to walk all the way home. I stopped at a convenience store and stocked up on the basics – whisky, coffee and frozen pizza – and planned a quiet evening in.

Saturday night was clear, with a full moon. Not exactly textbook conditions for breaking and entering. I spent some time considering how to dress. Dark colours seemed like the obvious answer to the problem of camouflage, so I selected a pair of black trousers, and a black jumper to go on top. Simon had left behind a black beanie, rightly assuming he'd have no use for it in Sydney's sub-tropical climate, so I put that in my pocket. I considered my reflection in the mirror. Not

exactly David Niven's gentleman thief, but I hoped
that nobody would be checking.

Eddy and I had a plan of sorts. Fortunately for us,
the building we were intending to break into wasn't
alarmed – the benefactor's generosity hadn't extended
that far – but a security firm patrolled periodically.
The people who owned the Roadblock building also
had another one nearby. We'd planned around that.

We met at a pub on Camden High Street, one of
the noisy, heavy-drinking ones where nobody would
particularly notice two men in black. We each had a
beer for Dutch courage, and then went up the street
to the scene of the crime. The building was set off the
street, and to reach it we had to take a narrow cobbled
lane through the market. The back entrance to the
building was up a flight of metal steps. At the top of
the steps was a high brick wall, but it had a gap so
that the people who work there can take a short cut
through to the market. It was useful to us because,
from the lower level, it was possible to see how often
the guard came by. We chose a place under an abandoned market stall and settled down to wait. There
are a few restaurants and cafés nearby, so we could
hear voices and footsteps and smell food cooking, but
at this hour nobody came up this far to bother us.

'I'm freezing,' Eddy said after about half an hour.
'What are we doing here, anyway? Breaking into my
own office, for God's sake.' The guard had been by
once, and we were timing him to see how long it took
him to get back.

I had been wondering the same thing. I was cold
too, and my legs were stiff from pins and needles.

What would my ex-family think if they discovered this was how I spent my empty Saturday evenings?

The guard came back. Eddy grabbed my arm. We looked at our watches. Half an hour. Not nearly enough time, but it would have to do. We waited another few minutes, then went up the steps. As my mother had always instructed me, I looked both ways before crossing the forecourt. No sense in being struck down by a speeding security guard. The window we had chosen was small – about two feet by two – but big enough for us to squeeze through. Eddy taped the glass, then knocked it with a rubber hammer. I held my jacket underneath, in case any stray glass made a noise that would advertise our presence. It came away easily and in almost one piece. We cleaned up the edges of the pane, and Eddy scrambled through, with me close after him. After my wall-scaling experiences of the previous week I imagined that I was getting better at this sort of caper, but maybe it was the adrenalin coursing through my veins that had so concentrated my effort.

'We're in!' said Eddy. His stage whisper didn't hide his jubilance. It was straight-up adrenalin shots all round.

He led me through the darkened building. Our eyes were becoming accustomed to the dark by the time we got to the Roadblock offices. The desks were chunky darker outlines against the floor; a computer terminal perched on top of each of them.

'This is where she sat,' said Eddy. 'The police took everything.'

I opened the drawers of Elaine's desk just to make sure. But Eddy was right. They were empty.

We went up to the mezzanine. Mark's door was locked, as we had expected. I brought out the tool that Stumpy had sold me and inserted it into the lock. I tried the door at the same time. Nothing.

'Can't you go a bit faster?' whispered Eddy.

I wriggled the small piece of equipment as Stumpy had instructed. I don't know what fit of madness convinced me that I had any talent for this sort of thing, I even have trouble with locks when I've got the correct key.

I jiggled it some more. Eddy hopped up and down beside me. Then somehow – perhaps it was my prayer to the lock god – the door handle turned and we were inside.

The office was as I remembered it. A desk stood in the centre of the room, and to one side of it a computer on a small table. The walls were covered with photos of Roadblock demonstrations, most of them blown up to poster size. There was a standard filing cabinet with three drawers. Eddy started on the desk drawers. They were all unlocked except the top one. I started on the filing cabinets.

'Hey, give me that thing,' said Eddy. I handed over Stumpy's method of ingress and he went to work on the lock.

I flicked through the files. Staff CVs, clippings files, social security details, the sort of thing you'd find in any office.

'Found something,' said Eddy. He'd got into the locked drawer and was holding up a floppy disk. It had Elaine's name on it.

'It's her handwriting,' he said, closing and re-locking the drawer with professional speed.

'D'you hear that?' I asked Eddy.

'What?'

I raised a finger to my lips. Motioned Eddy to crouch down behind the desk. We strained our ears.

A door opening and closing. Footsteps. This time we both heard them.

Chapter Thirty

'The door!' mouthed Eddy. We'd left the door to Mark's office open. If the security guard was observant, he might notice that that wasn't the way it had previously been.

The guard, or whoever it was, was moving about the lower level of the office. Up where we were, on the mezzanine, we couldn't see what he or she was doing.

We sat there, frozen. Not daring to close the door in case the movement was noticed. The guard wandered around the lower level for a couple of minutes, then we heard his footsteps on the metal steps that led up to the mezzanine. He climbed heavily, ponderously. But the beating of my heart almost drowned out his footfalls.

There was nowhere in the office that afforded any better shelter than the footwell of the desk. My mind raced through the possibilities. Should we try to rush the guard? But then he would see our faces. Should Eddy try to bluff his way out? It would have to be a convincing tale indeed.

We were stuck where we were. The footsteps were on the mezzanine floor. Eddie, who had curled himself into a ball to give me more room in that small space, had his eyes shut. I held my breath.

Static burst the silence. The guard's two-way radio.

'Yeah?' he said.

More crackle. I couldn't make out the words.

'OK. Be right there,' he said. The footsteps began moving away. Across the landing and down the stairs.

I thought I would never feel that happy again.

After waiting a few minutes more, we shut the door to Mark's office and crept back the way we had come.

We squeezed back through the window in record time.

'God, I could do with a drink,' Eddy muttered. We made for the metal steps that would take us back down to the market and street level.

Behind me, I heard a shout. I looked back. There were two dark shapes. The smaller one shot towards us at high speed.

'Run!' I urged Eddy. 'He's got a dog.'

Chapter Thirty-one

We flew down the steps three at a time, and into the lane which led on to Camden High Street. Stumbling on the cobbled surface, we veered left into a square. Eddy led the way.

'The canal. Down here,' he gasped as he crossed the square. I followed his sharp left turn on to the towpath.

I could hear the dog behind us, his nails clattering on the paving. I didn't want to think about what would happen when he caught up with us. Eddy knew the area better than I do. I prayed that he had a plan.

My lungs bursting, we sprinted for a hundred yards or so on the towpath. We were heading east, towards Islington and King's Cross. There wasn't much light on the path, which was below street level. The canal smelt dank and fetid. Behind me I could hear the guard and the dog. The dog was gaining. I wondered what defence my lawyer would use when my case inevitably came to trial. Not guilty by reason of insanity would probably fit the bill.

'Shit!' said Eddy. He'd stopped dead in front of me. In front of us a bridge crossed the canal. The towpath did not go under the bridge. The path went over the top. But at this hour the path was blocked by a high gate. Even in the half-light I could see that it offered no footholds for climbing. The walls of the nearby buildings were likewise impassable.

The dog, sensing that dinner was approaching, had quickened its pace.

I took in the gate, the dog, the canal.

'Give me the disk,' I said.

'What?'

'Give me the disk!'

Eddy handed it over. I put it under my hat.

'We're going to have to get wet,' I said, sliding into the canal.

'Are you crazy!' hissed Eddy.

'Come on,' I said, ignoring as best I could the freezing water. 'It's not deep.' The water came up to my waist.

Eddy jumped into the canal. I grabbed his arm and we began wading across to the other side.

The dog halted beside the water's edge. It hesitated, whimpering. 'Go on!' shouted the guard, bringing up the rear.

Eddy and I ploughed on. 'We're going to get diseases and die,' he muttered as a dead pigeon floated by.

The cold, the water weighed us down. Eddy stumbled behind me, sank up to his neck. I reached back to help him up. His thin shoulders began to shake with the cold.

The dog reversed, prepared to jump. The guard urged it forward. It whimpered. The guard shouted some more. The dog began its approach. The opposite side of the canal was only a few feet away. I tightened my grip on Eddy's arm.

The dog began barking furiously. It had skidded to a stop on the edge, its powerful leg muscles keeping it safely on dry land. The guard was just about upon him, shouting, gesticulating, but the dog wouldn't budge.

'Good on you, Fido,' I said as Eddy and I clambered out. There was more shouting, but we didn't stick around to find out what it was about. A rough track wound up the side of the bridge. Cars drove by but no one paid any attention to us. We ducked behind the balustrade of the bridge, so the guard couldn't see our faces in the street light, then, straightening up, walked as naturally as we could towards Kentish Town.

'We won't get a cab to pick us up in this state,' Eddy said. 'We'll have to walk back to my flat.'

Walk we did. It took about forty minutes. We were frozen, exhausted and bad-tempered when we got there.

'Next time you ask me out, I'm going to say no,' Eddy said as he let us in. The living room was small but cosy, with an even smaller kitchen through an archway. And it was warm, that was the main thing. Eddy went into another room and came out with a track suit.

'I'm gonna take a shower,' he said. 'Put this on and dump your clothes in the dryer. It's in the kitchen.'

I was sitting on the sofa with the disk on the coffee table in front of me when Eddy emerged from the shower. He went into the kitchen and came back with two beers and a large bag of corn chips. We fought each other for the salty triangles, all social restraints disintegrating after one night of law-breaking.

'Right, let's see if our possibly contracting pneumonia was worth it,' said Eddy. He loaded the floppy disk into his computer, which had pride of place on the dining room table. I pulled up a chair beside him.

'The fact that there's even something on this disk is suspicious,' said Eddy. All of our records are computerized, and have been almost from the start. We had been storing them in the hard drive, but there are too many. Recently we started downloading them on to CDs, which have a huge capacity. You can store all of the *Encyclopaedia Britannica* on two CDs, to give you an idea of how much they hold.'

I nodded, although not all of what Eddy was saying was crystal clear. Apart from my computer terminal at work, which is essentially a clever typewriter, the computer age has largely passed me by.

'But a disk is good for one thing,' said Eddy. 'Because while a file is in the system it can be broken into, in theory. If you're clever enough and determined enough you can get into anything. But you put something on a disk, hide it away, and nobody can get at it.'

'Unless they break in and steal it.'

'Exactly.'

'The problem with that is . . .' His fingers flew across the keyboard. The screen indicated it was checking for viruses, then it gave the all-clear. Eddy punched in more commands.

The computer screen said, 'I can't read this. Do you want me to read it?'

'Shit,' said Eddy. He punched the keys which spelled 'cancel' and ejected the disk. 'The problem is that not all computers are created equal. New software is being developed all the time. Sometimes it's compatible with what has gone before, but sometimes it isn't.

So even a computer with the same software may not always be able to read a disk from another computer. The software we have at work is very up to date. Mine is a few years old – the application programme is different. They're talking different languages, that's the guts of it.'

'What do we do now?'

'We find another computer.'

It was three in the morning by the time I got home. I was too tired even for a nightcap. I slept the sleep of the innocent.

On Sunday I awoke to a bright newish day. I ached in every little place. Exercise; it's worse than being beaten up. I made myself coffee and wrote a letter to Simon. Despite what I'd told his mother, I did want him to be settled and happy in Australia. That was the best thing for him in the long run. The fact that it wasn't the best thing for me I put to the back of my mind as I wrote. I told him about how he was learning early that life wasn't always going to be fair. It would be a tough lesson for a ten-year-old, but I told him that he was smarter than most. Then I threw in some guy advice, emphasizing the importance of rolling with the punches, making the best of it, all that stuff. By the time I got to the end of it I almost believed it myself.

Then I called Jerry and Mike. Their answer machine said they were out living the fun life of a young professional couple, and would return my call when they got in. I left a message.

*

On Monday the papers reported a minor break-in at the offices of Roadblock. The police weren't saying much about motive. They reported the canalside chase and said that the guard hadn't been able to get a good look at the pair. I called Eddy with the good news.

'Ready to face the day?'

'I'm nervous as hell,' he said. 'And I'm not a very good actor.'

'You don't have to act. Just tell yourself that you were never there. You don't have to act surprised because you'll have read about it in the papers. Call in early, to show that you're really concerned.'

'OK. Were you able to get hold of your friend?'

'Not yet. I'll try again today.'

'If we leave some time for things to cool off, I can take it into the office and read it. But I don't want to do that at the moment. It's too risky.'

Monday was also the first day of National Infertility Week. Felicia had planned a special slot in each morning's show to deal with the issue. We already had several on the shelf, but Felicia told me it wasn't enough.

'Get off your ass, Ridley, and come up with some ideas for a change,' she said before she went into the studio for the show. It was a challenge. I had no interest in the topic and not one idea of how to generate news on it. But indefatigable Andie came to my rescue once more, waving a stack of clips from magazines.

'You'll find something in this lot,' she said, before

she too disappeared into the studio. Blessing the day her parents met, I started making calls.

Mike returned my call in the afternoon. I explained my predicament.

'Come over,' he said. 'If my machine won't read it, then I can probably find one that will.'

It was five thirty before Felicia would let me leave.

'I have toiled in the fields of mammon,' I said. 'And now I'm off to safeguard the future of the Western world.'

'Be on time tomorrow,' she said. 'I have an interview on breast-feeding lined up for eight fifteen.'

I had carried the stolen computer disk around with me all day. It was in my inside jacket pocket when I met a very nervous Eddy at the Lancaster Gate tube station.

'You got through the day, then?' I said as we walked along Bayswater Road to Jerry and Mike's flat.

'Barely. It's so nerve-wracking. I tried to be calm, but I felt like everybody was looking at me. The trouble is, I've never done anything like this in my life,' he said. 'I don't even get parking tickets. Even Elaine, who was a wimp if ever there was one, used to laugh at me for being so law-abiding. Bills paid on time, taxes declared to the last penny.'

We turned into Queen's Gardens. 'Well, now you can think of yourself as a Renaissance man,' I said.

Mike was sitting on the steps smoking. I made the introductions.

'Hiya,' Mike said, jumping up in the depressingly energetic manner of one who spends many hours each week at the gym. 'Jerry won't let me smoke in the flat.'

He dropped the butt on the step and ground it out with his foot, then he picked it up and carried it inside.

Mike was a man who took computers seriously.

'Jesus,' said Eddy as he gazed upon them.

A large colour monitor dominated the cluster of electronic boxes and keyboards, printer and fax machine. On the screen a dinosaur prowled through thick, prehistoric woodland. Every so often it would roar. Mike sat down in front of it.

'Like my new screensaver?' he asked, showing childlike delight in his new toy. 'Or we can watch TV if you like.' He pushed a couple of buttons and the local news came up.

'The office of the high-profile environmental group Roadblock was broken into over the weekend. Police say nothing was stolen, but they haven't ruled out a political motive for the robbery—'

'Burglary,' I said, interrupting her.

'What?' said Eddy and Mike together.

'It was burglary. We're burglars, not robbers. Robbery is when something is taken by force. I hate it when they do that.'

Mike said, 'Sam, is there something you haven't told me here?'

'Well,' I said. 'I was getting to that.'

He nodded calmly while I told him. Then he turned back to the screen.

'Let's see whether all the trouble you went to was worth it.' He punched buttons and the pictures disappeared.

'What application programme is it?' he asked Eddy,

rightly assuming that he was the one who knew something about it.

Eddy told him. 'I thought it was worth a shot with mine, but it wouldn't play.'

'Well,' said Mike, 'it could be your lucky day.' He turned to me. 'Sam, there's some San Miguel in the fridge. Wanna grab it? I can only think while I drink.'

I went in search of the beer. When I came back the screen was blank except for a little square.

'It's locked,' said Eddy.

'Locked?'

'Whoever used it locked it. We need a password to get in.'

'Can't you hack into it?' I said, using the only computer term I was familiar with.

'I could, but I'd have to program it to take every conceivable letter and number combination. It could take ages,' said Mike. 'Much better if we do some brainstorming. Most people choose silly passwords, like the name of their partner or their pet. What would this woman, Elaine, have thought of?'

'Let's start with Albion, then,' I said.

Mike typed in the letters. The screen made a clinking sound, but stayed resolutely blank.

' "Roadblock" is pretty obvious,' said Eddy. Mike typed in Roadblock. The file didn't open.

We tried 'Mulberry' and 'Audrey' and 'environment' and 'protest' and 'activist'. We tried 'York' and 'Robert' and 'Elaine' and 'Rachel', which Eddy explained was Elaine's middle name. None of them contained the key.

'She named her daughter after a William Blake

poem,' I said. We tried various versions of Blake. The file did not respond to any of them.

'Albion had a favourite toy called Floppy Bunny,' said Eddy. Mike typed in differing versions of that with no luck.

After three-quarters of an hour with no success we decided to go away and think about it. Mike told us to ring him whenever we thought of something, and he would enter it.

Magnolia had phoned when I got in. She suggested I come over for supper and sex – not necessarily in that order – after her show had finished. I called her back at the Kit Kat and we arranged to meet at midnight. The most prudent thing to do was to pass the time – about four hours – resting up. But the devil had got into me. I had the urge to break the law. I'd caught the bug, and I'd caught it bad. I went to my wardrobe and selected a wire coat hanger. I straightened it out and made a small hook by bending one end. Then I bent it into a shape that would fit into my breast pocket. I locked the door behind me and went out.

It was a crisp evening, and my protesting muscles were not happy about the walk, but there was no sense in leaving unnecessary evidence, like the car whose registration is in my name, outside the scene of the crime.

I remembered too late that Elaine's flat was pro-tected by the heavy police padlock on the front gate. I had not taken it into account when I planned this outing.

'Damn,' I said. I had Stumpy's all-purpose lock-picking device with me, but I had the feeling that it would be about as useful as dental floss. I fiddled with it for a few minutes, but the lock refused to yield. I took hold of the gate and shook it hard. It seemed fairly stable; the hinges were strong. I went out on to the street to check that there were no witnesses to my impending crime. The street was deserted. Neighbours on either side couldn't see the gate because there were no windows facing it. The other side of the street was shielded by trees. No wonder whoever had attacked Elaine had been able to do so with impunity. I took a firm grip on the gate near the hinges, as my farming grandfather had always instructed me, and hoisted myself up on to the cross rail, which was about waist high. The top of the gate had a half-hearted representation of spikes, which were easily manoeuvrable. I delicately lifted my right leg over, balanced on the other side of the rail on my toes and lifted my left leg over. The gate creaked, but it held. I dropped heavily on to the concrete on the other side. There were four steps down to Elaine's front door. At right angles to the door was a wooden gate, which presumably led to the garden. I reached into my pocket for the coat hanger and straightened it out, leaving the hook at the end. I opened the mail flap and inserted the coat hanger through and up. Elaine's front door was not particularly secure. There was an old spring lock and a letterbox without a protective shield behind it. As any security company will tell you, an open letterbox means open house for burglars.

I inserted the coat hanger through the slot and angled it upwards towards the lock. I heard the sound of metal striking metal, twisted the coat hanger and felt it tug on something solid. I pulled sharply and the hanger came away. I tried again. And again. After about ten minutes I was about to concede that it wasn't as easy as it looked when the hook once again made contact with the lock handle. I pulled, more gently this time, and the lock came away. I pushed the door and it gently swung open.

Pulling a small torch out of my pocket, I went inside.

Chapter Thirty-two

The flat didn't exactly welcome. It was cold, dark and damp and had the oppressive feeling of a place that has been abandoned. I went through the hallway and into the living room, which looked out on to the street. I ignored the spot in the middle of the room where I had seen Elaine's body. Instead I made for a small desk set up in one corner. I muttered an apology to the dead woman, told her I was on her side, and started going through the drawers. There was the usual collection of bills and bank statements, newspaper clippings of recipes and old Christmas cards. She had brochures listing the virtues of a small town in Somerset, and a stack of old photos. Mostly they were of Albion, in various stages of infant- and toddler-hood. There was a fuzzy one, much older, of Elaine with her arm around Anna. Both wore dresses and make-up and high heels. Probably off to a teenage dance. I put the photos back in the same order I'd found them. There was no sign of any personal correspondence. I guessed that was in the police file. The fingerprint powder that was dusted over walls and surfaces was a reminder that the police had taken everything they thought would help them find Elaine York's killer.

Opposite the desk was a small built-in bookshelf.

The spines showed names like Thackeray, Austen, Dickens and Joyce. She had several reference books, a couple of works on green politics and consumerism. As I'd half expected, there was also a book of William Blake's 'Poems and Prophecies'. I opened it to 'Visions of the Daughters of Albion'. Unhelpfully, she hadn't written anything revealing in the margins.

I went into the kitchen. The noticeboard was still there, but a number of things had been taken off it, probably by the police. The bathroom and bedroom appeared untouched. The bedroom had two free-standing wardrobes filled with clothes, a dresser and a double bed. A baby's cot stood against one wall. It was even colder in here than in the rest of the house. I sat down on the bed. Elaine was not an easy person to get to know, especially in death. She hadn't left anything behind that told me anything other than the surface stuff, and it appeared from speaking to her friends that she'd kept her secrets, whatever they were, to herself. But maybe now she'd crossed over she'd changed her mind, and would be at least a little forthcoming.

I sat on the bed and imagined her living in her little flat, cooking meals in the kitchen, playing with Albion on the carpet, maybe even getting dolled up for the occasional date. She'd obviously liked to dress up; the night she was killed she'd been in a short black dress with high-heeled shoes, more fitting for the dining room at the Dorchester Hotel than a neighbourhood brasserie. Why had she gone to such trouble?

'Help me out here,' I said to her. 'Give a working hack a break.'

But if her ghost was in that cold place, it was silent.

I let myself out the way I came in. It was nearly eleven, too late to go to most pubs, so I walked up Golborne Road to the Rover.

Stumpy was there that night and he seemed surprised to see me. He'd no doubt imagined that an amateur such as myself would by now be languishing at Her Majesty's pleasure.

'No names, no pack drill,' he said, clapping me on the shoulder rather more sharply than my aching muscles would have preferred, 'but 'ow'd it go?'

I told him his device had performed beyond expectations.

'Designed it meself,' he said proudly. 'Did years of research before I got it right. Being in the nick 'elped, gives a man time for reflection, like.' He looked pointedly at his empty glass. I got the hint, and went up to the bar to order refreshments all round. Dean wasn't behind the bar and there wasn't nearly as much satisfaction to be gained from looking on the guy who was her replacement for that evening. I took the two beers and a packet of cigarettes back to Stumpy's table. We were chatting away, exchanging war stories like two old pros, when Max came in with Jenny. They went up to the bar and ordered drinks. They had their backs to us, and I imagined I could see the bulge around Max's waistband where his gun was stored.

Stumpy saw me looking at Max.

'You know 'im?' he said.

'I've had the pleasure.'

He tut-tutted. 'You'll be well done to keep out of 'is way. Drugs. It's all down to drugs. It weren't like that in my day, you earned yer money fair and square.' Stumpy sounded like a middle-aged matron talking about the decline of the younger generation, instead of a man who had devoted his life to crime.

Max turned and saw me. He whispered something in Jenny's ear then came over to our table.

'When's my reward coming?' he said.

'I'm working on it.'

'Yeah, you do that,' he said. 'And don' forget our deal.' He walked off.

'You made a deal with Max?' Stumpy gaped.

'Of a sort,' I said.

'Did you hear what I just said?' he said. 'Don't trust the bastard. 'e'd shoot his grandmother if he thought there was something in it.'

'Did you know his friend Shark?' I said.

'I 'eard of him,' he said. ' 'e and Max used to come in here some time. ' 'e 'ad Shark on a lead, all right, least that's what it looked like. Shark was 'is lapdog.'

'I'm trying to find out if Max knows anything about Shark's death.'

Stumpy snorted. 'Max has a temper, and not too many smarts. I remember one night – musta been, oh, over a year ago, they had such a fight in 'ere. You shoulda seen it. Over some woman, apparently.'

'Jenny?'

Stumpy shook his head. 'Nah. Dunno who it was.'

Max looked at his watch, then at the barman. The barman nodded and Max got off his stool and went into a back room.

Stumpy nodded in the general direction. ' 'e's seeing Rufus. Rufus 'as been here a lot lately. Moved in, by the looks of fings.'

Jenny sat alone at the bar, nursing a Guinness. I

excused myself from Stumpy and went and sat on the bar stool next to hers.

'I got in trouble because of you,' she said, keeping her face averted.

'I'm sorry to hear that, Jenny. I hear that Max has a real temper. Does he beat you up? A lot of little men do that, it makes them feel big and important.'

'Mind your own business,' she said, putting her head down to meet her drink. But when she lifted it, I got a look at her left eye. It was purple.

'I hope you hit him back.'

'Didn't you just hear what I said? Get lost.'

It was the best advice I'd had all day. I went to the other end of the bar, ordered another round for me and Stumpy. I put down a five-pound note, and when the barman gave me my change he handed me back my wallet. I looked inside. The money was gone, but everything else was there.

'Where'd you get this from?' I asked the barman.

'I don't do questions,' he said.

Magnolia was resplendent in a purple velvet dress, which was low-cut enough to put her in serious danger of catching a chill. I'd had to wait outside her flat for ten minutes, but that dress more than made up for it.

'Hey,' she said, as she jumped me in front of an ogling cabbie. 'How've you been?'

The cabbie reluctantly drove off as we turned to go indoors. Magnolia seemed a little drunk.

'Allow me,' I said as she tried for the third time to get the key into her front door. I took the key from her hands. Inserted it into the lock and turned. Then

I did the same with the other two. The door had been recently installed, and had not yet been painted.

'Itsh a good door, trouble is . . . trouble is, it keeps me out too.' She giggled and collapsed. I caught her and carried her into the living room. I lay her on the sofa.

'Let me get you some coffee,' I said. I know it's a myth about coffee sobering you up, but it gave me something to do.

'Coffee. Good idea. In the kitshen.'

I found some beans in the freezer and a grinder in a cupboard. I made the coffee and waited a few minutes for the mixture to steep. From the sofa, Magnolia had begun singing sea shanties. As I reached into the fridge for some milk, a bulletin board caught my eye. It was pinned with recipes, old theatre tickets, photos and spare keys, and because I'm naturally nosy I perused it. The first photo showed a tanned and handsome older couple standing on an exotic beach. The woman was enough like Magnolia for me to conclude they were her parents. The second photo, half hidden by the first, was of Mark, Magnolia and a pregnant Elaine at a summer picnic. Magnolia was in the middle with her arms around the other two. All three were holding champagne flutes. Mark and Magnolia were laughing into the camera. Elaine had a slight frown. None of the photos I had seen of her had shown her smiling. I turned it over; the date on the back was three years ago.

'Hey, where's my coffee?' I spun guiltily around, expecting to see Magnolia standing at the door, but she had called, monarch-like, from her couch.

'Coming, my liege. Got any digestives?'

'Cupboard over the hob.' I found the biscuit packet, slapped it on a tray along with the mugs, coffee and milk and made a grand entrance. Magnolia was still lying on the couch, but she had taken her tights and shoes off and thrown them across the floor.

I poured the coffee and handed her a cup.

'I don't really want thish,' she said. 'Bring me champagne.'

'This is what you're getting, kid. Drink it or else.'

Meekly, she drank it.

When we'd finished our coffee I made her take a couple of paracetamol and a large glass of water. Paracetamol is better than aspirin, I told her, because it doesn't irritate the stomach. I poured another large glass and put it beside her bed, in case she got thirsty during the night. Boozers know all the tricks. I helped her to her room, and undressed her.

'I suppose you want sex now,' she said, as I stood by her bed.

I'd be lying if I said the thought hadn't crossed my mind, but I shook my head.

'I'm not that kind of guy,' I said before I closed the door behind me.

I let myself out, slamming the door so that the deadlock would click into place.

I looked over at the Summerhill Estate as I walked home. It was hard to avoid; it dominated the whole area. I walked briskly, relieved when I reached the relative security of Ladbroke Grove. It was getting on for two in the morning, but the place was as lively as if it were midday. My stomach reminded me that I hadn't yet eaten, so I stopped at the kebab place just past the tube station. The place was full of clubbers. I had to fight to get up to the counter and have my order taken. I ate the kebab quickly and it lay in my stomach like a dead animal. At home I had a large glass of whisky to cut the grease, then another because I liked the first one so much.

Felicia was as good as her word. When I arrived at work at eight, a woman awaited me in the green room.

'Breast-feeding, remember?' said Andie as I sat wearily down behind my desk. I felt nauseous; I blamed the kebab.

'Oh, Jesus.' I hadn't remembered.

'I'll delay her,' said Andie. 'Read this.' She slapped a folder down on my desk. I read it while walking over to the coffee machine. Like most assignments I was required to undertake these days, it seemed straight-forward.

'You're gonna like this one,' said Lyall, soberly pouring himself coffee.

'What one?'

'This one. Your assignment du jour,' he tittered.

I was shocked. Lyall tittering? Lyall never tit-tered. He hardly ever laughed, except when he watched old re-runs of the TV show *Not Only but Also*.

'I don't get it.'

'You will.' He walked off, a smirk on his face.

I feared another set-up. I collected my tape recorder and walked apprehensively into the green room.

A dumpy woman sat on the sofa, reading through a file which lay on her lap. She was probably in her early thirties, but her choice in clothing hinted that she had rushed headlong into middle-age. She wore a cardigan with sheep embroidered on it, a calf-length denim skirt with a ruffle around the bottom, fluffy wool tights and shoes so sensible they could have been wearing horn-rimmed spectacles. But that wasn't the first thing you noticed about her. I don't think I'm saying this because I'm a sex-obsessed old goat. I think most people would notice this first off, without any prompting. This woman had huge breasts. I'm not exaggerating. Words like *melon* and *bazooka* danced in my brain. I slapped them about and put them in their place. I thought about Lyall and I started to smirk. *Cut it out, Ridley*, I told myself. *You're a professional*. I stepped forward to shake her hand.

Chapter Thirty-three

I seated her in one of the larger interview rooms and put the tape recorder on a table in front of us. I tested the microphone and asked her to speak a few words so that I could adjust the level.

'Certainly, Mr Ridley. My name is Martina Waters, and I'm here to talk to you about liberating the breast from its tyranny as a sex object.'

She was good. Intelligent. Forceful. She spoke clearly and without hesitation. Those are qualities you have to cultivate going through life as a 46DDD. The interview took less than thirty minutes. Afterwards I walked her to the elevators and said goodbye. When I returned to the newsroom all the male members of staff were doubled up with laughter.

I stopped. I looked at them. They continued to laugh.

'Oh, grow up,' I said, and went back to my desk.

I spent the rest of the morning prepping an interview for Crosbie about infertility. Some couple had agreed to come on the show and reveal their most intimate problems to the world.

Magnolia rang me at home that night.

'Did I make an arse of myself?' Her voice had

dropped an octave or so. She sounded sexy. She also sounded ill.

'You were your usual charming self, only more so.'

'I don't believe you.'

'It's the truth.'

She sighed as if the memory pained her. 'We had a flood at the club, so the show was cancelled. A few of us went round the corner for a few drinks. I hadn't had anything to eat; I never eat before a show anyway, so I went straight off the deep end. Do you forgive me?'

'Nothing to forgive. Anyway, I'm hardly the one to be casting the first stone.'

After dinner I decided to see Geoffrey. I caught the number 7 bus, which dropped me right outside the hospital feeling ill and discombobulated. On some of the less popular runs at night they trade the sturdy old double-decker Routemasters for their baby brothers which zip in and out of traffic. Most of the drivers behave as if they're getting in valuable practice before they're called upon to join the British Formula One team. If you're unlucky enough to have to stand, staying upright requires the balance of a world champion surfer and the stomach of a test pilot, as the drivers lurch from stop to stop with all the restraint of a child driving a dodgem. If you're elderly or carrying heavy shopping, as most of the passengers are, you don't stand a prayer.

My inner ear just about regained its equilibrium when I reached Geoffrey's ward. Jerry was sitting at his bedside, reading Keats. Geoffrey smiled broadly when he saw me.

'Good thing you're here,' Jerry said. 'The police

will be arriving any minute. They're taking Geoffrey's statement about the accident.'

'Are you OK to do this?' I asked Geoffrey. 'If you'd rather postpone it, just say.'

Geoffrey smiled. 'I am feeling quite refreshed,' he said. 'This hospital isn't as bad as I had first thought. I like the food.'

Some moments later two young police officers appeared at the door. They carried their hats in their hands, and seemed awkward. The man was about six foot six, with feet so big they must have challenged even the police shoe supplier. His side-kick, a dark-haired woman with acne, looked equally ill at ease. I went in search of extra chairs. I brought two back and tried to arrange them in a conversational grouping around Geoffrey's bed.

The male officer looked at Jerry and me. 'Are you sure you want these people here?' he said to Geoffrey.

'They're my friends,' he said.

The police officer took a notebook from his breast pocket. It had a pen clipped to one side.

'We'll start by ascertaining your whereabouts on November fifteenth,' he said. Geoffrey looked puzzled.

'That's Monday fortnight ago,' I said to him.

'You stay out of this,' the jolly blue giant snapped.

Geoffrey paused for some time before speaking. 'I remember that day,' he said, 'because I had been at the library, and I was making my way home. I was walking up Queen's Gardens. It was a lovely day, more like April than November, and I just popped into the garden for a few minutes. I'd planted a rosemary bush . . . You won't tell the garden committee, will you? They don't like unauthorized plantings. I wanted to see how it was doing, and take a couple of sprigs home. Then I heard a terrible noise, the sound of tyres squealing and a heavy thump. I looked out. A little girl lay in the road, next to a big car.'

Tears rolled down his cheeks at the memory of it. He stopped. One hand plucked distractedly at the bed linen. He seemed to will himself to go on. Jerry patted his hand.

'I ran out into the road to see what I could do to help. When I got there, the driver was reversing. He saw me. But he didn't stop. He . . . he backed down the street, drove off and just left her there.'

Geoffrey's voice dropped to a whisper. 'He just left her there.'

'What did you do then?' prompted the woman police officer.

Geoffrey blinked away tears. 'People started coming out of their flats. I heard someone say they had called for an ambulance, so I left. I couldn't stand to stay and look at her lying there. I knew she was dead. The expression on her face was . . . was peaceful. I walked around for some time, I can't remember exactly where.'

'Did you get a look at the car or the driver?' The woman's tone was gentle.

Geoffrey looked uncertain. 'I couldn't be sure. It was a foreign car, maybe German or Swedish, I'm not sure. I'm not very good on cars. Haven't owned one, you see, well . . . for a long time now.'

'The person behind the wheel? Did you manage to get a look at them?' The woman police officer continued.

Geoffrey shook his head. 'It all happened so fast . . .' There was a pause while he struggled to remember.

'Did you notice whether it was a man or a woman?' said the cop finally.

Geoffrey paused. 'I . . . no . . . I don't think I noticed anything like that.'

'Did you notice anything about the car, something that may have struck you as unusual?'

Geoffrey silently shook his head. 'The little girl wore a blue coat. An old-fashioned one with a velvet collar.'

'What about the licence plate? Did you recognize any of the letters?' asked the policeman.

Geoffrey screwed his face up as if it was an aid to thought.

'A letter, maybe, or a number,' the female officer said. 'Take your time, think carefully.'

Still he said nothing. He closed his eyes and leaned back against the bed. Jerry patted his hand again. For a moment or two I thought he'd fallen asleep. The cops looked at each other. I could see they were preparing to go. The notebook snapped shut. We sat silently.

Then, as the cops got up to go, Geoffrey stirred.

'I saw it all,' he said finally, in a voice so low that we hardly heard him.

Both cops looked like a brick had been dropped on their toes.

'You did?' they said in unison.

'I'll never forget that licence plate as long as I live,' said Geoffrey. He leaned over to me. 'Sam, my throat is dry from all this talking. I wonder if you'd be so good as to pass me a glass of water.'

*

I left the ward with Jerry and caught the bus for another nausea-inducing ride home. Like a drunken sailor I lurched up the stairs to my flat. I collected a whisky on the way through the kitchen, and flopped in front of the television. There was news on. There's always news on these days.

This news was about a rape in a shopping centre. Some louts had snatched a woman as she went about her business, but because the shopping centre was rigged with enough cameras to broadcast the World Cup live, they were able to catch the guy.

A lightbulb went on above my head – these things really happen sometimes. I left my whisky, grabbed my coat and car keys and went in search of the Renault. It was parked where I had left it and it still had the radio in. The gods were good. I got in, fired her up and headed for the pub where some cops I know drink.

The cinema was doing brisk business because the alley was filled with cars. I took the same route I had the night Roger Fitzgerald had told me in his own inimitable way to stay off his patch. I turned off the street into the lane and walked down towards the cinema. Again there was the feeling that I was being watched. A couple approached the lane from the other end, giggling and groping. The guy tried to get his hand up the girl's shirt.

'Don't,' I heard her hiss, 'someone's there.'

'But I want you now,' he said thickly.

I walked past them, eyes averted.

'He's gone now,' said the guy.

'Not him,' replied the girl. 'There's a closed-circuit

camera. We don't want to end up on one of them videos they sell in W.H. Smith's.'

And there it was. A little silver beauty, mounted on the corner between the lane and the cinema back entrance. And it swivelled, following me as I walked.

Chapter Thirty-four

The cinema manager didn't like the look of me, I could tell by her barely suppressed irritation. But I took no notice. I explained my predicament.

'Oh yes,' she said, tapping a pencil on her blotter. The cinema's advertising which adorned the walls of her office seemed to have a far stronger pull on her attention than I did. 'The police have already been in touch with us about that. We handed the tape over.'

Damn it. Roger Fitzgerald had been quicker off the mark than me. Sometimes the race is to the swift.

'Tall, redheaded chap? Funny moustache?' I asked, although I knew what the answer would be.

'Yes.' The manager's eyes went dreamy. 'Very charming.' She pulled Roger Fitzgerald's card out of a drawer.

'Can I speak to your security people?'

'I think,' she said, 'you'd better speak to the police.'

'Look,' I said. 'The police are part of this problem. Did you get a chance to compare the face of the cop and the face of the guy who was doing the assaulting? It's the same face. That's why he was so keen to track it down.'

The woman picked up the phone. 'Sandy, can you ask Bernie to come in here, please.'

In came a guy who probably weighed twenty-five stone. He was as wide as he was tall. He wore a checked shirt the size of a home county and the crotch of his trousers swept down below his knees. His feet, the size of frying pans, were encased in carpet slippers. A name tag perched jauntily over his breast pocket identified him as Bernie O'Flaherty.

'Bernie. Can you tell this man what happened with the police officer?' She spoke slowly, as if to a child or a simpleton.

Bernie opened his mouth to speak; it created a tsunami effect on his many chins. 'You asked me to give him the tape, so I did.' He spoke so softly I could barely hear him.

'And what did he say about the tape?'

'That it was needed for evidence in court.'

'Did you make any copies?' I asked, clutching at straws now.

Bernie looked at the manager before replying. 'No,' he said.

'Satisfied that we're not holding out on you?' said the manager sweetly.

'More than,' I said and got up to leave.

'The detective promised it would be returned.'

'Right,' I said. 'After it's been accidentally waved near a strong magnetic field. I bet you a barrel of your overpriced popcorn that you never see that tape again. But if you do, here's my card.'

There were no messages on my answer machine when I got home and I deduced from this that the password to Elaine's disk remained a mystery. I knew that I hadn't been paying as much attention to it as I should have. I needed to sit down and think about it carefully, because if I did that, something would fall into place. I poured a whisky and sat on the couch in quiet contemplation, hoping that something would shake loose. It didn't, so I went to bed. I do my best thinking lying down anyway.

'Geoffrey's checking out of hospital today,' Pat said as she delivered my scrambled eggs on toast the next morning. 'Four o'clock.' She went away and came back with the coffee pot. 'You'll be there, won't you?' She slopped some coffee into my mug.

'If I can get off work I will. Otherwise I'll go over to his place in the evening and check that he's OK.'

'The boys are gonna drive him home,' she said, in a manner which indicated that she hadn't quite made up her mind about Jerry and Mike. 'I'm gonna go over to the house, clean and cook dinner. Make sure he gets a decent meal. That's half his problem, he doesn't eat.'

'I'll be there,' I said.

'Just make sure you are.' She stomped off.

Replete, I caught the bus to work and was inside the doors on the dot of eight.

'Your friend made the papers,' said Andie, dropping the *Daily Telegraph* on my desk. I'd told her about Geoffrey. There was a short story about an eye-witness testimony leading to the arrest of a BMW owner. He was to be charged with hit-and-run driving.

It was one of those days. Nothing happened. After the show we sat around listlessly, squabbling over the papers and making excuses to pop out for coffee. Felicia seemed wearier and crabbier than usual. I thought I'd catch her at a weak moment. She was leafing through a file when I made another approach at peace.

'Hey,' I said in the nonchalant and charming manner for which I'm known, 'the sun's practically over the yard-arm. Let's step out for a drink.'

She looked up from the file, but didn't stop leafing.

'How about a quick coffee?'

She was silent, leafing some more.

'OK, OK, my last offer – mineral water. Let's step out for a nice big glass of water.'

Felicia slapped the file down on the desk. 'Ridley, go and play somewhere else. I've got work to do. And come up with some story ideas, for once in your god-damned life.'

I went back to my desk, chastened and indignant at the same time. I have lots of story ideas. I get story ideas every day. It's just that they're not stories *Female AM* listeners would be interested in. I looked at my watch. It was a respectable hour for lunch. Lyall was free too, so we went together.

'So you're saying it wasn't Felicia, then,' he said as we walked around the corner to the pub.

'What are you talking about?'

'She acts like a woman scorned. You didn't bonk her and then promise you'd call, did you? What have I told you about that?'

'Lyall, you're just going to have to trust me when I say that I have not had relations with Felicia in the carnal sense. I know it's boring. I know it's not what you want to hear, but that is the truth.'

'Oh,' he said. 'Who, then?' Lyall has the monogamous person's desire for vicarious sex.

'Nobody you know,' I said. 'But if I play my cards right, you might get to meet her some day.'

That satisfied him so much he bought me a pint and a pie.

The day dragged on. I applied myself to several tasks which in other newsrooms would be classified as meaningless. I flirted with the notion of kidnapping Felicia and holding her to ransom until the station agreed to put me back on hard news. The idea wasn't without its charms. In this manner the day passed.

'I'm leaving early,' I said to Felicia later in the afternoon. 'I have to pick a friend up from hospital.'

'I didn't know you were a boy scout in your spare time,' she said.

'Oh, shut up,' I snapped. And left.

The hospital staff handled Geoffrey's send-off with all the ceremony of a state funeral. It seemed every nurse within a five-mile radius had gathered to say goodbye. Two of the nurses had composed a telegram, which they read out to much laughter. There were presents and flowers. Come back next week and they'd have started a cargo cult in his name.

He sat in the middle of it all, slightly bewildered by the attention but beaming and wiping the occasional tear from his eye.

Jerry had collected Geoffrey's few things, and the procession made its stately way out of the ward and down the corridor. It had thinned somewhat by the time we reached the front entrance, where the car was waiting, but there were still five or six nurses in the cortège. I was making the most of my good luck, trying to draw some of the female attention away from the man who least appreciated it.

Eventually we were allowed to take our leave. Jerry brought the car round and we pulled out slowly, with Geoffrey waving from the back seat like royalty. At Queen's Gardens, Pat and Mike waited on the front steps. Everybody offered to help him up the stairs, but he shook us off. He strode ahead, and we straggled in his wake.

Pat must have spent the whole afternoon scrubbing, because the flat looked like someone else's. The carpets were dust-free, books were on shelves, windows sparkled and fresh flowers stood in large glasses. She had dug out covers for the furniture and given them a clean, too. Mike had made a 'Welcome Home' banner which he had strung from the ceiling.

Geoffrey stepped gingerly over the threshold and spent a few minutes wandering wordlessly from room to room. Pat and Mike followed him around anxiously.

'It hasn't looked like this since . . . a long time,' he finally said when he came back to the living room.

Pat sighed with relief. 'I'll put the kettle on,' she said.

Mike and Jerry wandered into the kitchen while I helped Geoffrey to unpack his books. He'd brought a suitcaseful back from the hospital, but there were barely any gaps on his well-stocked shelves.

'Did you get through all these in hospital?' I asked him while he decided which shelves we should put them on.

'Oh, no,' he said. 'I had to have them with me. They're my best friends.'

As if to prove his point, he picked up two editions

248

of Blake that were practically identical. 'This one is a first edition,' he said. 'And this one Eleanor gave me.' Eleanor was his wife. It was the first time I'd heard him speak of her.

He handed the book to me gently. It was a well-worn paperback, smooth and yellowed. The spine was broken and some of the pages were loose. It fell open naturally.

'She loved Blake too,' said Geoffrey. 'That's how we met. At a lecture.'

Maybe the book had talismanic powers. It felt good to hold. As best friends go, it didn't quite measure the same on the conviviality scale of someone who would go to the pub and buy their share of rounds, but I could imagine the fascination. I handed the book back to Geoffrey. As I did, one of the loose pages fell out and I stooped to pick it up. On it were printed the words from one of Blake's most famous poems.

I had a brainstorm.

Mike and Pat were putting cups and saucers on a tray.

'I think I've got the password to the disk,' I said. We dashed downstairs.

'Elaine wanted to move to the country,' I explained, as Mike pushed the disk into the computer. 'She'd begun to plan it; she'd arranged someone to train as her replacement at work, and she had all this information about a village in Somerset. Eddy told me she wanted the natural life – cows, grass, space for her kid.'

'What does that have to do with the password?' said Mike.

'Heaven on earth,' I said. 'Her utopia. Blake had a

similar idea. She liked Blake, so she used his word for it – Jerusalem. You know – how does that poem go?'

> '*I will not cease from mental fight*
> *Nor shall my sword sleep in my hand*
> *Till we have built Jerusalem*
> *In England's green and pleasant land*'

Geoffrey quoted. Mike typed in 'Jerusalem'. The computer blinked and the screen opened.

Chapter Thirty-six

We crowded around the screen. The file consisted of spreadsheets of accounts for Roadblock. They were dated three years back and showed the financial concerns of a very small organization. The amount of money coming in was modest, as were the wages going out. We looked at the spreadsheets. We looked at each other.

'Perhaps we need Eddy,' said Mike finally.

Eddy arrived about forty minutes later.

He went through them once, sighed, and looked over them a second time.

'They're legit,' he said. 'What do we do now?'

Inadvertently, Felicia supplied the answer to that question the next day.

'The old codgers want to do a follow-up on the Campaigning Grannies story. I said you'd pass on your notes and interview,' she said at the end of the morning, which I had devoted exclusively to the question of whether aliens were conducting sex experiments on British women.

'Fine,' I said. The 'old codgers' was the name we gave to a once-a-week show called *Issues for the Third*

Age, which ran on Sunday mornings. The show had almost no budget and only one producer, who was mostly reduced to begging for material from other shows. He was a desperate and bitter man, eagerly awaiting the day when the programme director fiscally acknowledged demographic surveys which show Britain has an increasingly ageing population.

He was going to love me for this. I dug around in my desk until I found the tape with Esther's interview on it, then flicked through the notes I'd scrawled while speaking to Mark and Esther. They were almost illegible, even to me, so I started to type them out.

My mind in neutral, I read and I typed. Then I had a bright idea.

I called Eddy at work. 'I can tell you why Mark hid that disk,' I said.

When we met up at Mike's flat later in the day Mike had the file open.

Eddy leaned over his shoulder, looking at the spreadsheets. 'I don't get it,' he said. 'It looks perfectly OK.'

'That's the point,' I said. 'It *is* in order. Money coming in, in the form of donations, and money going out, mostly in the form of wages. Now, what did the Roadblock people say to you almost from the day you arrived?'

'Uh, that I . . . uh, hadn't been there in the beginning when it was harder . . . and . . .' he looked up at me, 'they worked for no money, as volunteers.'

He looked puzzled. 'I don't get it. Why would they

say they didn't pay their staff when these records show that they did?'

I said nothing, waiting for the penny to drop.

'Ha!' he said. 'Social Security fraud. They were claiming the dole as well as being paid. That would make sense, because this year we applied for charity status, you know, so that donations are tax deductible. Elaine must have found out about this when she started going over all the old records.'

'There's no charity status if your ecologically sound organization is practising fraud,' I said.

'She and Mark were having some ding-dong rows in his office. I bet she didn't want to go ahead with the application and Mark did, something like that. He probably wanted to hide it. She liked to play by the rules; she wouldn't have worn this at all.'

'You have no proof that they were claiming benefit,' said Mike.

'That shouldn't be too hard to get,' said Eddy. 'I'll do some discreet asking around. There's a guy who left after he and Mark had a difference of opinion. I'll bet he can tell us.'

Chapter Thirty-seven

'We didn't come to blows, but we got pretty damn close.' Jonathan Maxwell pulled two pints and put them on the bar in front of us. We were in a pub in Hammersmith. It was quiet; apart from us there was only an elderly couple playing cards.

He was a quiet man with thinning black hair and horn-rimmed spectacles that gave him an intellectual air.

'I thought he was a vainglorious, publicity-seeking pain in the arse. And he didn't think that highly of me, either. We started the organization together, back in the days when we liked each other. It was a damn good idea, to help co-ordinate and organize people who wanted to protest in an effective manner. We were supposed to be like publicity consultants, advising but essentially taking a back-seat role.

'But Mark took over almost from the beginning. He wanted to do things his way or not at all. In the end we were fighting all the time, and the organization was starting to suffer. We had one final big row, can't even remember what it was about now, and I was out of there. I'm not sorely missed, I'm sure.' He pulled a beer for himself. 'I'll tell you one thing, though. He was damn good at raising money. The stuff flooded in right from the start.'

'Where did it come from?'

'From a very odd source, actually. We got a lot from very conservative country types. The ones who drive Land Rovers and want to see England preserved just the way it was in 1954. And of course Mark's mother is a charity fundraiser, so he had the contacts.'

'Seems like an odd constituency to be donating to a radical protest group.'

Jonathan shrugged. 'Not that radical. The issue's crossed party political lines now. Everybody wants to save the planet, even Conservatives.'

'Did you know Elaine?'

'Yeah, I did. We overlapped for a bit. She was a sweet girl. It was too bad what happened to her.'

'So how long did you stay at Roadblock?'

'All up, about six months. Elaine had just arrived as I was leaving. Mark probably had the idea that something was up, so he started bringing in the replacements.'

'Mark said you all worked as volunteers in the beginning.'

He laughed. 'Yeah, I've heard him say that in interviews. That was part of his historical revisionism. At first we did, before we got properly organized, then we pulled off a big stunt and someone sent us money. So we set up Roadblock with that.'

'And you were paid wages?'

'Yeah, we paid ourselves. All unofficially, of course. It was sweet bugger-all, though, so we kept drawing benefits.'

'Why?'

'Why not? We were out for everything we could get from the government at that stage. They were wasting taxpayers' money on grandiose road-building plans. We saw it as the least we could do to drain the coffers for a good cause.'

He sipped his pint. 'Not that they'd thank me for reminding them of that now that they've gone all respectable and worthy,' he said. 'Cheers.'

'What do we do now?' asked Eddy as we drove back to my place. 'Go to the police?'

'It's not exactly conclusive evidence,' I said.

'Well, what, then?'

'Talk to Mark, find out what his story is.'

'Think he might come right out and admit it?'

'I doubt it. But if we put him under a little pressure, he might be able to come up with a better explanation for his behaviour that night.'

Eddy said, 'There's just one thing. How are you going to do that without revealing that you broke into his office and stole something?'

'*We* broke in, Eddy. We're in this together, remember?'

'Right,' he said. 'That's what I meant.'

When I got home there was a message on my machine from a hesitant-sounding chap called Bernie. He reminded me that we'd met at the cinema manager's office and asked me to ring him back, which I did.

'It's about the tape,' he said. 'I think I can help you.'

Heart full of hope, I rescued the Renault from the

dodgy side street I'd parked it in and drove to meet him. The place he'd chosen was a dingy café near Leicester Square. Bernie was already wedged in between the table and a wall when I got there. We ordered a big pot of tea. The waitress slapped it down like a woman who wasn't fulfilled in her chosen line of work. Then two chipped mugs skidded across the table to join us. Bernie caught them like he knew they were coming.

'I couldn't say anything in the lair of the dragon queen,' Bernie said. 'We don't get on.'

I sipped my tea. It tasted like an industrial by-product.

'She's tried to have me fired, you know. It's nothing to do with how I do my job. It's because I'm fat. She doesn't want to have to look at me, that's what it boils down to.

'So I knew something was up when she came over all sweetness a week or so back. The police wanted to talk to me. That guy, the redheaded one, came to my office. He wanted the tape. I didn't like him much. I stalled. Told him to come back. Then I looked at the tape. And I couldn't help noticing why it was he wanted it.' He reached down below the table and produced a VHS. 'So I made a copy. Just in case.'

'You didn't.'

'He called me "fatso",' he said.

I took my precious cargo home. I put it in the machine. Pressed the play button and there we were. Roger Fitzgerald with his fist in my stomach. Roger Fitzgerald with his other fist in my stomach. There was no mistaking it. No way he could plead mistaken identity. I rewound the tape, watched it again and I felt better than I had done in a long while.

I called Charlie.

'I feel pretty, oh so pretty, I feel pretty and witty and wise . . .' I sang when he picked up the phone.

'Ridley, you've got nothing to be cheerful about,' he said tartly.

'My dear Charles, that is exactly where you are wrong. Life is very good indeed. Gooder than good. Couldn't be better.'

'Are you on drugs?'

'Next best thing. I've got Fitzgerald by the short and fucking curlies.'

'You've got Fitzgerald?' Charlie sounded sceptical.

'He beat me up, he scratched my car and a security camera recorded everything.'

'Does he know this?'

'He thinks he's got the only copy. He won't know what's hit him.'

Charlie sighed. 'Jesus, Ridley. Think the cops care about this? He beat up a hack reporter, so what? Think he hadn't done this before? Think nobody knows that's how he behaves when he gets a bit put out? There are units that'd give him a bloody promotion if they saw that tape.'

'Charlie,' I said. 'Your cynicism has touched my heart. But I'm still going after him.'

'No matter what you do, he'll make you sorry. He's like the fucking Terminator. He never gives up.'

Happy to know that men such as Roger Fitzgerald were guarding the nation securely, I went downstairs and knocked on Everard's door. He opened it wearing his habitual at-home garb – a silk paisley robe. I could hear his stereo playing soft classical music and smell the aroma of a good-quality cigar.

Everard had once lived stylishly in South Kensington, but he'd lost a lot of money speculating on derivatives, or futures or selling short when he should have sold long. One of my other neighbours said he'd been a Lloyds name, but nobody knew for sure and none of us felt free to ask. Whatever the truth, he was now making the best of it in seedy Ladbroke Grove. For the first time I wondered how old he was. He had very little hair, and despite the slab of extra pounds around his waist, the skin on his face was firm. At the moment that face was set in the pinched manner of a well-bred person looking on something he doesn't care for – usually anyone not listed in *Burke's Peerage*.

'Yes, can I help you?' he said in a manner which clearly indicated that he didn't want to help me. I debated briefly about whether to ask another neighbour, but I pressed on. Everard hated the police; he saw them as slackers who spent their time cosseting drug dealers when they should have been patrolling our street in an armoured car, blasting away undesirables like Rastafarians and single mothers.

'I'm hoping you can,' I said and I told him about the tape.

'If this is something illegal, then I'm not interested,' he said.

'It's not illegal. It's evidence that I want to use in a case against the police.'

That piqued his interest. 'What is it? Drug dealing? Corruption? That doesn't surprise me. They're all corrupt around here, you know.'

'I know,' I said, assuming the look of a person who's just signed the State Secrets Act. 'And I have the evidence here,' I held up the tape, 'that's going to blow this town wide open. Wide open. But,' I tapped the tape significantly, 'it is important that I keep it somewhere safe. Vital. Can you look after it for me? I don't want to run the risk of someone finding it at my place. They're desperate people we're up against. Desperate.' I held out the tape.

He took it lovingly. 'Yes, yes, of course. Now, let me see. Where shall we put it?'

He led me down the hallway and into his living room. Everard came from the type of people who inherited their furniture rather than bought it. In his case the ancestors had favoured the depressed Victorian look. Everything was dark, overstuffed and covered in plush velvet. There were sombre, gilt-framed paintings of fat Georgians. A brandy goblet stood on a table beside one chair, and a book on opera beside that. There was nothing in the room to indicate we were in the twentieth century, except for a very expensive stereo which I was able to see because the doors of the cabinet which housed it stood open.

Everard walked into the middle of the room holding the tape in both hands. Then he bent down on one knee and pulled back the oriental runner. He pulled out a pocket knife and delicately lifted a floor-board. Underneath was a grey metal box, long and narrow.

'I'd appreciate it if you didn't tell anyone that this is here,' he said. 'I've had a couple of burglaries.' He produced a key from his pocket and opened the box. Inside were bunches of papers tied with ribbon and several other smaller boxes. Everard rearranged them, laying my videotape alongside. The fit was snug, but the lid closed. He returned the box to its hole and placed the floorboard and the carpet back.

'Thanks,' I said. 'You won't be sorry.'

Everard was quite excited by this stage. 'Do keep me informed,' he trilled, guiding me back to the door. 'And don't forget the house meeting next week. We'll be discussing geraniums.'

'Geraniums?'

'For the windowboxes.'

'Windowboxes. Right.'

'Unless you've got any better ideas? But we do need something hardy for the north-facing wall.'

'Geraniums sound fine,' I said. 'Colour. That's what we need around this place.'

I left him with his mouth hanging open. I climbed the stairs to my flat and let myself in. I grabbed the whisky from the kitchen cupboard and the ice from the freezer and sat down to reflect. I hadn't had any luck with murderers, but at least I'd managed to nail a thug. All in all, it didn't seem like a bad day's work. I poured a second whisky. Then I felt something cold on the back of my neck. It was the same feeling I'd had a few days ago in Vauxhall. I twisted my head round to get a better view. It was a gun all right. A big one with a long barrel.

Chapter Thirty-eight

'Hello, Max,' I said. 'I'd offer you a whisky but it's too good to waste on someone like you.'

'Rufus wants to see you,' he said. He waved the gun in a way that made me very nervous indeed.

'Put the gun away, Max. Haven't you heard that most accidents occur in the home?'

'C'mon, let's get going,' he said, waving the gun some more. 'He's waiting at the Rover.'

I collected my coat and keys while Max leaned against the table, idly playing with the gun. He followed me out of the house and down the stairs, putting the gun away when we got out to the street. I opened the driver's door of the Renault and got in. He seated himself beside me and pulled out the gun again.

'For God's sake, Max, you've been watching too many movies. Those bloody things are dangerous.'

He looked at the gun and then back at me. 'Just drive,' he said.

I started the car and drove down to the Rover. It was late and the pub was packed. To my relief, Max put the gun away. We squeezed our way through the bar and into a back room.

Rufus was sitting behind his desk, the same one that had been in the house in Bayswater.

'Mr Ridley, good of you to make it.' He rose to shake my hand like a bank manager who'd invited me in for a chat about my overdraft.

'It's the twentieth century, Rufus. Next time let your fingers do the walking.'

'Whatever do you mean?' The faux Cockney accent was gone tonight, replaced by the unforgiving vowels of the upper classes.

'I don't appreciate gorilla-grams,' I said, nodding in Max's direction. 'Especially when they carry big guns.'

Rufus, who'd picked up the Glenmorangie to do his duties as host, pointed it at Max.

'Is this true?'

Max looked sheepish, then defiant.

'You said to bring him,' he mumbled.

'Give me that thing.' Rufus held out his hand for the gun. Max handed it to him.

'Wait outside,' Rufus said. Max left. Rufus looked at me and shrugged as if to say he just couldn't get the right kind of staff these days. I sat down and accepted a generous shot of whisky. As if to emphasize the informality of our little get-together, Rufus perched on the edge of his desk. There was silence for a moment while we sipped our drinks. The man knew his single malts.

'Let's talk about changing your drinking habits,' he said, smiling in a false but jolly way.

I studied the amber in my glass. 'Can't afford this stuff.'

'I meant the Rover.'

'At first sight it probably doesn't have much to recommend it, but I admit the place is growing on me.'

Rufus rolled his whisky glass between his palms while he studied me. 'The Rover has a very select clientele,' he said at last. 'I can't emphasize that enough. Very select. Not really your sort of place at all.'

'It serves alcohol. I'm not choosy.'

'Apparently not,' said Rufus. 'But the trouble is the company you attract. Like the cops. They've been around rather a lot lately. It makes the customers nervous. They can't relax when they don't know who's going to walk through the door.'

'Why don't you save me some time, then,' I said, 'and tell me what you know about how Shark died? You remember Shark, don't you? Did you send someone to do it? Or did you do it yourself? There, I've given you a multi-choice option. Should be easy enough for someone as clever as you.'

'I've told you everything you need to know,' said Rufus. 'And you won't find out any more by sniffing around here.'

'Probably not. Shark is dead and Max has the look of a man who's been bought off. You are nothing if not thorough, Rufus.' I got up. Time to go.

He shrugged like I'd paid him a compliment. Pointed to the door. It seemed a shame, leaving the whisky like that.

I wasn't expecting Rufus to hit me. He seemed like the type who'd get someone else to do his dirty work. But on this occasion, apparently, I was wrong. Maybe I should have been more deferential, I thought as he sucker-punched me. I fell backwards over the sofa and crashed to the floor. Before I had a chance to get up, I was yanked to my feet, spun around. Both arms were pinned from behind. Max must have been waiting outside the door.

Rufus looked like he was going to hit me again so I figured I had nothing to lose.

'Cops giving you too much heat?' I said. 'You killed Shark, didn't you?'

Rufus hit me a second time. In the head this time. It hurt a lot more.

'Stay well away,' he said. 'I'm a dangerous man. Ask anyone.'

'I don't take veiled threats,' I said, running my tongue around my jaw to feel for broken teeth.

Rufus turned away. 'Get rid of him,' he said to Max.

'How?'

'Any way you like.'

'I think he means you should call me a taxi,' I said as Max propelled me down a short corridor.

'Yeah, right,' he said. 'Jeez, you're a fucking smart-arse.' He kicked open a fire door that led out on to a lane. Unfortunately for me it was deserted.

'Rufus pressganged you into paying off your debt, Max?' I gasped because I felt a bit rough at this stage. 'Or has he bought your silence? Maybe you know too much about what happened to Shark?'

Max's only response was to twist my arm further up my back. He pushed me through the fire door with a sharp show of force. My arms were too weak to break my fall. I banged my head on the pavement. For a second everything went black. I came to in time to see Max's boot travelling in a slow arc towards my head. I rolled to one side and the boot went clear past. By this time I'd had enough of being pushed around for one evening. I put a nearly useless arm up and grabbed his ankle. A slight twist and I had him off-balance and on the ground. I put one foot on his neck and bent his leg backwards to what I hoped was an uncomfortable angle.

'Who killed Shark, Max?'

'Fuck you,' he said.

I bent the leg back and to the side a little more. I didn't think it was going to make Max talk, but it was fun anyway. 'Is Rufus blackmailing you? Did he find out that you killed your mate? Or maybe you and Rufus were in it together from the start.'

'I don't know nuffin', Max said.

'You and Shark had a fight, I heard. Over a woman. Did he try and steal Jenny away from you?'

Max squirmed, trying to break my grip.

'Fuck you,' he said.

I bent the leg back till he squealed. 'Just a name, Max. Who was it?'

'Me sister,' he said at last. 'He was screwing me sister.'

'Sam! What the hell is going on here?' It was Dean, standing in the doorway with a sack of rubbish.

I got up, pulled Max with me. Pushed him towards Dean.

'Ask Rufus,' I said. 'You may find your security arrangements are more expensive than you first thought.'

I rang Charlie Hobbs when I got home.

'Bloody Ridley,' he said. 'Leave me alone.'

'Don't be like that,' I said. 'Tell me about Shark.'

'He's dead.'

'He's dead and what else?'

'He's staying dead for all I know.'

'Charlie, I know you've been around the Rover. Tell me what's up.'

'What's it to you, Ridley? You're not on the beat any more.'

'That's why you can trust me not to put it on the radio, old buddy. Besides, it's my hobby case.' I could hear Charlie sigh down the line.

'Just asking a few questions, shaking a few trees, seeing what kind of creeps come loose.'

'Any creeps I might know?'

'This is off the record?'

'But of course.'

'Rufus is setting himself up in the protection racket. With all the armed drug dealers running around that part of town, he figures it's an expanding market. The Rover is owned by a woman.'

'Dean.'

'You know her?'

'I get around.'

'Anyway, she's starting to get threats and fights and things are getting rough, with people beaten up outside her place. Even with the kind of crowd that she has, it's not that good for business. But she's not gonna call the cops, or any bloody security agency. Obviously not, that's gonna make her clientele equally nervous. So she goes to the most influential guy she knows. Rufus. And she asks, pretty-please, for his help.'

'And Rufus is a sucker for a woman in distress.'

'He's also been thinking along the same lines, so he moves his operation to the Rover and starts expanding his business. Only his other clients don't get quite so much choice in the matter.'

'That's too bad.'

'Right. So I start thinking, this guy has fifty different kinds of alibis for the night Harkness was killed, but what the hell, I'm gonna rattle him a bit, just for a laugh. Keep my mind open to the possibilities.'

'What if he really didn't do it?'

'What if the world's flat? Jesus Christ, Ridley, ever heard of henchmen? Just 'cos he didn't have his finger on the trigger don't mean he doesn't know a man who did. Now tell me how come you know so much about the Rover?'

'I've experienced the new arrangement first hand.' I told him about my meeting with Rufus.

'Interesting,' he said at the end of it. 'What sort of flowers do you want on your coffin?'

I went over to Stephanie Adams' flat in Bishops Bridge Road. I knocked on the door for several minutes. There was no reply.

It was past midnight and I was in need of some solace so I called Magnolia.

'Hi,' I said. 'It's late notice, I know, but are you free tonight?'

She seemed distracted. 'I . . . ah, no, I'm not.'

'Oh. Someone with you?'

There was a pause; brief for her, a lifetime for me. 'Yeah,' she said at last. 'I'll ring you.'

She didn't sound like she meant it. I hung up the phone, checked the mirror to see if I'd sprouted any leprous growths. Everything appeared normal. I decided a drink or two would take my mind off things.

On Saturday I thought about Magnolia a lot. It's often difficult to tell with women, but something was definitely up with her. In my experience when they don't want you around any more they rarely come right out and say it. Instead they kill you with a thousand half-hearted gestures. I know guys that can carry on for years like that, but I'm not one of them. I need to know, even if it does mean getting the 'let's-just-be-friends routine'. Judging by her offhand manner on the phone yesterday, Magnolia was sizing me up for friend-reappraisal.

I went for a walk while I mulled all this over. When I got in, there was a message on my machine from John Baker, City's political editor.

'Sam. Hi. Don't know if this is anything to do with what we were talking about, but the transport white paper due out in a couple of days is going to signal a big change of direction for government policy. From now on we're all going to be green, in theory, anyway. Don't know if that's any help to you. Let me know if you need any more information. You know where to reach me. Cheers. Oh, and by the way, the son, Mark Matheson, is going into the family business. He's put himself up for a safe Labour seat in North London.'

My eye fell on a stack of clippings nestling under a pile of newspapers on the coffee table. It was the Mark Matheson file that I'd pulled from the library. I opened it again. There were several articles that I'd put aside for later and had forgotten about. Most weren't of much interest. At the bottom of the stack was a clipping from a series in a Sunday newspaper which looks at famous couples. It was called 'How We Met' and this particular one was about environmental campaigner Mark Matheson and his dancer girlfriend Magnolia Trevenet.

'Well, I'll be damned,' I said out loud.

Chapter Thirty-nine

We met three years ago, at a picnic on a riverbank in Oxfordshire organized by a mutual friend, the article quoted Magnolia as saying. *She'd told me about this guy, how she'd known him at university. I don't think it was a set-up, though; I mean my friend knew I was seeing someone else at the time. Needless to say, he didn't last much longer.*

The first thing I noticed about her were her eyes, Mark said. *And the second, the fact that she smoked more than anybody I'd ever known.* We were obviously talking about the same Magnolia. I read on.

He flirted outrageously with me, said Magnolia. *But I didn't take him seriously. It's hard to take good-looking men seriously. We didn't meet up again until about six months later, when my friend had a party to celebrate getting a job. He was there and that was that.*

I like the fact that she's a belly dancer, Mark enthused. *It's so wild. So like Magnolia. She is a person who forges her own path.*

I skimmed the rest of the article and discovered that they shared an interest in Algerian rai music and had lots of arguments, but usually made up quickly. I wondered where Elaine had fitted into all this. I wondered where I fitted in now. Magnolia and Mark had obviously not been a couple at the funeral. His time had been taken up with the slender blonde, and I had no reason to suspect she had been two-timing him with me. Or maybe she had. God knows, I've misjudged women's characters before.

I thought back to our first night together. She had called me up. She had quizzed me about the murder case. Maybe she had recognized me from the night of the killing, thought I knew something and she wanted to find out what it was. It was a less satisfying scenario than the one in which she had fallen for my animal magnetism, but it seemed to fit better.

I picked up her phone, dialled her number. It was engaged so I got my coat and went out.

The evening was mild but wet. I smoked as I walked to the faithful Renault. Magnolia's house was close enough to walk to, but I needed cover. I ignited the car and drove to Mulberry Avenue. Like I said, it always starts first time. Her lights were on, which confirmed that she was at home. I parked the car opposite, next to the Summerhill Estate, and turned off the engine. I looked at Magnolia's windows some more. The heavy curtains were drawn, so I couldn't tell if anyone was in the room with her. I imagined Mark Matheson, playing out one of their famous make-up scenes, but I didn't much care for the thought of it.

I sat there in the car for an hour, maybe two. Nothing happened at all during that time, except that I got stiff and cold. The colder I got, the more I realized that I was behaving foolishly. Time to inject a little dignity into proceedings.

I had reached out my hand to switch on the engine when I saw Mark Matheson leave her flat. He hurried down the steps, hunching his shoulders against the drizzle. I watched him walk around the side of the flat, and a couple of minutes later he returned wheeling a bicycle. He got on and pushed off up the street. I slid down in the seat, but he didn't look my way. I got out of the car, locked it and walked over to Magnolia's front door. I pressed the buzzer. Without asking who it was, she buzzed me in. When I climbed the steps to her floor, she was standing in the doorway with a tie draped over her hand. She had her mouth open to say something, but whatever it was, when she saw me it became kind of redundant. So she said 'Oh,' instead.

I smiled pleasantly. 'Mind if I come in?' There wasn't much she could do. She stood aside, allowing me to enter.

Chapter Forty

I sat on the couch, she sat on the chair. We looked at each other in silence.

'So,' I said, still pleasant. 'Tell me a story.'

'There's nothing to tell.'

'Oh, I think there is. I mean, lots of questions spring to my mind.'

'Really,' she said, tucking one knee under her and lighting a cigarette. 'Like what?'

'Like why you latched on to me.'

She smiled coolly and blew smoke. 'Come on, Sam. You're a grown-up. These things happen.'

'You wanted information. You wanted to find out what I knew about Elaine's murder.'

'You have a low opinion of your physical charms,' she said, smiling still. 'Never heard of the demon lust?'

'You want to know what I think? I think you've been lying to me from the moment we met. Who are you protecting? Your boyfriend or yourself?'

'You come into my house and accuse me of murder. You've got real cheek, Ridley.'

'I'm fed up with being given the runaround. Straight answers only, please. Elaine had proof that Roadblock was defrauding the tax man. The Inland Revenue doesn't look kindly on that sort of thing. If it got out, it would put a dent in Matheson's political ambitions.'

'I don't think so,' she said, stubbing out her cigarette and lighting another without pause. It was clear I wasn't getting far. I tried another tack.

'Did you steal Mark away from Elaine? At the picnic.'

She laughed outright at that. 'It was nothing like that, believe me.'

That was the funny thing, I still did want to believe her.

'Tell me,' I said.

She got up. 'Fancy some wine? It'll calm you down.'

'This isn't a social call, Magnolia.'

She went into the kitchen and came back with two glasses and a bottle. She poured wine into both of them. I looked at mine, but I didn't touch it.

'Scared I've poisoned it?' she said nastily.

'Mark and Elaine,' I prompted.

'They were an item for a while. Then they split up.'

'Was this before or after she became pregnant?'

'I don't know. About the same time, no, a little after.'

'So is Mark Albion's father?'

She shrugged. 'He told me he wasn't.'

'Doesn't mean he told the truth.'

'Look, I don't know, OK? And I don't want to know.'

'Why were they picnicking together if they had split?'

Magnolia looked a little ashamed. 'She was trying to get him back. She brought me along for moral support.'

275

'What lousy judgement.'

'It wasn't like that. Mark and I didn't get together until months later. By that time she was over him.'

'Why were they having dinner the night she died?'

'I really don't know. Why don't you ask him?'

'Why did she go and work for Roadblock?'

'Mark felt sorry for her. She'd been temping at some big law firm and hated it. She was on her own with the kid, she needed a friend. Mark is a very fair man, which you would discover if you'd stop accusing him of all these preposterous things.'

'I haven't accused him of anything.'

'Well,' she said, getting up, 'we can sit here splitting hairs all night, or you can leave.' I didn't move.

'Did Elaine often try and get Mark back?'

'No, she knew it was over. It had been over for years.'

'Or that's what he told you. Did you find out he was lying and decide to teach her a lesson?'

She stood up. 'Get out,' she growled.

'Thanks for the memories,' I said as the door slammed behind me.

It was a damn shame, that's what it was.

I drove home, making a mental note to tell Simon to stay away from women at all costs.

I called him when I got in. His mother answered the phone.

'Hi, Mary, it's Sam.'

'I know who it is.'

'Is Simon about?'

'No.'

I paused just long enough to let her know I thought she was a first-class cow.

'Where is he?'

'What does it matter where he is? He isn't here.'

'Well, when he gets in, tell him his mother drives a hard bargain.'

'That's just bloody typical of you, Sam,' she said and hung up. I sighed and sat down on the sofa, allowing myself a moment or two of self-pity. Then I had a brace of whiskies, strictly for anaesthetic purposes, before turning in.

Chapter Forty-one

Monday morning, my head felt as if someone had taken it apart and distributed bits of it around the city, leaving me with an empty skull. Fortunately Felicia seemed to have forgotten my existence, and I was able to regain my equilibrium perusing one of the seedier tabloids, a steaming cup of coffee welded to my right hand. When I reckoned I had at least half a dozen neurons fired up, I called Mark Matheson.

'I need to speak to you. It's about Magnolia and Elaine,' I said.

'It's not a good time,' he said.

I persisted. He relented. I told Felicia I was off to do some research into serial adultery, and caught a bus to Camden Town.

I came straight to the point. 'She told you something important that night. What was it?'

'None of your business,' he said.

'I know about the Social Security fraud you practised. I don't need to tell anyone, but I will if I have to.'

'How . . .? Oh, never mind. This is blackmail.'

'Yes, it is a tangled web we weave. Now, let's start with Albion first. She's your daughter, isn't she?'

Mark had the look of a man whose life has suddenly become way too complicated. 'Yes,' he said in a very quiet voice. 'I . . . you know, I thought she might have been. The timing was kind of right, but Elaine had always insisted that she wasn't. There was another guy about the same time, which was the reason why we split up.'

'That's why you gave her a job?'

'Partly. She was a good person. I . . . She needed help. Even though she told me that Albion wasn't mine, I thought, you know, she could have been. I wanted to help her.'

'And what did she think of Magnolia and you?'

'She didn't like it much.'

'But she put up with it.'

'Look, we didn't shove it in her face.'

'And why did you go out for dinner? Was she black-mailing you with the accounts?'

'No, she didn't care about anything like that.'

'What happened, then?'

'She . . . she wanted us to get back together.'

'And you said no.'

'Yes I . . . It was all so messy.'

'Too messy for an aspiring young politician?'

'No! She wanted a more secure environment for Albion. Said her family had been bugging her about not bringing the kid up right. She finally told me the truth – that I was Albion's father. It was a bit of a shock, being confronted with a bald fact like that. I didn't know what to say. But I told her that I didn't think we should get together just for the sake of the kid. I told her she was going about it all the wrong way. She got upset. Well, when I mean upset, she got into a sulk. I hated her sulking. Used to really get on my nerves. So when she stormed off I thought "bugger you". I got on my bike and rode home as fast as I could.'

I decided to try a clever little bluff, to see what happened. 'That's not what Magnolia said.'

'What do you mean?'

'You didn't go straight home. You went to Magnolia's. You told her what happened.'

'No . . . I, she didn't know.'

'She didn't know what?'

He opened his mouth to say something and then shut it again and shook his head.

'You're protecting her.'

'No!'

'You went to Magnolia's, told her what happened. She got steamed up, jealous, and killed Elaine. You gave her the motive and she killed her.'

'Magnolia, she's no . . .' His body slumped. 'She's not capable of it.'

'But you must think she is, otherwise you would have told the truth about that night.'

'Look, I wasn't sure, all right? But I didn't go over there. I rang Magnolia when I got home.'

'Why weren't you together at the funeral?'

'I . . . it's complicated. I don't know. We had words. I did wonder, you know. If she did go over there before she said she did.'

'Tricky. Especially as she was thinking the same thing about you. A mutual accusation of murder would be a severe trial for most young love.'

He wanted to grin louchely at that, but it came out wobbling and finished up more like a sneer. There was a charming veneer struggling to reassert itself, but also a streak of coldness that got an outing less often.

He and Magnolia were a lot alike in that respect. Hot and cold.

'I'm sure you'll be very happy together,' I said, getting up. 'Now that your misunderstandings are all in the past.'

By the time I got back to the office a fragment of another memory had been dislodged. Mark at the funeral – chatting up an attractive young woman. The one who'd read a poem at the funeral. I searched my desk drawer for the funeral programme, found her name. Helen Smith. Well, that should be easy to track down.

Felicia was clearly upset that I'd been away so long. 'Well, who would have thought it?' she said, standing over me in her own special way. 'The elusive Sam Ridley is actually at his desk.'

'Cut it out, Felicia, I'm working on a story. It's about how to deal with harassment in the workplace. You're going to like it.'

She muttered something unprintable and stalked off. Then she stopped in the middle of the newsroom, turned back towards me.

'And return your bloody files. You've got the pornography file, the infertility file and the Roadblock file. And the library wants them bloody back.'

Lyall ambushed me at the coffee machine. 'Her name means happy,' he said, nodding in Felicia's direction. 'Ironic, isn't it?' He poured a cup of coffee and handed it to me. 'Bring your girl over for dinner, reassure her that you've got at least some respectable friends.'

'You should have asked me last week,' I said.

*

Anna resumed her regular phone-in show that morning. The lines were jammed with callers, all wanting to talk about their problems: relationship problems, money problems, sex problems, everybody had goddamn problems. I had one too. I had to find Helen Smith.

I ran Anna down after the show. Told her I wanted to speak to Helen Smith.

'Why?'

'I'm terminally nosy.'

Anna shrugged, got out her diary. 'She's known Elaine for years,' she said, scribbling down a phone number. 'We were all at school together.'

Helen Smith had that fragile blonde beauty that made you want to move in with her straight away and protect her. Her straight, fine hair hung to her shoulders. She wore little make-up, there was no real need.

She was sitting at a window seat in the café we'd agreed to meet at, which was in Hammersmith. She told me she'd be wearing a white suit, and so she was. A white suit, beige shirt and shoes, and a single gold chain around her throat. No gold band around her wedding finger. I felt suddenly happy as I pulled up a chair and introduced myself.

'Thanks for taking the time,' I said after we'd both ordered coffee.

'I've got time,' she said brusquely. 'I'm an actor.'

Her voice was well trained and throaty. It made me want to skip the preliminaries and invite myself back to her place.

She leaned forward, putting both elbows on the table. 'So what do you want to know about Elaine? We went to school together. Best buddies from the third form through to A-levels. She was a riot. Sort of person you should hate – clever and good looking – but she was just so damn nice. I was infatuated with her from day one. And I still am, I suppose. God, I miss her.'

'I wanted to find out what her relationship was with Mark Matheson.'

'First love,' said Helen promptly. 'They met when she was too young to know any better.'

'You didn't like him.'

'I didn't dislike him. But I thought she could have done better. You know he tried to chat me up at her funeral. At her bloody funeral!'

'I do know. I was there.'

'He thinks he's God's gift to greenies, but he's just a showman. I think that group is merely an expensive superstructure for his ego.'

'I heard he's going into politics.'

Helen smiled sweetly. 'Well, then, won't that be nice?'

'Why did Elaine not tell him that Albion was his daughter?'

'Foolish pride,' said Helen sarcastically. 'Also, she couldn't really expect to be welcomed by his family. He said he'd made the break from those High Tory bastards, but I think you'll find that Mummy still supports his little ventures. Can you imagine them welcoming someone of Elaine's background into the fold? Single mother? No job? Darling, it just wouldn't be done. Mark may screw in the demi-monde, but that's as far as it goes.'

'He's seeing a belly-dancer at the moment.'

'I rest my case. In five years' time, though, you'll see him with the regulation blonde wearing the regulation horsy scarf.'

'Elaine wanted him back, didn't she?'

Helen shook her head. 'I don't think she knew what she wanted. About anything. Here's a woman with a first-class degree who works as a temp at a law firm and from there goes on to the dizzy heights of book-keeping at a two-bit pressure group. I mean, where's the sense?'

'Perhaps she didn't want a career.'

'No perhaps about it,' said Helen, calling the waiter over for more coffee. 'But she lacked confidence as well. Timid. Too, too timid.'

Helen's eyes had filled with tears. She hastily wiped them with the cheap paper napkin provided by the café, and blew her nose. 'Sorry. I can't believe I'm crying in front of a stranger. But you do have the look of the father confessor about you.'

I supposed what she meant by that was that a hot role in the hay was out of the question. Dammit, I wanted to say to her, I may look like a father confessor, but on the inside I'm a sex god.

'Mark said she had been seeing someone else about the time they broke up.'

'I don't know. She was always a bit vague about that period of her life. I was away a lot, during one of my rare periods of employment. She didn't talk about it much and I often wondered whether she made the story up – about there being someone else – to get Mark's interest.'

'Odd thing to do.'

Helen shrugged. 'People do odd things. And she thought he was taking her for granted.'

'Her sister seems to think it was a casual encounter that resulted in Albion.'

Helen lit a cigarette – the pungent French sort that contravenes clean air laws everywhere – and discreetly blew the smoke away from me. 'What would Anna know about it?'

'That's what she said.'

'Here's some good advice: never believe anything that woman says to you. She's a lying, devious slut.'

I was stunned.

'I can see that I've shocked you with my injudicious choice of words,' Helen said bitterly. 'But it's the truth.'

'I've just never heard anyone talk about her like that. I work with her and she's pretty widely liked.'

'The caring therapist role is a big fat front. She was a monster as a teenager and she is still a monster. Selfish, greedy, manipulative.'

'Why do you dislike her so much?'

'I don't dislike her. I hate her. She's a little Nazi. She was always jealous of Elaine. She always wanted anything Elaine had. She couldn't bear it. Once, Elaine's mother gave her a brooch. It was a family heirloom, it'd belonged to Elaine's grandmother. Elaine got it for doing well at school. Anna was furious. She took the brooch and hid it. When Elaine confronted her, Anna threw it out into the garden. We spent hours hunting for it. She refused to apologize – she just laughed.'

I felt the teasing tug of a half-recovered memory. 'What did the brooch look like?'

'What? Oh, it was nothing special. A few coloured stones in a filigree setting. Just paste, actually, but for Elaine it had sentimental value. She loved her grandmother.'

'I thought Elaine and Anna were the best of friends.'

'Like I say, Elaine didn't like to rock the boat – for her mother's sake. But she always distrusted Anna and resented her interfering in her life. God, you should have seen Anna after Albion was born. She's got no kids. Spent thousands on the treatment, but got nowhere and suddenly she's the expert on child development. She wanted to put Albion in kiddy music lessons, kiddy language classes. Elaine refused outright. She didn't want any of Anna's snobbery rubbing off on her kid. And so Anna would go and buy half of Hamley's, bring it round. "I want my niece to have nice things about her." ' Helen's imitation of Anna was spot on. 'Elaine told her to take them back. She didn't want her child spoiled. She held her ground. One of the few fights that she ever won.

'And she did a great job raising her. Albion is a wonderful kid, although I fear for her now that Anna's finally got her hooks into her.' She stopped, lit another cigarette. 'What's the matter? You look as if I've just told you the Pope's a paedophile.'

'It doesn't sound like the Anna I know.'

Helen shrugged. 'The Anna I know trapped me and Elaine in a cellar at school. We were fifteen. She left us there for hours. We were terrified. It was cold, we had no food and we couldn't see a thing. When she let us out she persuaded Elaine not to rat on her – Anna would get expelled if she did and it would break their mother's heart. Elaine agreed because she was so terrified of upsetting her mother.'

'Why did you go along with it?'

'Because she asked me to. She begged me to, actually. I think Elaine hated her from that day on too. She was scared of the dark, so you can imagine what being in a damp cellar did to her brain. And we had a big chemistry exam the next day. I reckon that was why Anna did it. She always hated that Elaine was brighter than her. That was one thing she couldn't snatch away.'

She signalled for the bill.

'I heard Elaine was considering moving to the country,' I said, putting down some money to cover the coffees.

'She was. And we have some old school friends who live in rustic bliss Somerset. She was thinking of joining them. Making a break from the family.' She slipped on her coat. Pocketed my card.

'You never met her, did you?'

I shook my head.

'Too bad. You'd have liked her. She was fun.'

Chapter Forty-two

'Sam? What are you doing here?'

Robert answered the door wearing an apron. Albion peered coyly out through his knees. 'Anna's not here. She's at City, actually. I'm surprised you didn't see her there.'

'I wanted to speak to you alone,' I said.

'Oh, right. Sorry. Didn't mean to sound unwelcoming. I'm in chaos here. We're creating works of art with playdough, but come in. Albion wants me to make her a rhinoceros.'

We went downstairs to the kitchen. An antique oak table filled the room. It was covered with toys, colouring books and modelling dough.

'We went on a bit of a spending spree,' said Robert sheepishly. 'A lot of her old toys had her mother's . . . blood on them.' He mouthed the word so that Albion couldn't hear it. 'We thought it best to burn them. Fancy some tea? I was just about to make some.'

'Sure,' I said. I sat at the table and Albion pulled up a chair beside me. She grinned engagingly. ''noceros,' she said, pushing some dough my way.

'I've taken a couple of weeks off work, to help her with the settling-in process,' said Robert. 'It was just too mad otherwise. And since I work for my father, he was practically forcing me out of the door.'

'Dam! 'noceros!' said Albion, prodding my arm. I'd made little progress with the dough. Robert set a cup of tea down in front of me. Albion saw it.

'Want juice,' she demanded of Robert.

'OK,' he said, opening the fridge door. 'Apple? Orange?'

'Apple,' said Albion.

'Apple what?'

'Apple, please,' said Albion, drumming her heels against the back of her chair. 'Please, apple, please, Robbit-bobbit,' she chanted. She picked up a wodge of dough and threw it across the table.

Robert filled a child's cup with juice and placed it in front of her. He picked up the dough. 'Thank you,' said Albion, grinning wickedly. She was a child secure in her charms.

Robert sat opposite me at the table.

'What can I do for you?' he said. 'Not still working on the Elaine story? She seems to have dropped from the news.'

I felt bad about busting into this man's house and asking this question. But I had to get it straight.

'Did Anna and Elaine get on?'

Robert looked startled. 'What's this to do with?'

'Were they friends?'

'Look, I don't understand what you're driving at.'

'I spoke to Helen Smith. She said there was bad feeling between them.'

'Ah.' Robert leaned back in his chair. 'Helen and Anna have been fighting over Elaine's favour for years. Strange thing. It goes back to school, according to

289

Anna. Sure, to answer your question, there were times when they didn't get on, but that's family, isn't it? I don't know any families that are sweetness and light all the time.'

Robert picked up the dough and expertly moulded a tiny rhinoceros. He set it on the table in front of Albion, who recognized its beauty.

'Fancied myself as an artist once,' said Robert. 'Long time ago.'

'Ridley, where the hell have you been?' Felicia, as usual, was unamused.

I sat behind my desk wearily. 'Frolicking amongst the wild flowers,' I said.

'You're supposed to be doing an interview in Harley Street, for Infertility Week. Here's the file. Guy's name is Sturges and he's the best in the country. You're already late, taxi's waiting outside.'

I raced downstairs, dived into the taxi, spilling the file as I did.

Ronald P. Sturges's premises spoke success, even to the casual visitor. They were expensively but discreetly appointed. It was like stepping back in time. There was no sign of computers or faxes or any other twentieth-century ephemera.

The secretary showed me into Ronald Sturges's office. He was a glossy, satisfied man. He glowed from the crown of his shiny head to the tips of his shiny brogues. The bits in between were clad in expensive grey suit. He had an unseasonal tan and an accent that sounded South African.

He suggested coffee and I accepted. It appeared

several minutes later, borne in on a silver tray by the assistant. The coffee pot was also silver, the cups bone china. I set up my tape recorder on the coffee table, taking care not to scratch the cherrywood surface. Not for the first time I decided going into journalism had been a mistake.

Business was booming for the good doctor. Infertile women beat a path to his door, begged him to take their money if, in return, he would furnish them with their heart's desire – a healthy baby.

'What lengths will they go to?' I asked, hoping for a snappy soundbite.

Ronald P. Sturges leant back in his chair. 'They will do whatever it takes . . . Sell their house, take out a second mortgage, steal, defraud their employers. You name it.

'And there's no guarantee of success. That's the first thing I tell my prospective patients. I'm not God.' He gave a little smile which suggested that if he wasn't God, then he was at least high up in the Holy Trinity.

'And what if the answer's no after all that money and grief?'

'It often ends in tears. One couple ended their marriage right in front of me. The woman got up, said something to the effect that if she couldn't have any kids she wasn't going to stick with the relationship. The pressure that the process puts people under often distorts their values,' he added.

Anna was just leaving when I got back to the office.

'Did you speak to Helen?' she asked.

'She told me a funny story about your school days,'

I said. 'About spending the night in a cellar. It was very amusing, the way she told it.'

Anna frowned. 'It wasn't at the time. They were playing a game with a ouija board and needed somewhere dark to do it. And they went down to the cellar and got trapped. The caretaker found them hours later, but not until after the whole school had been called out to search.'

'Helen remembers it differently.'

'I'm not surprised. After they got out I tore a strip off Helen. It must have been her idea. I was certain Elaine would never have done something like that on her own.'

I rode the lift to the newsroom, rattled off the story about the good doctor, but my mind was other places. Tossing up the two wildly different accounts of the same event.

I finished the story, took it over to Felicia. 'Will you do me a favour?' I said.

'Why should I do you a favour, Ridley?'

'Because your reward will be great in heaven.' I put a slip of paper with Ronald P. Sturges's number on it in front of her. 'I want you to dial this number and make an appointment to see the doctor. Tell the secretary that you heard about him from your friend.'

'Ridley, this is the guy you just interviewed. I'm not calling him. Besides, he'll recognize my voice since I've already spoken to him. And I do have an American accent, in case you hadn't noticed.'

I got down on my knees. 'I'll do anything you ask,' I pleaded. 'I'll do the story on the teenage vice ring.'

Felicia rolled her eyes. 'All right,' she said. 'But this

292

is only because the sight of you on your knees is so repellent to me.' She dialled quickly, her long nails clicking against the plastic.

'Hello? Is that Mr Sturges's secretary?' Felicia's mild accent had been replaced by something much more strident. She sounded like one of those fat tourists you see walking around parliament square in glowing track suits and trainers.

'Yeah, cool.' The way she said cool made it sound like it had two syllables. 'I was wondering whether it's possible to make an appointment to see the doctor? Oh? He's very busy? Well, when will he be free? That long, huh? Goddamn, that's busy. What a shame. I heard about his work from a friend.' Felicia clicked her fingers, waved at me, mouthed *What was the name of the friend?* I wrote Anna's name on her blotter. Felicia glanced at it, did a double-take but kept on talking. 'Yep,' she said. 'Mrs York-Baines. She spoke very highly of the doctor's work.' There was more talking on the other end. The doctor employed an extremely chatty secretary. 'Well, OK, then,' said Felicia. 'I'll call back next month. Thank you so much, you've been so kind.'

She put the phone down. 'Mind telling me what the fuck that was about?'

'Playing a hunch,' I said. 'What did she say?'

'She said it was always nice to receive recommendations from other patients.'

That night I went to my local for a whisky and a think. It was, as usual, smoky and busy. But I didn't talk to anyone. I thought about what Helen had said about Anna's grasping nature. I'd seen Anna wearing the brooch that Helen said was Elaine's. Maybe Anna had seen Elaine's baby and decided she wanted that too. She'd gone for the treatment and had been told there was nothing more that could be done. But maybe Robert was right. That Helen had been motivated by jealousy. Maybe Anna had a similar brooch to Elaine's – you could buy them by the tray load at Portobello Market every week. And just because a woman was having infertility treatment it didn't mean she'd kill her sister so's to have her baby.

In fact, once I'd voiced the thought in my mind I realized how preposterous it sounded. I paid up and went home. The whisky had begun to make me think I didn't really care, anyway.

The next day, I stepped out on to the street and into a light drizzle. I turned my collar up and prepared to make a dash for the tube station.

'Ridley.'

I looked round. Roger Fitzgerald was leaning on his regulation-issue police car. He opened the door. Smiled like a wolf facing a three-course lamb dinner.

Chapter Forty-three

'Roger, you needn't have gone to all this trouble. A phone call would have done.'

'Get in.'

I got in. The car pulled out into traffic.

'I have to be at work,' I looked at my watch, 'in half an hour.'

'When you eventually get there you can tell them you've been helping the police with their inquiries.' He smiled, all chummy-like. I looked straight ahead. Then I remembered the tape under Everard's floorboards and I smiled too. The driver paid no attention to us. I studied the back of his neck. It was neatly shaven. I was dying for a cup of coffee.

'No chance of a cup of coffee, I suppose? I think so much better with a snort of caffeine.'

'Where's the tape, Ridley?'

'A slice of toast, perhaps? Anything will do. At this hour, I'm just not that fussy.'

Fitzgerald didn't reply, so we drove in silence for a bit. In a few minutes we had pulled up outside the Latimer Road tennis courts. The nets were down. Nobody wanted to play in this weather.

'Get out,' said Fitzgerald. 'We're going to talk.'

I got out, opened the wire gate and walked into

the middle of the court. I had played tennis once, an aeon ago. I know this because my mother has photos of me in baggy white clothing holding a funny, old-fashioned racket.

'I know you've got a copy of the tape. I spoke to the people at the cinema.' Fitzgerald stood about ten feet away from me. His body language suggested aggressive.

Bernie had been caught out. Still, it wasn't the end of the world.

'Yes,' I said. 'I've got a copy. It's no longer your word against mine, Roger. A respected officer of the law and all that.'

There was a pause. I wondered if Fitzgerald was going to go for my throat again. I looked over at the car. The junior cop was sitting inside. Presumably he wouldn't be springing to my defence. Fitzgerald was too close for comfort.

'I'll fucking break you, Ridley,' he said. 'Into little tiny pieces.'

'No, you won't,' I said. 'Because if even one little piece goes missing, my lawyer knows what to do. The tape's already addressed to ITN. Of course, it's a little bit dark in places, but they can fix all that now, I'm told. Don't worry, though, I'm sure they'll get your best side.'

This was going great. Just like in the movies. I was ad-libbing of course, but the bit about the lawyer could be fixed up soon enough. I felt better than I had done in a while. I smiled a secret and superior smile. The kind of smile that Paul Newman did well. The kind of smile that said, 'I'm in control.'

'And don't bother to have someone search my flat

while we're having this little chat,' I went on, 'because it isn't there.' Boy, was I on a roll. This was great, this was better than sex.

To my surprise Roger Fitzgerald didn't appear to be the least bit concerned about my threats. In fact, he burst out laughing. This didn't happen in the movies.

'Ridley, you're a complete pillock, you know that?' And he laughed some more. What a riot it all was.

'What's so funny?'

'I leaned on your friend, what's his name? Eddy? He caved in. Shipped you up the river. Breaking and entering! Har-har. Say bye-bye to your pathetic life, Ridley. You're going to jail.' He walked back across the court, paused at the gate.

'I want that tape,' he said.

And he left me there.

To say that my heart sank was to understate the case. As the car drove off, my most vital organ buried through the earth's core faster than a molten pluto-nium rod.

Chapter Forty-four

I've always wondered what I'd do if told I had hours to live. Would I proposition women in the street? Would I buy a magnum of champagne and drink it while dancing naked in a fountain? Would I do a dine and dash at Claridge's?

No. If today was anything to go by, I'd probably just get the next train to work. I'd suspected this about me, now I knew the truth. Faced with disaster and ruin, I take refuge in routine.

Latimer Road tube station was the closest, so I made for that.

It was raining heavily by now. I was drenched by the time I'd bought my ticket and got under cover. Around me, sullen commuters read papers and excavated noses and ears. Everyone has their morning routine.

On the train I brooded. There was clearly a choice to be made here; Fitzgerald knew that if he booked me I'd shop him. But if I handed over the tape I had no guarantee that he wouldn't double-cross me. Mind you, he had no guarantee that I wouldn't make a copy, or several.

A Mexican stand-off is what I believe it's called.

I deduced from the fact that we'd had our little

chat in private that Fitzgerald was willing to forgo my arrest in favour of keeping his good standing in the community. So he wanted me to stew a bit. The important thing was not to lose my nerve.

Fortunately Felicia was at hand with the means to forget my troubles.

'Where the hell have you been?' she demanded as I arrived about an hour later than the time agreed upon.

'I got delayed. The police wanted to talk to me.'

She paced around me like a show pony in her high heels. I expected to see her stamp her foot.

'I've had enough of this. I have a show to put out. You're not a police reporter any more. Can't you get that through your head? Why must we keep having this conversation?'

I could have been mistaken, but I think she was itching for a fight. If I'd thought about it, I probably was too. I was wet and mad.

'We don't keep having this conversation, Felicia. You only think we do. I think you'll find that most mornings I'm here on time.'

'Most mornings isn't bloody good enough. All my other staff, and myself, are here every morning on time. Why do you have a problem with punctuality? Is it a male thing? Do you think you're too important to have to come in every day at the hour you're supposed to?'

'Come on, Felicia. I told you why I was late.'

She jabbed a finger in my face. 'I'm speaking to Delaney about this. I can put up with your patronizing, your snide jokes, your superior-than-bloody-thou attitude, but this is too much. You're off my show as of right now.'

I did some jabbing myself. 'Great. I'm sick of you. You blow hot and cold. You're self-important. You never relax. You're no fun at all, Felicia. Sorry to have to be the one to break it to you.'

She was shaking with anger. 'And *you* are dead meat. I won't work with you any more.'

She went to her desk. I went to the coffee machine.

'You never give up, do you?' said Lyall. He poured coffee with a practised motion. He'd heard our exchange, as had most people in the building.

'She started it.'

Lyall poured another coffee for me.

'Listen to yourself. You sound like my kids. Are you sure you didn't bonk her?'

'I'd have remembered.'

'Something for you to think about: you can't pay child support from an unemployment cheque. If you don't pay child support then Mary will find a way to make sure you never ever see Simon again. Now go over and grovel before Delaney gets in.'

'I'll get another job.'

'In this market? They want twenty-five-year-olds with a double-first in journalism and tongue-proctology.'

'I can't work with Felicia any more. I'll throw myself on Delaney's mercy.'

'Clever strategy. Delaney thinks mercy is how the French say thank you. Think of something else.' Lyall loped off.

I read the newspapers, listened to the news, drank coffee and avoided Felicia's eye line.

Delaney didn't arrive until ten. He went to his office. He came out. He made himself tea. Felicia and I watched his every move.

Delaney walked back across the newsroom nursing his tea in a china cup. (He can't abide polystyrene, he says it's bad for the soul.) It rattled slightly on its saucer as he carried it. Without asking permission, Felicia followed him into his office and shut the door.

I watched them surreptitiously through the glass walls. Felicia gestured extravagantly. Delaney nodded sagely, his eyes on her breasts. After half an hour she came out.

I busied myself with the computer. The message light blinked. I pressed it.

'Can you come into my office?' it read.

Sighing, I got out of my chair.

Chapter Forty-five

I knocked on Delaney's door. He waved me in. The teacup, with the soggy bag glued to the side, sat on his desk.

'Felicia tells me we have a little problem here.' Delaney leaned back in his chair, his hands in the prayer position. 'I'd like to hear your side.'

That, at least, was something.

I nodded, gauging the situation, waiting for him to reveal how he felt about it.

'She says your attitude is bad, that you don't come up with any story ideas, you're never on time and you don't contribute anything constructive to the programme.' He smiled stiffly. He liked saying those things about me.

I decided on the mature, analytical approach, figuring Delaney had probably had enough raw emotion for one morning. He had water filters to sell, after all.

'Felicia and I got off to a bad start,' I said. 'That makes it difficult for us to communicate.' It also made it difficult for us to get through the day without ripping each other's throats out.

'Right,' he said, rocking himself gently back and forth in his executive chair. 'A personality clash.'

'That's all it is,' I said. 'I've done my best, and so has she. But it hasn't worked out.'

He rocked some more.

'You're on probation. You're supposed to be trying very hard.'

'Put me in another department. Think of it as a mercy divorce.'

'It's not that simple, Sam.' He smiled some more, but it had a mean edge this time. He was loving this.

'Alan, I was late today because the police wanted to talk to me about a murder investigation. Call Detective Inspector Roger Fitzgerald if you don't believe me. As for the other issues; well, I've done everything that was asked of me. I'm a police reporter. It's hard for me to get interested in fashion and showbusiness.'

Delaney reached for a pen and wrote something down on a pad in front of him.

'Felicia doesn't want to work with you any more,' he said when he had finished. 'I have to decide what we are going to do with you. We don't have any spare positions and we can't have you floating around the office like dead wood.'

No, I thought. You have to be promoted to management before you get to do that.

'I'll let you know by the end of the day,' Delaney continued. 'In the meantime, you can stand in for Lyall on the afternoon bulletins. He has a doctor's appointment, so he'll be out of the office.'

'At your service, sir!' I presented myself at Lyall's desk.

He looked up. 'Oh God, it's the cavalry.'

'Down to its last horse, and that one's limping.'

'How was it?'

'Bad.'

Lyall sighed. He stood up. 'I'll have a word with him, see what I can do,' he said. 'But this is absolutely the last time I stick my neck out for you.'

'Begorrah, ye'll be a friend indeed,' I said as I slid into his chair.

Eddy called.

'How did he get on to us?' I asked him.

'God, Sam, I'm so sorry.' Eddy sounded upset. 'He came to the office, questioned people about the break-in. Fishing, really, just seeing if it had anything to do with Elaine. I'm afraid I didn't do very well. I'm a terrible liar. He threatened all sorts of things.'

'Did he take you to the police station?'

'No, we talked in the car park.'

'Were there any other police around?'

'No.'

'Then don't worry too much. This is between him and me. I'll try and sort it out.'

'What if you don't?'

'Then we get one-way tickets to Rio.'

Delaney didn't get back to me by the end of the day. I finished my editing shift in limbo, wondering what fate the career gods would decide for me tomorrow. Lyall came back from the doctor. Then he spent some time with Delaney in his office with the door closed.

'We need a drink,' he said when he came back. 'Let's go.' All business, he marched out of the door, with me trailing in his wake. We stepped across the road to another pub, not our usual. One which isn't frequented by bikers and workmen.

'Why here?' I asked. Lyall and I have both agreed that we disapprove of the floral chintz decorating schemes favoured by most brewery-owned pubs and that, given the choice, we'll take good honest grime every time.

'Sit down there,' he said. 'I'm bringing you a drink.' He went up to the bar. I sat down in the chintz-framed alcove that he had directed me to.

In a few minutes he was back. He sat down and put the drinks in front of us. Every now and then he would look up at the door, as if expecting someone else.

'How did it go with Delaney?' I asked.

'I appealed to his self-interest.'

'Always a rich seam to mine.'

The door opened, a gust of rain blew in and so did Felicia. Lyall signalled her to come over.

'Sit down,' said Lyall firmly. 'I'm buying. What do you want?'

She looked at Lyall. She looked at me. She looked back at Lyall. She opened her mouth to say something and then closed it.

'Vodka tonic.' She took off her red coat and put it on a spare seat.

Lyall got up. 'Both of you'd better be here when I get back,' he said. And sure enough, when he got back, both of us were. We'd sat in silence, but we were still there.

'Right,' said Lyall. 'Here's the situation the way I see it. You are both hard-headed, stubborn, opinionated and impossible to reason with. And you're both used to having your own way at any cost.'

'I object,' I said.

'Shut up,' said Lyall. 'No one's asking you anything.' Felicia smirked.

'Now,' said Lyall. 'These are the facts of life. Sometimes, and when you grow up, children, you'll understand this better, but sometimes things don't go the way you want them to. And when that happens you have to deal with it by using what we grown-ups call maturity.'

'I don't have to take this,' said Felicia. She reached for her coat.

'Drink your vodka,' said Lyall. 'Now, we are presently facing one of those situations. And both of your jobs could be affected by how you handle this. So far it's only gone as high as Delaney, and that's a good thing, because he doesn't particularly care to deal with it. He's got other fish to fry, as we all know. But if you push it,' he looked at Felicia, 'it'll go higher, and there'll be serious consequences for both of you.'

'I'll do whatever I damn well like,' said Felicia.

'Of course you will,' said Lyall. 'Just be aware of what you're getting into, that's all. Now, a little quiz. Whose idea do you think it was that Sam go to your show?'

Felicia shrugged. 'Delaney's, I thought.'

'God's?' I ventured.

'Wrong. Think higher.'

'Marlowe?'

'Right. It was his idea. And he, not unsurprisingly, thinks it was a good one. The violence special worked out well, much kudos for the station there, and all round an interesting experiment. Now, what will happen if you go to him and say, "Daddy, we can't play together any more." I'll tell you. He won't like it even a little bit. He likes to look on the bright side. He doesn't want one of his subordinates telling him that one of his ideas wasn't the best possible solution to the problem at hand.' He was right about that. One of Marlowe's interesting little foibles was that he positively insisted on being right all the time.

Lyall drained his tomato juice. 'I have to go now. I leave you with this thought; kiss and make up.'

We were left staring at each other across the table. I ordered another round because I couldn't think of anything else to say. We sat there, not speaking, but not moving either. Felicia fiddled with a loose thread in the hem of her skirt. Her bright-red nails were exactly the same shade as the fabric.

'Which did you get first?' I said.

'What?'

'Which came first, the polish or the skirt?'

She stopped playing with the skirt and picked up her drink.

'You're weird, Ridley.'

'I had a good reason,' I said.

'For asking me about my polish?'

'For being late.'

'Ah,' she said. She was clearly thinking of something else. 'That shit Marlowe,' she said. 'He's trying to get rid of me. They used you as a Trojan horse, Ridley.'

'What are you talking about?'

'They knew we hated each other. That we'd start

scrapping from the first moment. But it was me he was trying to get at, not you. You were expendable.'

'Hardly expendable, and aren't you being just a little paranoid?'

'That bastard,' she said. 'Invertebrate swamp scum.'

'Why would they want to get rid of you?' I said. 'Don't tell me the chairman's daughter fancies a career in radio?'

Felicia flapped her hand impatiently. 'It's between Marlowe and me.'

'Ah,' I said. The way she'd said it made me think a revelation was about to follow. I put on my 'I-carry-secrets-to-my-grave' expression. It works every time.

Chapter Forty-six

'This goes any further and I'll make it my life's work to hunt you down and maim you, Ridley.'

'I get the picture. What happened?'

'You know I don't have any background in news?' she said. I had heard that, but it didn't seem particularly important, since *Female AM* didn't run any news.

'I got the job because I met Marlowe at a party. I was working in public relations, but it wasn't much fun. So I gave him the hard sell and he invited me in for an interview. It went pretty well and he offered me the job. As it turned out, there were a few strings attached. A while ago he invited me out for dinner, and I went, thinking there'd be other people there. I was quite chuffed, actually. Thought that the invite was some sort of recognition for my doing a good job. What a joke! There were just the two of us. It turned out that Mrs Marlowe was out of town.' She gulped down her drink.

'He got barking drunk and insisted on coming back to my place for a nightcap.' She snorted derisively.

'That old line!' I said, making a note not to use it in the future.

Felicia stirred the lemon in her drink with a fingernail. 'To cut a long story short, he made a pass at me, which is putting it politely. Actually he lunged at me, and wouldn't take no for an answer.'

'What happened?'

'I kicked him in the balls and threw him out on the street,' she said, angrily.

I conjured up the picture of our executive editor wandering half clothed and in drunken disarray through the streets of London. A broad grin spread across my face. 'My friend,' I said, 'let me buy you a drink.'

It was a few drinks later and we'd returned to the subject of Marlowe.

'Why don't you complain?' I asked. 'There're tribunals that deal with that sort of thing. And you'll get money in compensation.'

She glared at me. 'I fight my own battles, Ridley.'

'Right. Of course you do.'

'I don't need some tribunal to get back at him. I do that by turning up for work every day. It's just really, really hard. I get no backing from him – he's trying to freeze me out. There are days when I wonder if the struggle is worth it, but then I figure, what the hell. Stick it out for another year and then I'll have enough experience to land another job.'

'I had no idea. I thought you were the golden girl.'

Felicia smiled ruefully. 'I am. Which makes Marlowe hate me even more. He can't fire me for incompetence because *Female AM* is going better than ever. I mean, God, my life is such a mess. This is just not what I need.'

'What do you need? Maybe I can help.'

She laughed outright at that one. 'I don't think so, Ridley, but thanks for the offer.'

'Don't mention it. Any sworn enemy of Marlowe's is a friend of mine.'

'No, you can't help me with this one, Ridley.'

I had the idea that we hadn't reached the end of the evening's revelations. I checked my glass. It was full. I got settled in.

'I got myself into this mess and I have to get myself out.'

'That's usually the way it works. Blokes on chargers being in short supply these days.'

'Blokes on chargers. What I wouldn't do for a bloke on a charger. An unmarried bloke on a charger.'

'Unmarried. Right.'

'Ridley. I wouldn't tell you this except that I've had three vodkas.'

'Four, actually. One was a double.'

'I'm having an affair with a married man, Ridley. I am a living, breathing, walking cliché. I'm the Other Woman.'

I must have lifted an eyebrow because she shook her head. 'It's nobody you know, so don't start speculating.'

She snapped the loose thread off her skirt. 'Said he was going to leave his wife. I've been swallowing that line for a good two years now.

'I don't know why I hang on. It's so uncool, so desperate. I love him, I suppose. But I want other things for my life, too. Family, kids, the usual boring suburban aspirations. I'm thirty-five, my time is running out. You men don't have to think about these things. Just pick up a twenty-three-year-old. That's your answer to the biological clock.' She snapped her fingers and slumped back into her seat.

'Tell me honestly, do you think a twenty-three-year-old would have me?' I asked.

She leaned forward. Looked at me with one eye closed, a half-smile on her face.

'Well, I . . . ' she started to say.

Then it hit me. It hit me like a flying block of frozen urine from an aeroplane toilet.

I picked up Felicia's hand and kissed it.

'Have I got a story for you,' I said and jumped to my feet, knocking my stool over. The other patrons at the bar stared.

'Ridley, what the hell . . .?' began Felicia.

'I'll explain it all soon,' I cried over my shoulder as I dashed out of the door.

Chapter Forty-seven

I sometimes think that many of my problems stem from the fact that I hear but don't listen. Shark had tried to tell me what he knew, but I hadn't taken enough notice. That was about to change.

The night shift had started. The newsroom was quiet and dark because Ted, the night editor, wages a one-man campaign against fluorescent lighting. He says it rots the brain, which, if it's true, would certainly explain a lot of things about City Radio.

I took the tapes of Shark's calls to *Female AM* into an edit bay. I played them back. I listened hard. The recordings weren't as clear as I'd have liked, but that's why God created engineers. I went in search of one and found Gary lounging in the control room with his feet up doing the *Guardian* cryptic crossword.

'I have a problem,' I said.

'I thrive on adversity,' he replied. He followed me back to the edit room. I told him what I wanted.

'Think you can do that?' I asked. His look in reply was withering. Engineers can do anything. They pride themselves on it.

*

I went back to my desk. I rang Charlie Hobbs, but he wasn't in. I left a message.

'I've been looking all over for you.'

It was Anna. She stood in front of me, hands in the pockets of her expensive overcoat, smiling slightly. 'Robert told me you'd been over. We need to talk.'

'Yeah,' I said. 'You're wondering whether I believe Helen's version of the cellar story or yours. And she told me about the brooch. I've seen you wearing it. Did you steal it from your sister before or after you killed her?'

Anna jammed her hands further down into her coat pockets. 'You're obsessed with my sister's death because you identify with Albion. You know what it's like to have someone ripped away from you. It's your way of making sense of your own tragedy.'

I just laughed. 'Want to know what I think? I think the brooch was a big mistake, Anna. The police sealed her flat after she was murdered. How did you get it? There's only one way that I can figure. She wouldn't have given it to you. The brooch was a symbol of your relationship to Elaine. You were jealous of her. You wanted everything that she had. The brooch and Albion, you wanted them both very badly indeed.'

'You're accusing me of murder?'

'Someone has to.'

Anna sighed wearily. She put her hand at the small of her back as though to soothe a pain there. 'Listen to what you are saying, Sam. You're upset and confused. It's quite understandable. You've lost your son and you're compensating by projecting your sense of loss on to me. Think about it. Why would I kill my own sister to have Albion? She's my godchild. I could see her whenever I wanted. She lived just down the road.'

'Elaine had two plans. The first was that she wanted to get back together with Mark. The second was to move to the country. When the Mark option fell through she told you she'd had enough. Or maybe she was fed up with you meddling in her life. Or maybe it was a bit of both. That night she decided she was leaving Roadblock and leaving London. She told you and that made you flip out.'

Anna shook her head. 'That's quite a fanciful theory. Unfortunately I don't think it'll hold up in a court of law. There's no basis to these allegations. There's no proof. And I didn't see or speak to my sister the night she died.'

She turned and walked slowly towards the door, hand still rubbing her back. I stayed at my desk, head in my hands.

'You walked out on me. Where I come from that's called rude.' There was another woman standing over me: Felicia.

'What's going on?' she said.

'Do you think I'm crazy?' I said.

She shrugged. 'No more than usual. Why?'

'To cut a long story short, I think Anna York-Baines killed her sister because she couldn't conceive a child of her own.'

Felicia's eyes opened wide. 'Whoa!'

'She said I'm making it all up because I'm distraught over my son.'

'Wait a minute. Let me get this straight. You *told* her this?'

'I wanted to see how she'd react.'

'And what did she say?'

'She said I needed help.'

'Was that before or after she kneed you in the balls?'

'You think it's crazy too.'

'Well, it's not crazy. It's . . . improbable. My god, Sam . . . it's . . . it's . .!' She paused, searching for the adjective, and her face broke into an almost lascivious grin. 'It's a great fucking story! If it's true. What a fucking scoop.' She pulled up a chair eagerly. 'What proof do you have?'

'I . .'

'Oh, shit,' she said. 'You are crazy.'

The phone rang. It was Gary.

'Come in here. Got something for you.'

'God, I'm good,' he said as he spooled the tapes deftly backwards and forwards. He'd taken the tapes into the control room. He lined one spool up, finger poised over the play button.

'Ready?'

'Back it up a bit,' I said. 'I want Felicia to hear it from the beginning.' Gary spooled the tape back a few revolutions.

Shark's gruff voice filled the little room.

'I was there that night. I seen who dunnit.'

Gary paused the tape. 'Now you couldn't hear what she said in reply, because Crosbie drowned her out. But,' he spooled the tape back half a revolution, 'I did something a little bit tricky and,' he pressed the play button, '*voilà!*'

Anna's voice was slower, like a deaf person pronouncing words seen but never heard. 'What . . . do . . . you wah-un-tah?' she said.

'I think the lady said, "What do you want?" ' said Gary.

'What does it mean?' said Felicia, frowning.

'He's blackmailing her. That's what the conversation was really about. Her guard was down and she instinctively asked him what he wanted. Only Crosbie cut in. Unintentionally, Crosbie saved her arse. Shark called up about the reward, but somehow he twigged. Or maybe he already knew. He'd have seen her photo in the papers and recognized her. So he hit on the bright idea of ringing her on air in front of thousands of people. It put the fear of God into her. She thought the game was up. Look, later on,' I wound the tape forward, 'she says, "What do you suggest we do?" She's letting him know she's ready to do a deal.'

'Like, wow,' said Gary. 'What are you talking about?'

Felicia was still frowning. 'You're saying she killed her sister *and* this Shark character?'

'She had to. And it can't have been that hard. Shark wouldn't have thought a woman could overpower him; he was a big lad. All she had to do was arrange to meet him somewhere dark and deserted, which she did. Shark probably explained that while he'd been hanging around outside the Summerhill Estate that night he'd seen Anna go into the flat and that information like that was probably worth a good deal more than twenty thousand pounds. Anna didn't see it that way at all. So she shot him. Bye-bye, Shark.'

'I don't know, Sam.' Felicia shook her head. 'We can't use this. It's supposition. We need a witness.

Where was Shark all the time he was planning his campaign of blackmail? He must have laid his hat somewhere. He couldn't just vanish. Surely you could find a mate, or someone lurking in the . . .?' She stopped because I had grabbed hold of her shoulder and was gripping it hard.

'Of course! Max's sister, Stephanie Adams. The shoes. Come on.' I started out of the door.

We hailed a taxi. I directed it to Paddington. Felicia looked at me suspiciously, as though she feared I would pounce on her at any moment.

'Max told me that he and Shark had had a fight over his sister,' I said. 'So they must have been an item, or at least friends, at some stage.'

We knocked on Stephanie Adams' door. She slid open the peephole.

'It's Sam Ridley.'

The door opened silently and she stood there, thin and afraid.

Chapter Forty-eight

Stephanie Adams showed us through to her living room. It was tidier than the last time Felicia and I had called to ask about Max and Shark. It seemed like a long time ago.

'Want coffee?' Stephanie asked as we got seated. It was a welcome suggestion. All the alcohol that I had drunk with Felicia was still singing in my ears. And I needed a clear head.

'It's about Shark, isn't it?' she said when she returned with three mugs on a tray.

'Do you want to tell us what happened?' Felicia asked.

Stephanie nodded as she sipped her coffee.

'Shark came to stay with me after Elaine York was killed,' she said. 'He was strange at first. Wouldn't tell me why he was here or why he didn't want to see any of his mates. I assumed he'd done something illegal, so I didn't press him. Then he heard about the reward. He went out to get the papers one day and there it was on the front page. Twenty thousand quid. After he read that he started acting well pleased with himself. Kept telling me he was gonna be in the money. But he wouldn't tell me why. Eventually I wormed it out of him that he'd witnessed this murder.

But he wouldn't tell me what he'd seen. I told him he had to go to the police. He refused. Said they'd give him a hard time. So I suggested an intermediary.'

I pulled out a pack of cigarettes and offered her one. She accepted. I handed her my lighter.

'Turned out he'd seen you at Summerhill and reckoned you looked all right, so he agreed.' She exhaled a long smoky breath. 'Of course, like a moron he didn't keep the first appointment. Then he wondered why you didn't show up the next time.'

'Why didn't he turn up the first time?'

'Something to do with his debts. Shark wasn't long on business acumen, which was one of the reasons he botched this so completely.'

'Why did you take him in?'

Stephanie looked embarrassed. 'I . . . had a soft spot for him. So, anyway, he finds out about the call-in – on your radio station. So he rings, one day when I'm not there – I would never have advised him to do a stupid thing like that – and after that he starts acting all secretive and crafty. He won't tell me anything. He refused to ring you back and starts making calls from the phone box on the street. When I raised it with him he went right over the top, claiming that I only wanted the money. And the cheeky bastard was standing in my flat while he accused me of being mercenary. I didn't want his bloody money. I just wanted to know what he was doing. Then he goes out one night and that's it. Last I see of him.'

'Did he give you any hints, any suggestions at all?'

She shook her head. 'I tried everything. I even searched his bag. He had nothing except a few news-paper clips about the dead woman. That was the other thing. He started buying every newspaper he could find. I didn't even know he could read before that.'

'Have you got the clippings?'

'Yeah.' She went into another room.

'It's not enough, Sam,' said Felicia. 'She doesn't know any more than we do.'

Stephanie came back with the clippings in an envelope. She handed it to me.

'Didn't you tell the police what you knew?' asked Felicia.

Stephanie shook her head.

'Why not?'

'Don't like them.'

'Ah.' Felicia raised one eyebrow.

I perused the clippings that Shark had culled. He had collected photos of all the main players, including a studio portrait of Anna that the station had issued for publicity purposes.

I turned the envelope over. It bore a City Radio logo and was addressed to a Mr Smith.

'Not very original,' said Felicia.

I picked up the photo. Anna smiled back at me.

'He wanted to make sure he'd got it right,' I said.

'It's late. I'm going home,' said Felicia when we left Stephanie's flat and went out on to Bishop's Bridge Road in search of a taxi. 'We should call the police.'

'I want to check something out first,' I said.

I put Felicia in a taxi and started to walk home. But I got diverted. Before I knew it I was in Holland

Park. It's peaceful in that part of town at night. The traffic thunders by on Holland Park Avenue but that's a couple of blocks away and can't be heard. I stood under a tree on the opposite side of the street from Anna's house. I don't exactly know what I was doing there.

A big black Mercedes passed me and parked on the street. An overcoated figure got out. It was Robert. He crossed to the passenger seat and helped Anna out. She unstrapped a sleeping Albion from her baby seat. She looked up. Saw me, and put her other hand on Robert's arm, urging him inside, handing over the kid. He hesitated a moment before going in. He fitted a key in the front door and an oblong of soft light fell on the steps. Anna crossed the road. Stopped about ten feet from me.

'Go home, Sam.' She spoke softly but her voice carried in the still night.

'It won't work, Anna. I'm going to the police.'

Anna closed her eyes briefly, as if trying to decide something hard. 'You don't deserve to know this, but I'm going to tell you anyway, so you'll go away and leave me and my family alone.'

Instantly, I knew what she was going to say. It could have been a trick of the light, but it was more likely the way she was standing, with her hand in the small of her back. I'd seen her standing like that before.

'I'm pregnant, Sam. Twelve weeks. Sorry about your theory.'

Chapter Forty-nine

Anna was right, that was the problem. I'd lost my son. Albion had lost her mother. You didn't have to be Carl Jung to figure the connection. With not enough real stuff to fill my waking hours, I'd worked overtime concocting whistle and bell-laden theories.

I was at work half an hour early the next day. I bought an extra cappuccino and put it on Felicia's desk, to bolster the new spirit of accord.

'So what's happening with our scoop?' she asked after she'd given me a story to do about men who sleep with their girlfriends' mothers.

'Anna's pregnant,' I said.

'What?' Felicia gaped.

'I could have told you that,' said Andie, who happened to be passing. That girl had hearing like a bat. 'Bit of a miracle, from what I could gather. She and her husband had, like, a million quid's worth of in-vitro and nothing, then they give up and it happens.'

'How do you know?'

'I asked,' said Andie nonchalantly. 'Couldn't help noticing how she was back and forth to the loo. It's a sure sign.'

'Really,' said Felicia. 'Nice theory, Ridley.'

I went to the pub round the corner from work at

the end of the day. There seemed little point in anything else. I drank to forget that I'd made an arse of
myself. And I did a good job of it. After a while even
the bartender became concerned.

'Might like to have something to line the stomach,
mate,' he said. 'Or you're gonna be outside parking a
pavement pizza.'

He had a bold Antipodean accent, which gave me
something else to add to my litany of self-pity.

'I need another,' I said, slapping down some
money. 'Because you've just reminded me that my son
is going to grow up sounding like a bloody foreigner.'

The barman didn't understand what I meant, but
from his expression I could tell that he was used to
drunks speaking nonsense.

'Sam! Thought I'd find you here.'

I looked up, eyes struggling to focus. It was
Delaney. I struggled to unfocus.

'A glass of mineral water,' said Delaney primly,
pulling up a chair next to mine. I looked the other
way. I was too drunk to care about things like keeping
my job.

'I thought it was too expensive,' I growled as the
mineral water made its appearance. 'Dearer than
petrol. That's what you said.'

'What? Oh yes, heh-heh. Well, can't always be
choosy, since I don't drink and I can't have coffee
after about three in the afternoon. It really does make
me . . .'

'Was there a chase you wanted to cut to?'

'Chase? Oh yes. Chase. Right. I'm organizing a little
get-together. A few mates, you know. Thought you
might like to join us.'

'Delaney, whatever you're trying to sell me, I'm not interested. City Radio pay barely keeps me in whisky. I don't have anything left over for fancy extras like water.'

'Oh, this isn't to do with that. No, this is something else. You know, men who get together over a weekend and talk about their experiences. Put the humdrum behind them and learn how to relate to each other as men. I've done one before and let me tell you, Sam, it's empowering. Modern life doesn't leave much time for us guys to think about who we really are, define ourselves as men, particularly now the women's movement has so much to say for itself. This weekend group deals with important issues, Sam. We get together on Friday afternoon and spend two whole days in each other's company. I've done it once before and let me tell you, I feel a better person for it.'

'Fascinating,' I said.

'And it's only seven hundred pounds, all meals included, of course.'

'A snip.'

'So, can I sign you up?'

I am constantly amazed at the strength of Delaney's rapacity. We have never got on, but every time he comes up with a bright new idea his brain thinks it's Year Zero and we can begin again. Base a glorious friendship on my gullibility for shonky products.

'No,' I said, lurching off my stool. I'd meant to get up decisively but the whisky surfing through my blood system had another idea. 'I'm not free. I've arranged to spend that weekend in a traffic jam on the M25.'

The cool air felt good. Leaving Delaney behind felt

good. I walked to Tottenham Court Road tube station and rode a smelly, crowded train to Notting Hill Gate. Don't ask me why. The whisky was calling the shots.

I came out of the tube and tottered down Pembridge Road. Before I'd had the chance to register what I was doing, I was right outside the restaurant where Elaine had eaten her last meal with Mark. It stood on a busy intersection and two roads flowed around it. I stepped on to the pedestrian crossing without thinking, which was silly because drivers like to work up a bit of speed on that little narrow street. They genuinely seem to resent people trying to use the crossing there and make it their mission to try and stop them.

A car screeched to a stop. I stopped too, mid-crossing. The driver gesticulated and shouted words that would have got him sacked from City Radio.

I could see I had an audience inside the restaurant. A waiter carrying four large plates of pasta. As he slid the plates on to the table he glanced up and I saw a spark of recognition in his eyes.

I hopped up on to the pavement. The driver, still swearing, drove off.

I pushed the restaurant door open and went inside.

Buddhists say something about life being a wheel. I suppose that's why, at the end of it, I was at that restaurant. Time to say goodbye to Elaine.

I ordered pasta and beer.

'You nearly got killed out there,' said the waiter I'd seen through the window. He brought the beer.

'Lot on my mind,' I said.

'Happens a fair bit,' he said. 'That crossing. Drivers don't want to stop.'

I ordered another beer and a salad. Then I had tiramisu and coffee. After that I felt like a brandy, so I had one. The crowd at the tables had begun to thin. Soon I was only one of three left. I was at a loose end so I had another coffee and another brandy. The restaurant had a copy of the reward poster that the police had put about the neighbourhood. The waiter noticed my interest.

'She was at one of my tables. A real babe, people stared at her. In fact, when I saw you on the crossing tonight I had this wild sense of déjà vu. The night she was here some wally did the same thing. Held up the traffic staring at her.'

'What did he look like?'

'Dunno, it was dark. Don't even know if it was a he. All I saw was a great big bunch of flowers.'

'You tell the cops?'

'No. I just remembered it.'

I suppose if I hadn't drunk enough to float a cross-Channel ferry I would have made the connection a bit sooner. As it was I was halfway home before I realized what he'd told me. I ran the rest of the way.

'You're drunk.'

'Yes, madam, I'm drunk. But in the morning I'll be sober and you'll be . . . you'll be . . .'

'I'll still be your boss, Ridley. So you'd better have a good reason for calling me like this.'

'I've got it right. I've worked it out.'

'For God's sake, Ridley. Worked what out?' asked Felicia.

'The killer . . . Elaine . . . I know . . .'

'Ridley, please stop with this already. Take some paracetamol. Take a *lot* of paracetamol and get a good night's sleep. We'll talk tomorrow, it can wait. Besides, you're in no condition to go charging off.'

She hung up on me but I barely noticed. I was drunk. Delusional. That was my last thought as I passed out on the sofa.

Chapter Fifty

'You look like shit,' said Felicia as I placed another cup of coffee in front of her. I was in work early. I was on my third cup of coffee, wooing my hangover. I was sober. Well, sort of sober. And I had a plan.

I'd made a call. Spoken to a secretary. Then I called Charlie.

I explained my plan to Felicia. 'You're fucking crazy, Ridley,' she said. 'And I won't do it.'

'It'll be quite safe.'

'Safe? Two people are dead, Ridley. That's a risk in my book.'

'We'll get the story.'

'A scoop?'

'Sure. We'll be the only ones there. Just think, it'll make Marlowe about as comfortable as a barium enema.'

She rolled her eyes, but I could see that I had her hooked.

I went into the control room where Gary, the engineer, was reading a journal about electronics.

'Do we have a radio mike?'

'No,' he said, 'but I can make you one. What sort of range?'

'About a hundred yards.'

'Come back after lunch.'

I went back after lunch. Gary had two small bundles of transistors, a walkman and batteries and wire wrapped in gaffer tape.

'Right,' he said. 'This bit, the transmitter, goes on the person you're miking. Tape it on, let the wire hang down the back. The microphone goes in the pocket or tie, *c'est ca*. The receiver is connected to the walkman, which is tuned to the right frequency. I've tuned it and stuck tape over the button, so no fiddling. Stick a cassette in to record. Any one will do. Use these headphones. I must emphasize, Sam, that these are my personal headphones. You don't bring them back and I wire up your flat so that you die in a flaming fireball and it looks like an accident. You die and I get off scot-free. Got that?'

'Got it. Will this work?'

Gary looked hurt. 'You criticize my life's work?'

Felicia and I prepared for the next part. She dressed down. Paint-stained jeans and a faded blue sweatshirt with no university address on the front. She tied her hair back and stuck a baseball cap over it. We went to Stephanie Adams's flat together. Stephanie had the baby under one arm and an overnight bag in the other. Another woman stood behind her.

'I'll be at my friend's,' she said. 'I've left the number on the pad by the phone.'

I walked them out to the car, made sure no one was watching. But I wasn't too concerned. Because as I explained to Felicia, I didn't think the killer knew what Stephanie Adams looked like. That was the basis of our plan. I got Felicia wired up and then we waited. She played patience. I drank coffee. The hangover was still perking my brain cells. Just what I didn't need.

'What if the killer doesn't call?' she asked after about ten minutes.

'Relax. Remember how we found her? She's in the phone book.'

We waited an hour or more. It got dark. It started to rain and then stopped again. Felicia and I watched the news on the television.

At ten past nine the phone rang, interrupting a story about Bosnia.

'Hullo?' Felicia's American accent had vanished. She had Stephanie's flat, almost sullen tone dead to rights. She nodded a bit, wrote a name on the pad by the phone and told the person on the other end she'd call her back tomorrow.

'One of Stephanie's friends,' she said. 'Still, good practice for the real thing.'

We watched more television.

The phone rang again at ten thirty.

'Hullo?'

'Stephanie?'

'Yeah.'

'They tell me you have some information about Elaine's murder.'

'Yeah,' said Felicia. 'You'd be surprised at how much I know.'

'What are you planning to do about it?'

'My options are open,' said Felicia. 'I've got expenses, know what I mean? And there's no love lost with the Old Bill.'

'Perhaps we should meet and, er, discuss your options?'

'We can discuss it right now. I want seventy-five thousand quid.'

There was spluttering on the other end of the line. 'There's no way I can raise that sort of sum.'

'Fine. The way I look at it, it's still cheaper than a life sentence.'

'OK, but I can only give you a down payment at the moment. How does fifteen thousand sound? And I'll go to my bank in the morning.'

I could see that Felicia was completely immersed in her hard-bargaining mode, and probably wanted to haggle him up, so I grabbed the phone pad and wrote 'For God's sake say yes!' She looked almost disappointed.

'OK. Fifteen thousand will tide me over. But we meet somewhere crowded. I'm not making the same mistake as Shark. I'm smarter than him.'

'I'm sure you are,' the caller said smoothly. 'Where would you like to meet?'

Felicia named a pub on Westbourne Grove.

'How will I recognize you?'

Felicia described what she was wearing, then she put the phone down.

'We have half an hour.'

'You deserve an Oscar,' I said. 'I'll call Charlie.'

'Well, bugger me backwards,' said Charlie when I told him about the phone call.

'We're meeting at the Cock and Hoop in half an hour.'

Charlie sighed. 'Bloody Ridley. You're interfering in police work, placing me in a compromising position. I could bloody get the sack. I've got a wife and kids to feed, you know.'

'Just be there,' I said. I was depending on Charlie, because of course I had no idea what we would do.

We double-checked the equipment. Felicia had the mike pinned to her shirt, under her sweatshirt. The aerial hung down her back where it couldn't be seen.

She set off. I followed about twenty yards behind with the walkman attached to my belt, Gary's little headphones in my ears. I dropped back a bit further, but could still hear her clearly reciting 'Mary Had a Little Lamb' in Stephanie Adams's voice.

'Help the homeless. *Big Issue.*'

A street seller had approached Felicia. I could hear their exchange more clearly than I could see them.

'No, thanks.'

'Go on, luv, it's me last one. Only seventy pee. Help the homeless.'

'I said no thanks.' Felicia, right into her role, was still doing Stephanie's accent. The street seller put his hand on her upper arm. Felicia went to shake him off, but couldn't.

'If you don't want to buy my magazine, then you'll have to come with me, Stephanie. I've got a gun and I will use it, you know that, don't you?'

It was Robert.

Felicia nodded. She and Robert turned off Bishop's Bridge Road down a side street, walking quickly. I followed at a respectable distance. It was dark and cold and there were few people around. Felicia and Robert looked like a normal couple. I couldn't think of any rescue attempt that would not endanger Felicia's life. I couldn't think of any plan at all. All I knew was that I had to keep them in sight. Robert, fortunately, did not seem to have considered that he would be followed. He didn't look around once as he hurried Felicia along. Cars whizzed by but nobody took any notice of them. Nobody except me.

'What are you doing?' Felicia asked.

'Taking you somewhere where we can get to know each other better.'

'What about the money?'

Robert just laughed. 'No money, my dear girl. Surely you worked that out from what happened to Shark.'

'Why did you kill him? If you'd given him the dosh he'd have gone away.'

'You don't see,' he said excitedly. 'I did it for Anna. To save our marriage. She'd forgiven me for the affair with Elaine. She even covered up some of the evidence from Elaine's killing. But she wasn't very happy with me. No. Then when Shark contacted her, I had to do something. He thought Anna had killed Elaine, but she was just trying to protect me. Our family, every-thing we'd built up together.'

'I'm all choked up.'

'I can't work out whether your death should be a statement,' mused Robert. 'You read that these days – killers using their work as art. I wanted to be an artist once. My parents didn't think much of the idea. Perhaps I can make amends now. Unfortunately, all I have is this gun.' He waved his hand around in the pocket of his voluminous overcoat.

'Just make it quick,' said Felicia. 'Truth is, I'm a little bored with your company.'

Felicia had guts, trying to antagonize an excitable man with a gun, but Robert didn't seem to care.

'Did Elaine get sick of you?' Felicia went on coolly.

'We were thrown together when she came to work for me, at the family firm. But then she told me she didn't really love me. She'd only done it to get back at Anna. But I didn't believe her. I couldn't believe that.'

'So she told you that Mark was the only one for her?'

'I think she wanted me to see her with that little prat. Having dinner with him. She knew I walked past that restaurant, you see, on my way from the underground to her mother's flat. I thought she had set it up because she wanted me to be jealous, but I misread the signals.'

'It's so easy to do,' said Felicia drily. 'Perhaps you were right. If we killed people when they got tired of us then we wouldn't have to worry about bumping into them around town.'

Robert shook her violently. 'Don't joke about it. What we had was special.'

'You've been listening to too many love songs, you know. All you had was a bit on the side.'

We were in a street with houses on one side which faced on to a high brick wall. Beyond that were the rail and tube lines for Paddington Station. Robert tugged Felicia to the right. At first I thought he was taking her on to a raised pedestrian footbridge which crossed the tracks. But instead I heard a metallic rattling.

'Here's one I prepared earlier,' said Robert with a

flourish, pushing Felicia through and shutting the gate behind him. The gate's heavy padlock had been attacked by something heavier and was hanging drunkenly off.

There was a person coming towards me on the street. A stooped figure carrying two plastic shopping bags. I stopped her.

'Please call the police. There's a man with a gun on the tracks and he's got a woman hostage.'

'Pervert,' she said, crossing to the opposite side of the street.

'Please call the police,' I implored her as she hurried away. She didn't look back.

Robert was prodding Felicia across the train tracks. There were three or four sets for the mainline trains and then a narrow concrete gully where the underground trains went through.

I took the footbridge. I ran across it as quietly as I could, to the point just after the drop to the underground tracks. There was a Portakabin next to a bridge support. I could get down without Robert seeing me.

'So what's your plan, Robert?' asked Felicia, picking her way across the tracks. I could hear her breathing shortening. It was the only sign that she was nervous. 'You gonna get dressed up in a black cape and tie me to the tracks?'

'Keep walking, please. Don't forget not to step on the live track.'

I got ahead of them on the overbridge. There was a thick blue pipe overhead. I jumped up and grabbed it and swung myself up on to the top of the steel walls of the bridge. Almost directly beneath me was the Portakabin. Between them and me an underground train rattled into view.

The bridge support prevented Robert from seeing me. The train masked the sound of my landing on the roof of the hut.

I dropped. Rolled over and dropped again. Solid ground. Too solid, judging by the pain in both my knees. I peered around the side of the cabin. Felicia and Robert had cleared the electric tracks and were on the edge of the underground channel. He had the gun out now and had jammed it into her back.

'You don't expect me to jump,' said Felicia. 'I failed athletics in school.'

But Robert had noticed the bulge in the small of her back. 'Oh dear,' he said. 'Now what is this?' Using the gun barrel, he lifted up the back of her sweatshirt. Even in the sulphurous half-light, he could see what she had taped to her back.

Inexplicably, he began to laugh. He laughed as he raised the gun to her face. He laughed some more as he tightened his finger on the trigger.

Chapter Fifty-one

I charged out from behind the Portakabin. Yelling, 'You fucking bastard!' or words to that effect. Drawing fire, I think it's called. And I took a running jump across the underground tracks. There was more sound. Another train. Above ground this time, behind Felicia and Robert.

I was jumping for a long time, it seemed. Maybe the gods were with me that night. Maybe they'd given me a special dispensation from the laws of gravity. Whatever it was, I sailed through the air for the longest time. Below me was a canyon with two silver tracks leading straight to death. In front of me Felicia, turning slowly, slower than slow motion, to the man and his monstrous laugh.

I landed. Lunged for the two people who'd now become one in the struggle for the weapon. Robert lurched it away from her, pointed at the second nearest thing. Which was me.

All I was conscious of was sound. The aftermath of the shot, the high-speed train receding and me bellowing like an animal in pain. I couldn't actually feel any pain but from the dark stain spreading across my jacket I knew the evening had taken a turn for the worse. The impact of the bullet spun my torso, sending me off balance. I took a couple of steps back. The second put me right back at the edge of the underground track. Ten feet down, probably. But it wasn't the drop that would kill you, it was having all your creases ironed out by a lumbering, old-fashioned London tube train.

Instinctively, Felicia came towards me. Robert grabbed her by her collar, yanked her back.

I was losing blood. It was increasingly hard to work out whether I was balanced or not. I swayed, Felicia gasped.

'Give it up, Robert,' she said, faster now. 'You can't kill both of us.'

'Why not? I've got the gun.'

'The police will be here any minute. They have phones on trains these days.'

'Quiet, woman. I'm trying to think.'

'Just put the gun down and go home. I need to get Sam to a hospital. Can't you see he's about to pass out?'

'I said *quiet*, you stupid bitch!' screamed Robert. He struck Felicia on the side of the head. It was a fatal move. Nobody calls Felicia a stupid bitch. Her nostrils narrowed. Neatly, and without telegraphing it, she snatched her elbow up and jabbed him in the Adam's apple.

Robert stepped back, gasping from shock and lack of oxygen. I lunged in what I hoped was the right direction.

Somehow, I grabbed him round the waist. An impressive tackle, given the circumstances. We went down, Robert underneath. He struck me repeatedly on the head with the gun. I could feel viscous blood

making tracks down my face. For a skinny little guy
he was surprisingly strong. I tried to grab the gun,
but he wriggled away. I lunged for his foot. He kicked
me in the shoulder. That was the cue for my body's
post-shock anaesthetic to give out. The pain, hot and
sharp, nearly made me pass out. Robert saw his
chance, leapt to his feet. Struggled to get both hands
on the gun. When I next looked up, he had it pointed
at me.

'Get over. Both of you stand together. Right by the
tracks.'

I reached out my hand for Felicia. I needed some
support.

'Come on! Come on!' He was dancing like a boxer
on the balls of his feet. Beside that nasty little gap
there.' Felicia tightened her grip on my arm. We edged
towards the tube train tracks.

'Now,' he said. 'Which one of you wants to go first?'
He was like a goblin, moving, flying, feet not even
touching the ground. Things started to get hazy. I
thought I could hear another train. I thought I could
hear Felicia yelling at Robert. I couldn't make out the
words. The sound was coming in stereo now. Two
trains, overground and underground. One on either
side. Or maybe it was just me losing my grip on con-
sciousness.

He took one step too far. On to the live track. In
front of an oncoming train. Felicia screamed.

The image will stay with me for quite some time.

The police arrived soon after. It was lucky they did
because I was having some problems walking and

Felicia made it pretty clear that she wasn't going to carry me.

'I told him to look out,' she whispered, her face aged by the evening's events. 'I told him to look out.'

They never did find the knife that Robert used to kill Elaine. My guess is that it's resting in the silt at the bottom of the Thames, waiting to be discovered in two hundred years' time, like a Viking broadsword. But the gun that killed Shark was the one that Robert used to make a bullet-shaped hole in my shoulder. Robert's father had brought it home from the war after he took it from a dead German.

Female AM did a follow-up called 'Killer for Love'. It had just the right balance of sensationalism and prurience – Felicia and I knew exactly what we were doing. Crosbie interviewed me on the programme, which put me in the rather bizarre position of having to answer questions that I had written myself. The blokes upstairs loved it.

Albion went to live with her grandmother.

They patched up my shoulder and I had the pleasure of having physiotherapy from a delightful woman who was deeply impressed by my bravery. I hoped to be able to translate that into the odd dinner date.

City Radio gave me my old job back. Marlowe realized that since Felicia and I had learned to get along there wasn't much amusement value in my being at *Female AM*. But I think the clincher was that Rick got a job somewhere else. His plastic heart was no longer with the gritty reality of the crime beat after he was offered a weather presenter's job on a local TV station.

'A stepping stone,' he said when he broke the news to his gleeful colleagues. 'On to bigger things.'

'Right,' we all said. 'Bigger things.' We had a whip-round to buy him one of those little pointer sticks that weather people use to show ridges of high pressure.

It was about a week later when I rang Detective Inspector Roger Fitzgerald to discuss some outstanding business.

We arranged to meet in Trafalgar Square. I waited for him in front of Nelson's statue and watched tourists feed the pigeons.

'If I go down, I'm taking you with me,' I said when Roger showed up. 'Now, we both know that's not going to happen.'

'Out of my hands, Ridley. If Roadblock press charges.'

'They're not going to do that. Too much stuff would come out that wouldn't show them in a good light; the leader's got political ambitions. And I know that you've kept this as our little secret. Only me and Eddy.'

'There's no deal unless you give me the tape.'

'I'm keeping the tape. It'll never see the light of day unless you forget your end of the bargain.'

'What guarantee do I have?'

I smiled. 'My word as a gentleman.'

He knew a *fait accompli* when he saw one.

'All right, then. Deal.'

We shook hands, for what it was worth.

'Oh, and Roger?' He'd started to turn away. He stopped.

'I don't expect to get any grief from you after this.' He shrugged.

'And I'm sending you the repair bill for the car.'

I made my way back to the office. The sky was low and grey. The streets were crowded with commando shoppers. London is not at its best in December, when all we have to look forward to is months of short and gloomy days. I can only forgive the city again in March, when the first crocuses appear in Hyde Park. The time in between is tough. Only the hardy survive.

I turned into Oxford Street where I knew there was a travel agency.

'Where's good at this time of year?' I said.

The bright young thing in a light-blue suit rattled off the usual list of low-rent destinations in the Mediterranean. I didn't feel like joining hordes of my fish-and-chip-eating compatriots on the Costa del Sol.

'How about Sydney?'

'Long way away,' he said. 'But I can do you a deal.'

Ten minutes later I walked out with a round-trip ticket to Australia in my inside pocket.

That night I rang my son.

Chris Niles

Run Time

What follows is the first chapter of
Chris Niles's new novel, *Run Time*,
featuring Sam Ridley.

It is available in Macmillan hardcover,
priced £16.99.

Wednesday 8.00 a.m.

I woke in a strange room in a strange town and felt like death.

Not just any death. Not some quick-but-merciful-chop-across-the-carotid artery death. That I would have almost welcomed. No. This was more the slow-painful-expiry-at-the-hands-of-a-torturer-who-loves-his-work death. Slow roast over a low flame, hang 'em up by the thumbnails death.

I suppose the headache had something to do with it, although to call it a headache was to call the Grand Canyon an interesting geological feature. I had a hangover only a football team or a very large mammal could have done justice to. A creature with the body mass of a blue whale could maybe, just maybe, have coped with the nausea, the dry shakes, the feeling that if my brain had the gall to offer any instructions to my body, it would get a 'closed' sign in response. My stomach felt as though it was auditioning for the part of a storm-tossed ocean. My tongue was so dry I could have used it to shave paint. My eyes felt as though they were about to make an audacious escape bid from my skull.

Record this day, I said to myself as I edged my fingers towards something that would give me purchase, *because as of this moment, I am never, ever, drinking again*.

It felt good, to make a decision like that, and so early on in the piece. It gave me the strength I needed for the next stage of the morning's activity, which was to open both my eyes.

The shimmering pain around my head had diverted me from the fact that the rest of my body was in a very odd position. When I prised my lids open and got focused, all I could see was white. White tiles, white porcelain. Something hard and round jabbed into my back. I looked up. A cistern loomed above me. I groaned.

I'd passed out in the toilet.

My arm slithered around the floor, pushed up, found the door handle. It was an odd position to be in, but I was more confident now. I had to show this hangover who was boss. The bowl was close, in case I needed it. I had the feeling I might. My knees found the floor. This was good. This was real progress. Taking all the time that I needed, I hauled myself into a crawling position. The minute I did that I could have sworn that someone began sawing into my skull with a rusty blade. I closed my eyes, tried to get some control. The sawing went on. Back, forth, ear to ear. Perhaps there were two of them. One pushing, the other pulling. Perhaps even another one, shouting encouragement, like a cox.

It didn't bear thinking about. I stood up.

Uh-uh, said my stomach. *Baaad idea*. I sat down on the toilet. It wasn't much better. I leaned my head against the cistern, to reassure it that everything was going to be OK. It was then I realized that the room wasn't familiar. The clues were simple but obvious. The room was clean. Tasteful. Both of which immediately ruled out my place. White walls, white floors. A little frosted window, partially open.

The smell was the other thing that stuck me. Sweet and fresh. And it was quiet. No humming thrum of traffic. Just birds. Birds singing brightly, without a care.

Nature, I thought. Terrific. Just what I need.

I lay back some more. The ceiling was white, but there were blue and orange spots before my eyes. I thought I could hear Talking Heads singing in my brain, but maybe it was the hangover.

This is not my beautiful house.

But if not, whose?

I made another manful attempt to sit up. Ignored the sawing in my head. I thought hard. I'll remember everything in a minute, I thought, overcome by a burst of irrational optimism. I sweated my brain. Start slowly. It'll come. Relax.

I put my headache on hold, grabbed the door handle. I pulled the door open slowly. Since I was naked, I didn't want to frighten the natives.

There was a house attached to the bathroom. A nice house, by the looks of things, with hardwood floors and elegant art work. A corridor led to an open-plan living area with a breakfast bar attached to a cooking site. It wasn't entirely unfamiliar. Fragments of the previous evening began to emerge. I remembered a blonde woman called Michelle. And lots of bottles of a champagne called Bollinger.

French doors gave out onto a wide wooden deck that surrounded the house on two sides. I opened the doors and went out. The tropical air smelt sweet but the light was way too bright.

In the distance I could see a glint of sunlight on water. Could smell the frangipani, hear the boom of boats on the harbour. I'd seen that harbour, last night. I was in Sydney. Half a world away from my home.

The timpanist inside my brain was sounding long, slow strokes that reverberated around my skull. My cells were screaming for caffeine. I went inside, searched for the drug that helps my brain to work in these situations. There was a jar of instant coffee in the cupboard. I'd make it do. I put some water in an Alessi kettle and plonked it on the stove.

I moved a handbag which had been left sitting on the breakfast bar. It was glossy and expensive and bore the initial of a label synonymous with sophisticated travel. And then I noticed there were clothes on the floor. Tangled clothes. Some of them were mine.

Outside it was clear, inside my brain it was foggy but the caffeine would help, I promised myself. I concentrated on the gurgly sound that the kettle made. Ready to snatch it before it burst forth into song.

Song was the last thing I needed.

I found a cupboard with some cups, put five teaspoons of coffee in one and poured myself a restorative jolt. I looked at the bag as I drank and I looked at the clothes on the floor that weren't mine. The beautiful young woman who'd been wearing them came into clearer focus. Along with me, she had drunk quite a bit the previous night. She'd probably need a gallon or two of coffee as well.

It was the least I could do. A way of saying thanks

for giving me a hangover that even I would mark as a milestone.

I poured a second cup. Put it on a tray and took it to her room. Put my hand up to knock. Then I paused. If she was in anything like the state I was, the sight of a naked man might not be what she wanted first thing. I took the tray back to the living room and got reunited with my clothes.

I knocked on the bedroom door. Silence. She was probably still asleep.

I knocked again. Still silence. She'd probably sleep till lunchtime. I should really get going, I thought. Get a place to stay. See some of the sights. Make the most of any weather that wasn't a British winter. After all, I was on holiday. There was no time to waste.

'Michelle, it's Sam. Brought you some coffee. If you feel half as bad as I do, you could probably do with it.'

There was no reply. I knocked again, half-hoping that she'd sleep on. The idea of not hanging around picked up speed. Maybe I should just write her a note and leave. Explain that I'd had a really great time and that I'd call her. Last night had been one thing, but what would we say to each other in broad daylight when our lust had faded and the only frisson left was born of awkwardness?

The silence from Michelle's room stretched out as I debated with my inner weasel.

I waited a minute, then I eased the door open with my shoulder because I didn't have a hand free.

When I did that, I knew I should have listened to the weasel.

Michelle was in far worse shape than me. I just felt like death. She was dead.

Her face bore little resemblance to the laughing woman I'd met the previous evening. She'd been bludgeoned with something heavy and blunt. The result was pulp. Her features merged in a purée of blood, skin and gristle. The beating had been so savage that one of her ears was separated from her skull, her nose had been flattened. The bedclothes were soaked in blood. There was blood sprayed around the walls. Despite this, Michelle had put up little resistance. She hadn't been able to. Her hands were tied to a rail on the bedhead.

I took it all in and my hands began to shake. I tried to get some control over my limbs. I took the tray and the coffee back to the kitchen. Placed them down carefully. Shook my head to dislodge the horrible image. Went back to where Michelle lay.

She was so mangled by the beating she didn't look human. There was no face to connect with my hazy memories of the night before. There was nothing.

This isn't happening. This isn't happening.

I decided to make a deal with the gods. This wasn't real. I had had an atrocious, alcohol-fuelled hallucination. And this was the gods' funky way of telling me to straighten out my life. Not to have one-night stands. To find a nice woman, settle down. Participate in a loving, mature relationship. They were right. Absolutely right. I promised never to do it again.

But the deal didn't make the body go away. And in the humid Sydney heat it had already begun to smell. I gingerly checked under the bed, half expecting to see blood dripping from the springs. A ghastly, blood-soaked face stared back at me. I jumped, my heart set up a steady tattoo. It was the primitive art statue that'd been sitting in the living room last night. A statue that I'd touched. That had my fingerprints on it.

I dashed out on the verandah, desperate for a reality check. The world had tilted on its axis. I was in some parallel universe that looked just like this one except in one crucial detail. I gripped the balcony rail till the wood hurt my hands. Acceptance began to seep into my brain. A woman had been killed yards from where I slept. How had this happened? Why, even as drunk and jetlagged as I was, hadn't I heard anything? What the hell was going on?

I checked the doors and windows. As an occasional housebreaker myself, I knew that the place would have posed no serious barriers to anyone who wanted to get in. All those French glass doors – might as well leave them open. There was no sign of forced entry, but the locks on the doors were so flimsy that they would have provided no real challenge to an intruder, especially one who'd remembered not to leave home without his credit card.

The wooden deck gave out onto the garden and a path right around to the front gate. The gate was six foot high and made of wood. In these discreet, leafy streets everyone had a similar fence to the one that Michelle had, shielding them from outside eyes. The lock was intact. This was bad. This was very, very bad.

I went back inside. The birds were still singing, the

air still smelled sweet but the picture didn't hold much charm for me any more.

Very soon the police would come. They'd look the place over. They'd talk to a few people. They'd conclude that most murder cases are pretty open and shut affairs. Most women are killed by men that they know. They'd ask around some more. They'd find that a gormless English tourist had been seen out with Michelle just hours before her death. Drinking, dining, clubbing. The whole population of Sydney'd be lining up to testify. The police wouldn't be looking too hard for whoever had done this.

They wouldn't have to. They had me.

We got drunk together, came back to her place. I wanted to have sex. She said no. A fight ensued. I beat her. I killed her. My fingerprints were on the murder weapon.

And what would I be able to say in my defence? *I didn't do it, officer. You have to believe me.*

Yeah, he'd say as he bundled me into the cell. *And I'm a sucker for Father Christmas and the tooth fairy as well.*

I went back to the kitchen and took a desperate mouthful of coffee. I had to think what to do. I squashed the panic. Told it to wait its turn.

Think, Ridley!

I didn't kill her, that much I knew. It didn't narrow the field because I didn't know what the field was. I didn't know the first thing about this woman. I was tired, hungover and my whole body hurt. Might as well just sit here. Wait for the police to come and collect me. Let them take me off and put me in gaol. At least that way I'd get some sleep. In fact, I'd have more time than I knew what to do with. I wondered how often they'd let Simon come and visit.

Simon.

'Oh, Jesus,' I said out loud, looking at my watch which told me it was eight thirty. My kid. He was due here in Sydney any time. He didn't expect to see his father in a striped suit and leg irons. I didn't want him to see me that way.

I had to find some way out of this mess.

SIMON BRETT

A Nice Class of Corpse

Pan Books   £5.99

Mrs Pargeter's arrival at the Devereux does not exemplify
the decorum which the hotel's genteel owner, Miss
Naismith, had come to expect from her guests. But was
that any reason to blame her for the untoward incidents
which followed?

Namely, the discovery of one frail resident's body at the
foot of the stairs, closely shadowed by the appearance of
a second corpse.

Unfortunate accidents, claimed the upstanding proprietor
of ancient nobilities. *Murder, said the altogether more practical Mrs Pargeter* . . .

SIMON BRETT

Mrs, Presumed Dead

Pan Books   £5.99

'Living in a house where a murder had taken place did give it a certain social cachet . . .'

Intrepid detective Mrs Pargeter, sixtysomething (and a little bit more), has risked almost everything with a daring move to the well-to-do housing estate of Smithy's Loam. Yet something rankles about her new neighbours.

Do they all have to behave as if a body in the fridge is a perfectly *normal* event? Does every bored and lonely housewife have a guilty secret behind the fixed smiles and the endless round of coffee mornings?

As Mrs Pargeter soon comes to realize, Smithy's Loam might be perfect for social climbing – but it's also perfect for murder . . .

SIMON BRETT

Mrs Pargeter's Plot

Pan Books   £5.99

'I'm afraid, Mrs Pargeter, it does look as if my client has been – as he himself might put it – very thoroughly stitched up.'

But Mrs Pargeter was not so easily daunted. 'Well then,' she said with a sweet smile, 'it's up to us to unpick the stitches, isn't it?'

The indomitable Melita Pargeter has decided to build her dream house on the plot of land left to her by her husband, the much-loved, much-missed 'business man' Mr Pargeter. And there is only one person she could possibly trust to make this dream come true – her talented builder Concrete Jacket.

Scuppering her plans, however, are the dead body lying in her new wine cellar – and Concrete's arrest for murder . . .

SIMON BRETT

Mrs Pargeter's Package

Pan Books   £5.99

**'It was remarkable, Mrs Pargeter reflected, what one
would do in the cause of friendship . . .'**

Mrs Pargeter had not reached the indomitable age of sixtysomething (and a little bit more) by neglecting her
friends. Even if two weeks in Corfu – self-catering – was
probably just about as far as she was prepared to go.

Joyce Dover had recently lost her husband. She needed
the company. Yet the hot sunshine soon revealed an
unsuspected dark side to the widow.

For Joyce Dover came to Agios Nikitas to die. But,
wondered Mrs Pargeter, was it really suicide? Or
murder . . . ?

SIMON BRETT

Mrs Pargeter's Pound of Flesh

Pan Books   £5.99

Although she's never felt the need to change her own ample form, Mrs Pargeter could see nothing wrong with joining her weight-conscious friend at Brotherton Hall Spa.

While Kim strained to lose her excess inches, Mrs P would enjoy a luxurious rest in the health farm's mud-baths. A pleasure entirely spoilt when, in the dead of night, she watches the body of a young girl being mysteriously wheeled away.

The death sets Mrs Pargeter off on a furious trail of detection. Because although slimming might be murder, *covering up the evidence demands a suitable revenge . . .*

All Pan Books are available at your local bookshop or newsagent, or can be ordered direct from the publisher. Indicate the number of copies required and fill in the form below.

Send to: Macmillan General Books C.S.
                Book Service By Post
                PO Box 29, Douglas I-O-M
                IM99 1BQ

or phone: 01624 675137, quoting title, author and credit card number.

or fax: 01624 670923, quoting title, author, and credit card number.

or Internet: http://www.bookpost.co.uk

Please enclose a remittance* to the value of the cover price plus 75 pence per book for post and packing. Overseas customers please allow £1.00 per copy for post and packing.

*Payment may be made in sterling by UK personal cheque, Eurocheque, postal order, sterling draft or international money order, made payable to Book Service By Post.

Alternatively by Access/Visa/MasterCard

Card No.

Expiry Date

Signature _____

Applicable only in the UK and BFPO addresses.

While every effort is made to keep prices low, it is sometimes necessary to increase prices at short notice. Pan Books reserve the right to show on covers and charge new retail prices which may differ from those advertised in the text or elsewhere.

NAME AND ADDRESS IN BLOCK CAPITAL LETTERS PLEASE

Name _____

Address _____

_____

_____

_____

8/95

Please allow 28 days for delivery.
Please tick box if you do not wish to receive any additional information. ☐